ALSO BY TA]

WORK FOR IT

A SMALL-TOWN M/M ROMANCE

TALIA HIBBERT

NIXON HOUSE

For everyone who needed Olu's story.

ACKNOWLEDGMENTS

The themes of this book turned me into a weepy mess for weeks at a time, so thank you to my family and friends for putting up with me. Thank you also to Kia Thomas, Zahra Butt, Mina Waheed, Jack Harbon, and Therese Beharrie for invaluable edits, critique, and advice.

Thank you to Jhenelle Jacas, Rosa Giles, Adina Taylor and Ellen Baier, who were some of the first to hear about this book, and whose excitement made me smile through the more difficult scenes.

Finally, thank you to the readers who love Olu as much as I always have.

Please be aware: this book contains mentions of depression, anxiety, parental death by suicide, past sexual trauma, forced outing, and intimate photographs being shared without consent.

Olu

I can't remember what it's like to be happy.

It's not as though I didn't see this coming. I have been slightly… *distant* all my life, so these recent changes are a natural escalation. I don't feel the things I used to, can't catch the cold echoes of emotion I was raised on or the flashes of intensity I used to hunt down and leech like a vampire. Which means it's finally happened; after thirty-eight years of fighting it, I have become an alien species.

And tonight, like any self-respecting alien, I have left the safety of my flat to study humanity.

I blame my ludicrous thoughts on the night club's temperature. This place is hot enough to tease all my anxieties to the surface, like a sauna sweating out toxins—but these toxins don't come clean. They stick to my skin in a fine sheen of cursed, clammy uncertainty. The club's high-octane dance music has a drumbeat as loud and constant as my self-loathing and almost as jarring. All around me, a mixture of gorgeous and average and awkward men scream along to lyrics they wouldn't know if they were sober.

I eye the dancefloor like it's a corpse. Once upon a time I would've dived right in, blissfully arrogant and secretly desperate to be touched. Now I skirt the edges of the crowd, jerking away from flailing, distracted limbs. I'm afraid I might give someone frostbite.

Is that all you're afraid of, Olu?

I have years of practice in ignoring errant thoughts. Experience tells me that the key is to focus on one's surroundings, so when I finally reach the gleaming bar, I lean my bare forearms against it. The surface is cool, sticky, slightly wet in places, and my lip curls. I stand up straight.

New focus: the flash of the strobe lights, a blinking, toxic rainbow. There's a mirrored wall behind the bar, partially hidden by shelves of alcohol, and I see myself lit in a wash of deep, nausea-green. It's strange, looking handsome, when I feel the way I do. But I am—handsome, that is. So much so that people barely notice I'm cold.

Exhibit A: the man easing his way through carefree bodies toward me, hard-jawed and golden-haired like Captain fucking America. Tall, lean, with the kind of open face that signals a certain lack of complication. He is used to getting what he wants. Eyes like drills and the insistent angle of his body suggest that he wants me. He could choose any normal, messy, *human* man in this place, but he will take the alien because it looks divine.

Men, in case anyone on earth has somehow failed to notice, are pigs. I can say this with supreme confidence, since I was a man before I was E.T.

He draws closer, and I steel myself. A shudder wrestles with my rigid spine, trying to take over, but I don't let it. Emotions are not allowed to rule my body and feelings are not allowed to affect my reality; it's a game I like to play called Keeping My Shit Together. I try not to lose. Not in public, anyway.

Yes, it has occurred to me that I make an alien of *myself*. But now is not the time for Introspection Hour.

When the stranger reaches me, I am perfect.

"Hi," he shouts into my ear. "Come here often?" His easy grin says that he believes he is being ironic. Kitsch. Uniquely corny. His hand curls over my hip, his breath spreads over my cheek, and just like that, parts of him are clinging to me like slime. Something in my chest cringes and shrinks away, and I'm disappointed despite myself. It's always like this, now. Before, strangers were my sexual bread and butter. Now, they terrify—

Now, they disgust me.

"Hi," I mouth, giving him a nod, knowing I should pull away and go back home and write. I'm no longer sure why I came here; my old tactics haven't worked for over a year. Other peoples' bodies are not my safe, exchangeable shells anymore. It isn't too late to make a healthy choice, to head home without hurting myself, to pour meandering rubbish into my smallest journal, the one labelled with an *F* that I can't admit stands for *Feelings*. Yes. That sounds wonderful—or maybe it sounds like weakness. Like I don't want to test my battered boundaries again, because I'm afraid of the fallout.

Alright. A compromise, then.

I lean close to the stranger and holler over the music, "Come home with me."

He is a little bit surprised, a lot satisfied, and a touch smug— because I look the way I do, and I'm still gagging for it. He's the cock of the walk and this is his due, so he doesn't question, even for a moment, why I would immediately want such a thing. As far as this man is concerned, he deserves to put his hands on me.

The strobe lights flash and my expression in the mirror is android-blank, but I am still handsome.

His name is Mick, or so he tells me in the taxi. By the time I drag him home and slam my front door behind us, the cracks are starting to show—not in him. In me. When he presses me up against the wall and puts his tongue in my mouth, I slide a hand toward his arse, grab his phone from his back pocket, and put it on the sideboard.

He jerks away, and my horrified heart rate slows in relief.

"What are you doing with that?" he asks, privately annoyed but willing to be amused. He wears a smiling frown, the warning shot of human expression.

"Don't want to smash it when I rip your clothes off," I tell him, and he sniggers and returns to the matter at hand. I don't want to say that he kisses me again. When I'm like this—when disgust seeps from my pores like ectoplasm—words like *kiss* seem wrong. If I were writing this down in my journal, I would call it a *happening*. Like the title of a horror story.

We stumble through the flat, just like desperately aroused people do in films, both of us breathless for different reasons. I tense my stomach muscles to stop the roiling in my belly, wishing his tongue weren't jabbing past my teeth so I could clench them. I don't know if he tastes sour or if it's simply how I feel. We fall onto my bed, and I resent it when we land.

I'd thought taking him to my flat would help; that the disgust might not follow me here the way it follows me into hotel rooms and nightclub toilets. But that was a grave miscalculation on my part: I had Jean-Pierre at home, too, after all. I had the bastard everywhere, and he still sold pictures of our intimate moments for nothing more than a small mountain of coke. I mean, for fuck's sake, Jean—I would've *bought* you the coke.

I doubt his high lasted half as long as my current low has.

After five more minutes of heavy petting, revulsion succeeds in strangling me, and I am forced to admit that taking Mick home is a bust. *Quelle surprise*, as Jean would say. I tell Mick that I've changed my mind, and when he pretends not to hear me, soldiering through my pesky 'No's, I punch him in the balls. Even that, his soft, vulnerable flesh crushed under my knuckles, makes me feel disgusting. But I maintain my composure, staring blankly at the shadowed bedroom ceiling, while he yowls like a wounded animal—goodness, the melodrama—and curls up like a wood-louse at the foot of my mattress. The presence of his weight makes my stomach squirm. His jerky, gasping sobs make me want to shudder. So I shove his body clean off the bed, and I have no regrets.

Faster than I would prefer, he recovers enough to stand and catches his breath enough to tell me what a disgrace I am. "Fucking nutter," he mumbles, snatching up his shirt, stabbing his legs into his jeans, hiding his tear-stained face from me. "What's your fucking problem?"

"My problems are myriad and varied," I drawl. "So are yours, I presume." Lounging naked on the bed in front of this creep is making my skin crawl, but I've decided to stay nude anyway in a show of dominance. Olumide Olusegun-Keynes does not scrabble about on the floor for clothes; my middle name is Dignity. And besides, I look incredible.

Mick gives me a poisonous glare with a hint of uncertainty, as if something about me disturbs him deeply—mission accomplished. I think he's unnerved by the fury in my eyes, in my voice, rushing hot through my veins and smoking all around me. He doesn't know it's been simmering for months, ever since my first failed one-night-stand. He's probably worried I could snap at any moment, that I'll hack him into tiny pieces and hide his cubed remains in my freezer. It's always the pretty ones; isn't that what they say?

I'm silent and still for a moment. Then I whisper, "Boo."

He actually flinches. "Fuck you."

"Cheerio."

Thirty seconds later I hear my front door slam.

As soon as he's gone, I'm opening my bedside drawer, fumbling through its contents for the little journal marked *F*. I stay on the bed as I crack it open and write, trying to make the unclean clean again. I stay naked too, as if I hope to reconnect with my strange body: here is the soft smell of leather, the sweet rasp of fresh paper beneath my fingertips, the ache in my knuckles as I clutch my pen too hard. The loss of time as I look down and see my own words crawling, sprawling, sprinting across the page, ink staining my skin. Dark, pure, pushing away the slime. Wishing I didn't have to.

I know it's perfectly fine, normal, healthy to *not* want sex. I know that. But it certainly isn't fine for *me* to feel sick at the prospect of my favourite thing. It isn't fine for my *F* journals to have gone from *I wish it wasn't so hard to find a connection* to *I touched a cabbie's hand as I passed him the fare and almost vomited.* I know it isn't fine, but I don't know what to do about it. So I write.

I'm not sure how long it takes me to finish, but when I'm done, when the night is nothing more than a story, I feel a little better. The fact that I *feel* at all makes me want to smile.

Then I put my journal away and lie down to sleep, and hear my father's voice in my head. *This is what you are,* he tells me. *A half-thing tied to pathetic survival techniques. Emotional. Weak.*

I already know that. I've always been arrogant, but not so arrogant as to believe that my handwritten ramblings mean anything but failure. I tell the voice that I'm aware I was a disgrace tonight, and it settles, satisfied. It lets me rest.

For now.

———

OLU

In the morning, nothing has changed; shit is simply brighter in the sunlight.

I wake up to texts from my sister and devour them.

Isaac took a picture of the sunrise for you this morning.

Come down and we can all watch it together tomorrow.

I know you're not busy Olu! Don't test me.

She's happy, and she doesn't need me, so I put the phone

down without replying. I refuse to give Lizzie my frostbite; she'll have to wait until I've gotten myself under control.

But after last night, progress is non-existent, and my Elizabeth is not a patient woman.

I sigh, stand, find my pyjama bottoms. God, my head aches, and I didn't even drink last night. As I wander into the living room, eyeing the ink on my hands, I accept that in the case of my disappearing humanity, urgent action is required. I've become a storm cloud, misery and electricity rolled into one, and soon, someone will notice. It might be my baby sister, or my perceptive best friend, Theo, or my nosy friend, Aria. In the end, it doesn't matter. None of them can learn about the problems I've been having, because when everyone around you is living out their dreams, burdening them with your bullshit is simply a crime.

So what, exactly, should I do?

My laptop is sitting on the coffee table, where I left it yesterday afternoon. I open it without examining my own thoughts too closely, log into my browser, and begin a search. Long minutes pass while I cling to denial: I'm not backsliding or abandoning the people who need me, I'm simply searching for somewhere to go, somewhere to visit, a little trip to take.

Anywhere but here.

The urge to run is an old one. I haven't exercised it since everything changed last year, since I was forced to come out of my very comfortable, handmade, bespoke closet. Back then, I roamed the world so I could be myself with men who barely knew me. I don't have to do that now. Last night proved I *can't* do that now. I keep typing anyway.

I need to disappear for a while, that's all. Just while I fix things. Just while I fix myself.

I am an expert at last-minute disappearances to interesting places, so my search starts with confidence—but this time, I have some unfamiliar limitations. For one thing, I'm no longer as wealthy as I once was. For another, my sister is pregnant. I'm not leaving the country. It's spring, so I decide to look for somewhere disgustingly English and twee, somewhere that will be rife with apple blossom and flat-cap-wearing locals who give me a wide berth.

For almost two hours, I scour forums and fall down rabbit holes and mix up questionable keywords. I know how to find out-of-the-way destinations no tourist would ever hear of, but when I stumble upon the strangest jackpot, even I am impressed with myself. The blog post is on the website of some popular cordial brand that's currently pride of place in Waitrose—the latest sober, hipster, health-based smash everyone will spend the summer choking down, regardless of whether it's good. I've never tried the drinks, but they have ridiculous flavour combinations that I assume taste hideous. People adore the unusual for its own sake.

But that's none of my concern. What catches my eye, at first, is the website's photography: it shows the sort of pastoral, rolling hills and lush, verdant plant-life I didn't think this grim little island was still capable of producing. The brand's logo is surrounded by drawings of daffodils and daisies and tiny white flowers. According to the blog post, those flowers need to be plucked.

ELDERFLOWER HARVEST, reads the headline.

Fernley Farm is nestled at the heart of Fernley, a tiny village filled with generous and hardworking people. Every harvest season, the locals help us gather flowers and berries by hand, the young and old all chipping in together. That's why Fernley Cordial tastes like home and heart.

They need a copyeditor. The use of 'heart' is repetitious.

Want to join in the Fernley fun? Anyone can help us pick, and we pay a pound per kilo. The farm is due to open for harvest in mid-May this year. Join our mailing list for updates!

I find myself smiling, though the action feels rusty and no-one's here to see it. This is absolutely adorable and astonishingly perfect, from the timing to the task to the location. Join their cute little mailing list? Oh, I'll do one better than that. My father is a piece of shit, one I try to forget exists, but I suddenly hear his voice in my head. *"Hard work cures all ills, Olu."*

God, I hope he's right.

———

Griff

It's a warm, sunny Saturday—proper lovely, bright enough to beam through my rose-printed curtains and paint my living room blood-red. Which, now I mention it, looks a bit weird. But still; this is a nice, spring day.

Now, ask me what I'm doing. Go on. Say, *What are you up to with your weekend, Griffin?*

Right now, I'm sat in the (creepy) blood-red living room, staring at my mother's candles on the end table. There's three of them, burned down to different heights, all as thick as my wrist, which is pretty fucking thick. They used to be black, but their colour is messed up by the thick layer of dust that's settled over the last ten years. Dribbles of wax cling to their edges, frozen forever, because these candles will never be lit again. Mum's not here to do it, after all. But I'm not thinking about that.

No; on this fine Saturday, I'm thinking about ginger, and all the ways it's causing me problems.

I stormed into the living room five minutes ago, because if I'd stayed in the kitchen, I might have tried to brutally murder a root. The twist in my latest cordial recipe, a rich orange and cinnamon spice I'm planning in time for Christmas, is frustrating the shit out of me. It's not right. It wasn't right on Monday evening, either, or Tuesday or Wednesday or the rest of the week, which is why I'm still fiddling with winter flavours in the middle of spring on a Saturday—because Rebecca reckons holiday options will keep the business's momentum going, and who'll

9

come up with those options if I don't? Definitely not our bloody boss. He—

Ah. *Ah*. I've fucking got it.

I jump up—or, rather, I get up slowly because this sofa hasn't changed since Mum died either, and it whines whenever I sit or stand. Doesn't matter. This is my, what do you call it? My eureka moment. Fuck the details. I stride back into the kitchen, pick up the wrinkled knot of ginger I threw down a while ago, and snag a red chilli from the little plant on the windowsill. If I can DIY some minor infusion, just as a test run—

Bang, bang, bang.

Aaaand *that* is the sound of my Saturday work session coming to a fast and definite end. I drop the ginger—at this rate, it'll bruise like a peach in protest—and smile in spite of myself. Only one tiny fist has ever made such a racket at my back door. To be honest, only one person in this village ever comes to see me at all, not that I'm complaining.

Rebecca lets herself in after three seconds of waiting, which she'd probably describe as *Oh my God like a fucking hour*, and stands in the open doorway, her hands on her hips. Behind her, I see my garden, a contained little fairy forest bathed in rich, afternoon sun. The light glints off Rebecca's hay-coloured curls and steely expression.

"Griffin Everett," she says to me, "you best not be working."

"Nope," I tell her. Not a lie. I've just started washing up.

"Oh, Lord, you are. This is what happens when I leave you to your own devices of a weekend." She throws up her hands. "Come on, you great lump. Let's go and have some fun."

I grumble and moan because that's what I do, and she ignores me happily.

Five minutes later, we're walking down the village's main road. It's called Fernley Road. The village is called Fernley. Yeah. It's that kind of village.

Since this is the only way to get anywhere useful, and since it's such a nice day, there's plenty of people out and about. They walk their dogs, call absent orders to their kids, give each other cheerful hellos, ignore me and Bex. That's part of the routine. We come face to face on the narrow path with old Mr. Holyrood and his five dachshunds, who all stop to greet Rebecca—probably because they're miniscule dogs and she's a miniscule human. My best friend and I are opposites, little and large, light and dark, mouthy and socially silent.

Mr. Holyrood, like everyone else in this town, watches me from the corner of his eye as if I'm one of those midnight monsters who creeps up on you when you look away. He greets Bex first, since her only crimes are 1. Being a bit *brash*, for a woman, and 2. Being best mates with me. The fact that she used to get with girls before she "came to her senses" and married a nice young man is seen as a teenage phase—by everyone but us, I mean.

"Rebecca," he says stiffly, nodding all slow and careful, like the pea-sized head on his long, thin neck might drop off and roll away. Then, through gritted teeth like I'm bloody Voldemort, he mutters my name. "Griffin."

Griffin. Even that part of me is wrong, in a place like this. My mother—my tragic, scandalous, blah-blah-fucking-blah mother —gave me a weirdo name, as far as Fernley's concerned. People round here are called John or Beth or James. People round here aren't born out of wedlock, people round here aren't unnaturally massive and unnervingly quiet, people round here aren't openly into men and completely fine with it. People round here aren't *me,* unless they have the bad taste to *be* me, in which case you'd better avoid them or tell them what a freak they are whenever you can.

Although, most people stopped choosing that last option once I hit 6'2.

"Afternoon, Mr. Holyrood," Rebecca says. The words are polite, right? But the way she says them, they sound like *Fuck you,*

Mr. Holyrood, wearing their Sunday best. That's her superpower. I don't have a superpower, or the patience to talk to people I don't like, so I just stand there in silence. I do that a lot, which might be part of my, er, image problem. Not that I care.

After a tense moment of awkward nodding and sharp commands at dogs, Holyrood skirts around us and fucks off. Once he's gone, Rebecca hooks her arm through mine—which is awkward, with the height difference, but I like it anyway—and drags me down the street. "Don't you want to know what we're doing?"

I seriously consider that. "Is it going to give me a heart attack?" Rebecca has a talent for wild decisions and for convincing me to go along with them.

"No," she laughs. The sound tinkles like bells. If you didn't know Rebecca very well, you'd think she was just the sweetest *doll* of a woman. "We're going to spy on Mrs. Hartley."

Maria Hartley is a war widow with three kids, and a teacher at the local school. She has a single shock of white in her brown hair and she smiles at me like I'm a normal person. When my mother was alive, Mrs. Hartley called her *Gemma, babe,* and looked her in the eye. Sometimes Mum sent me round to hers with jars of homemade jam. I'm right fond of Mrs. Hartley, I am, so I frown. "Spying why?"

"She's renting out her little flat again. To a Londoner, I heard."

Mrs. Hartley's flat does a not-so-roaring trade in historical tourists, usually snagging one a year. If that. "A relative?"

"Not that I've heard. Aly says—" Aly is Rebecca's neighbour "—that he looks like nothing she's ever seen."

I have no idea what that could mean, so I mutter dubiously, "Hm."

"Oh, go on with you." Rebecca smacks my arm. "This is why we're going to spy! To see if she's right!"

"Hm," I say again.

Rebecca laughs.

It takes all of five minutes to reach Mrs. Hartley's big, white house with its pretty hanging baskets and green-painted fence. Her kids are in the front garden, arguing over who gets the last choc ice and who'll have to make do with rocket lollies. The minute they see me, their eyes widen. I hover by the garden gate behind Rebecca and consider smiling at them. Then I realise I'm casting a shadow—a literal fucking shadow—over the garden. *Sigh*. My awkward attempt at a smile would probably send them screaming.

I don't know how to deal with people. Never have. Plants are easier anyway.

"Mam," the eldest shouts, already unwrapping the choc ice for herself, debate be damned. "Miss Becky's here."

A shout comes through the open front door: "Alright, Suzie." And then a moment later, there's Mrs. Hartley. She looks a little worn-out, I notice, her hair frazzled and her cheeks flushed pink, a tea towel in her hands. But she smiles as bright as ever when she sees us—both of us.

Mrs. Hartley is one of those people, like Rebecca, who makes the knot in my chest get looser instead of tighter.

"You two," she grins wryly. "Never apart, not for a second, not since you were small." Mrs. Hartley is only sixteen years older than me, but she sees me as a kid because she and Mum were almost the same age. And I call her Mrs. Hartley for the same reason.

Rebecca's parents are older than Mrs. Hartley, though, and Rebecca's not a socially awkward human statue, so she leans over the fence and beams, "Maria!"

"How are you, my darling?"

"Curious," Rebecca grins, and lowers her voice. "A little birdy told me you've smuggled a handsome man into the village." This is what Rebecca's like. She says shit like *We're going to spy*, but here are three things she can't do: keep a secret, lie, be subtle. People love it or hate it.

Mrs. Hartley whips Rebecca with the tea towel and rolls her eyes, but she's one of those who love it. "The gossip in this village, by God. He only arrived last night. And yes, he's handsome, madam, but you're a married lady."

"You lost me at *but*. Lewis knows how to share." The two of them laugh. The children edge closer, trying to eavesdrop. And me? I don't know. The conversation sort of fades into the background of my mind, like it always does when people laugh at jokes that don't include me. Like I said, I'm awkward. Don't know what to do with myself. My eyes wander up to the flat above Mrs. Hartley's garage, persuaded into curiosity by Rebecca's determination—which happens a lot. Sunlight flashes off the windows, and I squint. For a moment, I think I see something: a man. Just the slightest impression of a sharp, brown face, broad shoulders, a hand at the curtains. Then the light glints again, and he moves away, or maybe he was never there at all.

But it feels as though he was.

2

GRIFF

He's real, and I meet him the next day.

Fernley's a tiny place. I know the name of every family here, and everybody knows who I am. Sheep block the road often, but people never care. There's no post office or corner shop, and only one pub. So, the stranger isn't hard to spot.

Especially since he's currently *in* the only pub, sitting at the bar like a tropical flower.

"He's *ridiculous*," Rebecca tells me, clearly stunned. It's Sunday evening now, and we're playing pool. Well, I'm playing pool; Rebecca's got her knickers in a twist, has done ever since the stranger strolled in five minutes ago. She's on her tiptoes, trying to murmur in my ear, but since she's as tiny as this village—tinier, even—her mouth is level with my armpit. The pool cue in her hand's as tall as her. She whispers ferociously, "Everyone said he was handsome, but this is just *silly*."

She's not wrong. I study him subtly—I hope—trying to decide if he looks like a serial killer, because I always keep an eye on Mrs. Hartley's visitors. But I can't get a read on him, because he doesn't even look real. He's like a fucking sunset. Not that I'll be admitting that to Bex. I grunt, turn, bend, and pot a red.

"Oi," Rebecca tuts. "I wasn't ready."

My lips twitch at the corners. I didn't know Rebecca had to be ready for *my* go.

"Oh, stop smirking," she mutters. "I'm taking this turn." Rules mean almost nothing to her. Keeps me on my toes.

While she squints at a yellow ball and tests 95 different angles, I look up—and find myself staring into the stranger's eyes. He's turned away from the bar and stands with a pint in his hand, leaning against the polished wood, watching me without shame. His head is cocked to one side, like he finds me as interesting as everyone finds him. Could be, he heard Rebecca's awful excuse for a whisper. Could be, he noticed me because I'm hard not to notice. I look like God forgot to turn off my 'grow' switch. I look like I shouldn't be allowed to hold children or small animals in case I snap their necks—that's what a guy I once slept with told me. When I'm beside Rebecca, I might as well be a T-Rex. The stranger's probably wondering if I'm part gorilla.

I'm wondering if he paid for his face, the way people do these days. His skin is light brown, like autumn sunlight through sparse trees, and I suppose that must be natural. His hair, cropped and tightly curled, is a tawny shade that must be natural too, since his eyebrows seem to match. But the rest—the razor-sharp jaw, the soft, wide mouth and noble nose—surely no-one's born with all that at once, perfectly symmetrical and unnervingly striking?

Well, whether he bought it or not, it looks bloody good.

I turn back to Rebecca. "Shoot."

"Piss off, you're distracting me."

"From what?"

She gives me a dark look over her shoulder. "Griffin Everett, you cheeky bastard. You're watching a master at work, here. Prepare for a humiliating defeat."

I snort.

She sniffs, shoots, and pots two of my balls. "Crap," she says.

"Ta, Bex."

"God, you're smug." Her voice lowers, her frown fades, and she goes up on tiptoe again. "So, about this handsome stranger."

I raise an eyebrow. "Handsome?"

"Don't give me that. I think you should talk to him."

For a moment, I wonder what the hell she's on about. Then I catch the gleam in her eye that means trouble, and the penny, slow as ever, drops.

I give her a stony look. "No, Rebecca." When she gets these ideas into her head, I have to be firm.

"Why not? You haven't gotten laid in eight-hundred-and-seventy-five years."

Thanks for the reminder. Definitely needed that. Had totally forgotten. "I can't just *talk* to someone like him," I mutter.

"Why not? He's perfect!" She starts ticking qualities off on her fingers. She's painted little ladybirds on her nails. "Stranger, new in town, probably won't be staying, and he's absolutely gorgeous."

Yeah, like lava is gorgeous. From a distance. Even across the pub, I can feel his heat, and I'm not interested in getting burned.

"I don't do pretty," I mutter, moving around the table to line up my next shot.

Sadly, Rebecca follows and keeps talking. "You did Annabelle Cross."

"That was a one-time thing." All my things are one-time things. No-one ever keeps me. But some people—usually women —find my ugly mug a bit of a thrill, and when they want to misbehave, they call me over. Problem is, like I said, Fernley's a small village. Last couple of years, I've run out of one-time things to tap.

It feels like I'm running out of lots of things, lately. Like this place has nothing left for me to survive on. But I don't dare think of *that*.

"Griff," Rebecca sighs, like she's talking to a kid. "It's just a shag. You're not looking for a bloody boyfriend."

Aren't I?

No. You're doomed to be alone, and that's okay.

I've learned over the years that I have to be firm with forbidden hopes, just like I'm firm with Rebecca.

Although, I never last long against Bex. She has this dizzying mix of charm and 1-2-3 logic that I struggle to fight. Plus, she talks really fast, and it makes her sound smart. Already I can feel my remaining braincells toddling after her toward a cliff's edge.

Still, I put up one last show of resistance. "Doubt he's interested."

"He's staring a hole into you, Griff. No, don't look, you donkey. Trust me. Have I ever steered you wrong?"

I finally take my shot and fluff it. "Year 2, you told me to pick up that stinging nettle—"

"I thought it was a flower," Rebecca interrupts. "Don't be petty."

"Year 3, you convinced me to nab you a jam tart off your nana's counter, and we both got—"

"Griffin! Are you going over there or not?"

I sigh and stare at the green velvet in front of me, red and yellow balls dotted about. But after a second, that's not what I'm seeing: my eyes are full of the beautiful stranger. I study the memory of him, since I'm not allowed to look, and list his pros and cons.

The pros go like this.

1. Jesus Christ, I need a good fuck.
2. He's intimidating. I like it.
3. His bottom lip is the rounded curve of a plump, ripe peach, and that's my favourite fruit. I want to bite.

Yeah. The pros go off the rails pretty fast. I turn to cons.

1. He's out of my league.
2. I've never seduced someone I don't know. Fuck, living in a place like this, I don't think I've ever *talked* to someone I don't know.
3. The whole pub, also known as half of Fernley, will be watching the entire time, thinking about how I'm a changeling or a freak.

The cons are daunting, but that last one bothers me most of all—because it shouldn't have even made the list. I'm not supposed to care what the village thinks of me. Their shit doesn't belong in my head. That's how my mum raised me, or tried to.

All you can ever be is yourself, so try not to second-guess it.

Fuck. Okay. Fine. No second-guessing.

Nerves crawling over my skin like aphids on a rose, I hand Rebecca my pool cue. "You sure you don't mind?"

"Mind?" she echoes. "Oh, I'm sure, babe."

I huff out a laugh and start to turn away.

She grabs me. "Wait, Griff—roll up your sleeves."

"…Why?"

"You have really nice forearms."

My best friend is nuts. I do as she says.

Olu

I arrived in Fernley on Friday night and was promptly bored out of my skull. I remained in that state all weekend, dreadfully disappointed by the dullness of this rural eat-pray-love experience—then I looked up from my travel journal long enough to remember that, usually, in order to experience new things, one must leave the house.

It *has* been a while since I took a trip like this. Perhaps I've lost the knack of running away.

19

Whatever the case, I've finally dragged myself to the village's only centre of entertainment. And from the looks of things, I am about to be entertained.

The dark-haired giant moving toward me doesn't seem to fit in around here. Since meeting my hostess, Maria Hartley, and looking around the place, I've gathered that things in this village tend to be bright and quick and simply done. But this man is slow and steady and impenetrable, with eyes like black mirrors and a near-tangible reserve that makes me want to crack him wide open.

Not that I'd ever obey that urge. I've learned, courtesy of Jean-Pierre, that the more you know someone, the uglier they get.

But the giant is striding over with obvious intent, forcing me to wonder—if he starts something, if he flirts with me, will I respond? The old me adored flirting. The new me is tense, ready for familiar, creeping disgust to come along and ruin everything. If this were one of the London nightclubs I periodically haunt like a poltergeist, my skin would already be sticky with apprehension. For some reason, the feeling hasn't come yet, but it will.

I wait for it and watch the giant. He has the stride of a minor god, and the pub's patrons, with their muddy tweed and their well-trained dogs at their heels, part for him like he's a rabid animal. Their worry is understandable: the glower on his suntanned, well-worn face can only be described as ferocious. Beneath a trimmed, black beard, his jaw is hard as iron. I wonder if he really is coming over to flirt or if he's coming over to punch me. One blow with that meteoric fist and he might snuff me out like the dinosaurs, so I suppose I'll have to dodge fast.

But when he stands in front of me like a brick wall, it's not to throw a punch. All he does is look at me and say, "Hello."

One word, two syllables, in a quiet, rasping voice that makes me oddly aware of my own skin—skin that still doesn't feel heavy or sweaty or too tight for my body. I'm not sure why. Perhaps it's because this man isn't staring at me with avid greed, as if I'm a dead work of art or a cold clutch of jewels. Which is silly of him, since I am all those things and nothing more.

I brush off my confusion and murmur, "Evening, handsome." I'm misbehaving, since he's not handsome at all, but I can't help it. I've never quite known how to be good, and recently, I don't even care enough to try.

He breathes out through his nose like a bull, and his glower becomes an outright scowl, but he doesn't call me out. "I'm Griff." His words are hard enough to qualify as brute force. I'm not sure why he's still talking to me. Five seconds of conversation, and it's abundantly clear he doesn't want to be here.

Maybe this is some sort of game. I like games. My emotions reach me through a thick coat of cotton these days, but the curiosity he's stirring is sharp enough to prick at me. He's like a little dose of the antidepressants I don't take. "I'm—" *Olu*, that's what I almost say, which is odd. Strangers don't use that name. "Keynes," I finish, my gaze steady, daring him to mention my hesitation.

Brazen it out, that's always been my tactic. And who is more brazen than me?

Apparently, this man. After a moment, he asks, "You sure?"

Wonderful. A comedian. Though he's taller than I am, I look down my nose at him—it's a hard-won skill. "Quite sure. Are you capable of more than two syllables at once?"

A hollow pause, during which I study Griff. He looks… interesting. Oh, I don't know why I'm being polite: he looks as if someone hammered chunks out of a mountain, saw a man's likeness in the resulting craggy mess, and gave it life. He's all weather-beaten skin, wild, midnight hair that falls into his eyes, and a nose that could be called a beak if beaks were crooked. His mouth is a grim, finely carved line that my own would suffocate, and his shoulders are like boulders. His knuckles are like walnuts. If I'm frank, he's quite ugly, but there is something about him.

The fleeting urge to crack him open should have faded by now, but it's still there.

Finally, he says, "Yes. I'm capable."

"Well done," I breathe, obnoxiously astonished. "That was five!"

The look he gives me says, very clearly, *Go fuck yourself.* No wonder he doesn't speak much. His face does the job for him, when he wants it to.

"So," I begin, leaning harder against the bar, starting to enjoy myself. "What are you doing over here?"

His jaw shifts and his eyes flick to the ceiling for a moment, as if he's asking the heavens that very question.

"Am I in your way?" I prod, knowing that I'm not.

A tiny silence before he replies, "No."

"Have you come to tell me that well-groomed facial hair won't fly in this here village, and I've got until sunrise to pack my bags and leave?"

His gaze spears me, exasperated. His eyes are dark, dark, dark. "No."

I let a slight smile curve my lips and notice him noticing. That gaze is on my mouth now. His hands curl into fists, just for a moment, a heartbeat, before he smooths them out. I purr, "Are you shy, Griff?"

Another of his little pauses. I finally realise that he's simply slow to speak—as if he thinks carefully about each word that leaves his mouth.

My diametric opposite, then.

"I'm wondering," he says finally, "which ale you chose tonight."

The words are so unexpected, I almost miss the fact he dodged my question about shyness. Arching a brow, I ask, "Does my choice matter?"

"Yes." It's a single word in a flat-stone voice, but I think the silent giant is… teasing me. How thrilling.

"In that case," I say, "I'm not sure I want to answer. What if I get it wrong?"

"You care?" he asks. Then adds, as if remembering full sentences are required: "Do you care what I think?" He has a gentle country accent that almost makes me want to smile. I'm not sure why.

"What you think? Not exactly. But you're rather large, and I don't know anyone here, and I've heard people take the strangest things to heart in the countryside. I'd hate to be driven out of the village with pitchforks because I'm drinking Rock Mild."

"Rock Mild?" He blinks slowly, his lashes incongruously long and thick. "Hang on. My pitchfork's out back."

I laugh. It's a short, awkward bark, more of a "*Ha*" than anything else, but it counts. I did it. I'm clinging to it. And I was right—Griff is teasing me. His own mouth curls at the edges, not quite a smile but the ghost of one, and I find myself wanting to see teeth. It's natural that I'm curious about him: he's displaying strange behaviour. Men never tease me at bars. They coax me, they catch me, they relentlessly *desire* me. And, even before Jean-Pierre, I never really enjoyed that. Being desired is such a dull sort of danger. I'm so used to eyes picking me apart.

But this? This is starting to feel like being with a friend, sans the added weight of hiding my recent… struggles. It's an unobjectionable dynamic. Perhaps even a pleasant one. Maybe that's why I tease him back. "So, are you as scary as you look?"

Through the messy fall of his hair, I see his eyebrows rise. "You admitting I'm scary?" He's warming up to me. I do believe I like him warm.

"No. I said you look it." I take a sip of my beer, which is indeed awful, and watch his eyes go to my throat. The action… isn't awful. "I'm scary too, you know."

His gaze flicks over me, not dismissively but quick, perceptive, as if he's catalogued everything relevant in 0.25 seconds. Or maybe he already got an eyeful, checking me out from the pool table. He says, his voice dripping with scepticism, "That so?"

The cheek of it. "I may not be built like a lorry, like *some* people—"

"I prefer 'brick shit-house'," he interrupts mildly.

I refuse to laugh. "—but I've been told I have a terrifying aura."

"Would be more terrifying," Griff says, "if you didn't talk about auras."

"I'm beginning to see why your friend was hissing at you over there. You're incredibly difficult."

"Now you've hurt my feelings." But he's smiling again, that faint curve. I want to reach out and trace it with my fingers, which is such an unfamiliar feeling that it shocks me. And then, a second later, it excites me—because that feeling constitutes desire, and it's been a long, long time since I experienced anything like it. My odd reaction to him sparks a reckless sort of hope, a wild taste of possibility in my chest.

"If I've hurt your feelings," I murmur to Griff, "I'd like to apologise." I am clinging to this hint of lust with both hands, desperate for it to grow roots, to bite deep into me, to make me myself again. *Want him. Want him carelessly and carnally, and then you'll be fixed.* As if shagging him, someone, *anyone*, is a magic spell that will rewrite months of cold confusion.

"Bet you're good at saying sorry." Griff's voice is low, slow gravel, and my pulse warms tentatively, an experimental simmer. This is wonderful. This is excellent. I feel a tiny bit like my old self, but I don't dare examine it too closely in case this miniscule change is a sham. Quick, quick, quick; I have to be quick, before the moment passes and the idea of human contact horrifies me again.

I wet my lips and realise I'm nervous, which is hilarious and ridiculous and perhaps a little bit good. "Would you like me to show you how I apologise?"

His gaze skims over me again, but it's slower this time, steadier, spilling sensuality over my skin. Ah. Fuck. Too much. The strangeness rears its head, sloshing a puddle of acid in my belly, whispering vicious nothings in my ear. *What are you doing? You think you can have him? Ask yourself why he'd possibly be over here with you.*

I crush the voice with a firm fist. Griff is here because I'm gorgeous and he wants me.

Jean-Pierre wasn't. Jean-Pierre didn't. Your life is just as cold and false as you are.

Well, now, subconscious. That was hardly sporting.

Griff's slow reply drags me, blessedly, out of my own head. "I think most people would like to see how you apologise." A pause, one that zings like sharp, intense thought, before he speaks again. "Where are you from?"

He's not dragging me outside? Astonishing. I tell myself I'm disappointed rather than relieved. I'm making progress, here. I'm not allowed to be relieved. If I'm really getting better, I should be desperate for some dick in a back alley, like I used to be. Shouldn't I?

"I'm from London," I say, hoping he isn't going to ruin my grand sexual plans by asking where I'm *really* from. If he does, it won't take the strangeness to put me off him.

He doesn't. Instead, he asks, "What do you do?"

"Why do you care?" I shoot back.

"I'm a gold digger."

My laugh is another brittle bark, but this one comes easier. Now I'm sparking off him, my throat feels less raw. "I've recently come down in the world, so your timing is off."

"My timing?" Something's happened to his voice. It still sounds like tires creeping over gravel, but now each rumble rolls through my belly. "You came to me, golden boy."

Golden boy?! "I don't even know where to start with that."

"The beginning," he says patiently.

I splutter. I actually splutter. I haven't spluttered since the last time I argued with my father, although this doesn't feel like that —there's no helpless rage, or secrets like brick walls. Just confused amusement. "Fine," I manage. "First thing's first: I didn't come to you. I came to Fernley."

"And here I am." He's been standing in front of me as I lean against the bar, but now he puts a hand on the shiny, sticky-ringed surface to catch someone's attention. The action brings his arm so close to my side, I freeze.

He doesn't notice. He's caught the eye of the older woman who pulls pints, and he makes a sound that can only be described as a grunt, but which she seems to understand. "Got you, Griff. Just be a sec," she says, and spins away.

I suppose when there's only one establishment in the entire village, everyone's a regular.

Looking back at me—but not moving that arm—he says, "Second thing?"

Oh—I'd almost forgotten that I'm in the middle of telling him off. Sort of. "I'm still on the first thing. I did come to Fernley—"

"Because?"

I ignore him. "But I was minding my business over here when *you* approached *me*."

His lips curve. This smile goes further than the previous ones, until he looks almost rakish, and his eyes crease at the corners. "Did I?"

"*Yes*." I should be irritated. I'm amused instead. Amused, and wanting him again, ever so slightly. "As for the second thing— don't call me 'golden boy.'"

"Why not?"

"So, so many reasons," I say. "But the only one you need to know is that I'll barbecue your balls."

He studies me for a moment, like I'm a surprise, before saying, "You're not how I thought you'd be." There's a little frown creasing his brow, like he's thinking. Deeply. About *me*.

I should really nip that in the bud.

"Forget the drink," I tell him, putting my own on the bar. "Let's go."

He hesitates, or maybe he's just taking his time in that slow, heavy way he has. Regardless, I don't have the patience for either —not when it comes to this, not when the thread of desire is back but could disappear at any moment.

I put my hand on his exposed forearm, which is all corded steel and fine, raised veins and crisp black hair. The contact sends an electric shock skittering over my skin. It must hit him too, because his muscles go taut under my palm while my nerves turn to water. I think I've miscalculated.

Then he calls, "Leave it, Moira," and I lead him outside.

———

OLU

It's dark, but the spring air is unseasonably warm, fragrant with the fresh scent of green things and filled with the sounds of night-time creatures. I barely notice. There are whispers of worry at the edges of my mind: *You don't know him. He's a stranger. You can't trust him.* These things never used to bother me; now they trigger the disgust, slower than usual but undeniably there. The thick, toxic slime of it coats my skin, and I know I've missed my chance. I waited too long, or things got too real; either way, the desire is dead. My dick is apparently still attached to my body, but it might as well have flown to Australia. That's how far removed it is from feeling even the slightest interest in this man.

For fuck's sake.

The fact that this reaction steals my control, my choice to find pleasure, my favourite fucking hobby—it makes me angry. And, unusually, Griff seems to notice.

He frowns beside me, cocking his head. "Are you—?"

The moment I hear his voice, or rather, the concern buried within it, I decide to do this anyway. To make things between us

27

as breathless and humid as the night air, *now*, because my pride won't let this strangeness win again. Griffin may be a big man, but I'm no daisy myself, so I drag him down the nearest excuse for an alleyway without too much trouble. I suspect he lets me.

I press my own back against the side of the pub and feel rigid, crumbling bricks against my spine. They stick out so randomly, they must have been laid before geometry was invented. But it doesn't bother me right now, not when my pulse is a frantic drumbeat of *Do it do it do it before your brain catches up*. I twine my fingers in Griff's plaid shirt and drag him forward, and when his weight presses me into the wall, I know I should like it. I've always liked this. But my stomach tightens in the bad way, not the good.

You don't know him. You can't trust him. You don't want him.

Ridiculous. I've been shagging strangers for over twenty years, and it'll take more than a snotty Frenchman, some mild blackmail, and a forced outing to take that away from me. It's not as if my heart is broken, or anything foolish like that. I never had one.

Maybe that's why it was so easy for Jean-Pierre to turn on me. I had no heart to offer.

It doesn't matter, it doesn't matter, because Griff is here and huge and hard in front of me. *Focus on your surroundings*. I take a breath and sink my hands into his hair, the texture a delicious surprise. He's so grim, so tough, but his hair is so damn soft—like silk, like water, like sheer luxury. If he grew it down to his knees, I'd roll around in it like a blanket, or maybe wear it like a cloak. I tug him closer.

But this time, he doesn't come. Firm and flat, he tells me, "Stop."

I stiffen. The strangeness sings, triumphant. *See? You can't trust him. He's made you show your hand, made you want and need, made a fool of you, and you fell for it.*

It is entirely possible that I'm going to be sick.

"I'm not doing this," Griff says. "You're—"

Pathetic, spectacularly useless, worth less than a kilo of snow.

But what he says is, "You're shaking. Keynes, you're shaking." His tone isn't gentle, but his hands are. They curl around my upper arms, stroking up and down, as if to soothe me. My eyes flick open—when did I screw them shut?—and I stare at his outline in the darkness for a moment, floating between reactions, between moods, between decisions. For the space of a breath, I feel a warm sort of shock. Or maybe it's awe. Or maybe it's piss-yourself relief, or gratitude.

Then I take another breath, and I'm fucking furious.

It crackles through my veins—and if it feels a little bit like shame, if its edges burn and twist like they've touched something corrosive, well, who's to know? Who, except this dangerous man who has the audacity to notice things and say them out loud?

What is he trying to do, anyway, with all this soft *You're shaking* bullshit? Does he think I'm weak? I shove him away just to show him that I'm not.

He obviously wasn't expecting it, because he stumbles back and hits the opposite wall. My heart constricts for one ridiculous moment before he growls—literally growls, like an animal—and I realise that he isn't hurt.

"What the fuck?" he demands.

I can't answer that, so I think I should ask the questions. "What's your problem?"

His face is still in shadow but his confusion's easy to hear. "My—what—?"

"I didn't ask you to come over all touchy-feely," I snap. I sound different, colder, crisper, rather like my mother. I am about to be cruel. The burning in me has become a cold, white flame, which feels safer somehow. "Clearly you're not intelligent enough to grasp your purpose here, but I'll leave you with a tip for next time: mouth shut, cock out."

He's quiet for a moment, which I should take ruthless advantage of. Instead, for reasons I don't quite understand, I let him have his little thinking pause. And then I let him speak.

"I'm not a fucking stallion." The words are made even harsher by that voice of his, like knives glinting in the dark.

"No. You're a bull." And I'm a bastard. I'm making myself sick and I can't stop.

"Wait," Griff orders, which must mean I'm walking away. My legs simply started moving. Clever, clever legs.

I flick a look at him over my shoulder. "Goodbye."

"*Wait.*" The iron in him bends ever so slightly, his anger hidden away for a moment. "Are you—are you okay?"

As always, concern drips over me like disgusting, sickly pus. My laughter is dry and detached even as my stomach revolts. "I don't know what you think is happening here, but aside from my disappointment at your provincial behaviour, I am *absolutely* fine."

And it's true. It *is*. Because tomorrow, it will be Monday. When the sun rises, I'll head to Fernley Farm and offer my services; I'll work and sweat in a strange place and I swear, I'll be Keynes again. I will be myself. I'll slough off this fragility like a snake's skin, and beneath it all I'll be shining and deadly like I once was.

Griff doesn't reply, and when I leave, he doesn't stop me.

3

GRIFF

"You're in a shit of a mood, then."

Is that what I'm in? I haven't been able to decide, not since last night blew up in my face. I sigh. "What are you doing here, Bex?"

I'm halfway up a tree—one of my favourite places to be—checking the progress of our organic apple orchard. I don't technically have to be here, but climbing into these branches is like easing into another world, a cool, simple one where everything's alive but nothing speaks. Sort of like me. In the realm of soft pink-and-white petals, I'm not a man who spent last night tossing and turning over a stranger. I'm not a man with a little burning coal trapped beneath his breastbone that could be worry or resentment. I'm not a man who had to go home and Google the definition of 'provincial' before he could be properly pissed off, either.

I mean, for Christ's sake, did he have to insult me with Scrabble words? Couldn't he have just called me a tosser?

Beneath me, Rebecca shouts up, "I came to take pictures for the Instagram account." It sounds realistic, since she's head of marketing and a great photographer besides. But when I poke my head out of this sweet-smelling dream, into the harsh reality of morning spring sunshine, she's stood there with her hands on her hips and no smartphone or camera in sight.

My tone is sharper than it should be. "Come off it, Rebecca."

"You come off it. What are you doing, sulking up there?"

What a load of rubbish. I don't sulk; I brood. Like Batman. "Piss off," I mutter, and begin the climb down. I'm on a ladder, like a sensible and professional production manager who respects the cost of our insurance payments, but when I get home, I'll probably climb the old oak in my backyard with my bare hands. Burn off some excess energy.

"Things go south with tall, blond and handsome?"

The minute Rebecca says it, I'm back there. His breath is hot against my throat, his body's hard against mine, and he's shaking ever so slightly in my arms. That's how it happened, I swear it. But the more time passes, all I can hear is the derision in his voice, and all I can think about is the fact that I'm shit at reading people and generally arse-backward when it comes to human nature. He even told me as much—told me what everyone's always said: that I'm an idiot, I'm a freak, I can't grasp the basic threads of behaviour that everyone else is weaving with. Oh, and that I'm a walking penis. Can't forget that.

I decide, for the thousandth time since last night, that I don't care if he was upset or not. He's a prick, and if I never see him again it'll be too soon.

But why was he shaking?

I hit the ground, dust my hands off on my jeans, and shrug at Rebecca. She arches an eyebrow and gives me her familiar *Keep going* look, so I offer a grunt, too. She arches another eyebrow, which means, *Try again.*

I mutter, "Didn't work out."

"But you were getting on like a house on fire!"

Yeah. For a while, that stuck-up city boy actually made me smile, which just makes my stomach drop. Bex must see it on my face, because she scowls, suddenly in outrage mode. She's got her golden curls in pigtails today, and she looks just like she did when we were twelve years old: adorable and determined to defend me. "Griffin Everett! Did he *say* something to you?"

That's code for *"Did he point out what a weirdo you are?"* I can't answer honestly, because life isn't worth living when Rebecca Anna Baird's on the warpath. She'll storm over to Mrs. Hartley's, and it'll be pistols at dawn, so for the good of Fernley at large I say, "No."

"Griffin…"

"No, I said."

She looks at me for a long moment before approaching the ladder I just climbed down, already fishing her phone out of her pocket. But as she passes me, she catches my hand and squeezes. "Sorry, Griff. Better luck next time."

Luck isn't a thing I have. Still, I squeeze her hand back before I leave. Then I make my way out of the orchard, my mind on yield productions and preparations for the elderflower harvest. I'm so deep in thought that I make it halfway across Fernley Farm's courtyard before I realise someone is calling my name. The voice, plummy and brisk and familiar, is repeating "Griffin. *Griffin*," with weary impatience. It's Henry, my boss—or should I say, Lord Henry Breton-Fowler. I find him 20 metres to my right, standing on the long, dirt driveway behind the farm's main gate.

And then I see the man standing beside him.

It's Keynes.

If this is a hallucination brought on by my sleepless night, it's proper realistic. I can feel the warmth of the sunbeams filtering through the beech trees. I can hear wood pigeons trilling at me to calm the fuck down. Daffodils droop gently at my feet, reminding me of my mother with a migraine. The detail says reality, but I'm still clinging to my hallucination idea, because I really, really, *really* don't want Keynes to be standing next to my boss right now.

Only, I blink, and breathe, and he still is.

Shit. Fine. Okay. I walk toward the gate.

Henry is the same as ever: broad-faced, red-cheeked, and dressed in mud-stained clothes that look a thousand years old and probably cost thousands of pounds. He has the air of a man who's always pleased with himself, probably because he's always pleased with himself. He's a bit shitty—but just regular, rich-people-shitty, not kick-a-puppy shitty. I think. Honestly, I don't know him that well; he doesn't show up to work much. Even though he owns the place.

Beside him, Keynes is looking at me as if we've never met before, a slight smile tilting his full lips and polite distance in his eyes. No recognition, no regret, certainly no fucking apology. I notice that, just like I notice those eyes of his are the deep green of winter firs. I really wish they weren't. I like green things. He has a dusting of cinnamon freckles across his nose, which is a piss-take, because I like cinnamon too. The terrible lighting at the pub didn't do him justice, which is bad news for the rhythm of my heart. Thank God I don't like *him*, or I might be in trouble.

I come to a stop at the gate, leaning against it, eyeing him the way I would a shark and trying not to feel like a walking, tangled knot.

"Griffin," Henry says, "you're just the man I was hoping to see. You won't believe this, but I've bumped into an old school friend this morning!"

An old school friend, as in... Keynes? He's right; I don't believe it. Not the 'bumped into' part, anyway. No-one wanders into a tiny dot of a village on the edge of Leicestershire and stumbles across a fruit farm and discovers Henry's barely-there presence by accident. Surely this meeting was arranged. But Henry's acting like it wasn't, and he's my boss, so I just nod.

"This is Olumide Olusegun-Keynes," Henry goes on, "an old chum, a noted traveller, and a guest here at Fernley Farm."

My first though is that *Olumide* suits him better than *Keynes*, maybe because it's an actual first name that real people have instead of something out of those old *Famous Five* books. My second thought is that I can't believe I almost fucked a guy who's so posh his friends call him a *chum*. My third—what the hell is a 'noted traveller'?

I'm just rolling on to my fourth thought—how can a working farm have guests and why did no-one warn me he was coming—when a strong, brown hand is stuck out for me to shake. The same hand that ran hungrily through my hair last night. I look up and lock eyes with the man I definitely hate.

"Just Keynes," he says, "is fine." Like we haven't had this conversation before. Like we don't know each other. Then again, I suppose we don't.

His palm isn't rough, but it is tough, and his handshake is firm. I must be off my rocker because I find myself wishing he'd try to squeeze the life out of my hand, the way some men do. It would be a betrayal of emotion, or, I don't know, fucking *memory*. Right now, he's making me wonder if last night even happened, and it's starting to piss me off. That coal beneath my breastbone, the one he put there, is burning through things best left unburnt. Apparently, it's not worry or resentment: it's anger, and it's rising up my throat at a rapid clip. I clench my jaw.

"This," Henry's saying, "is Griffin Everett, our production manager. You're free to roam as you please, of course, but if you need anything, Griff's the one you should speak to. I'm not often here—"

"Oh," Keynes slides in easily, "I won't be any trouble. Really, Henry, I just came to see the harvest. And to say hello, of course. When *can* I meet your lovely wife?"

Henry points a finger at Keynes and does this weird "Ohhh-ho-ho-ho, you!" laugh, like he thinks Keynes is full of it but finds that fact adorable. Then he slaps him on the shoulder, right over the brown leather strap of the satchel Keynes is carrying, and declares, "We'll do dinner, my boy. This week. Anyway, I must be off—I told Kate I was leaving, and she gets rather anxious about me wandering home."

Kate is the aforementioned wife, 'home' is the manor looming across the fields to our right, and the ten-minute walk it takes to get there isn't anything to worry about. Still, I stay silent while Keynes makes the right 'goodbye' noises. Then Henry is gone, rambling down the drive and around a corner, and suddenly it's just… us. Me, and this man I've apparently never met. I wonder if he'll drop the act now that Henry's left.

The answer is no.

I'm still leaning heavily against the gate, clinging to this barrier between us more than I should. He ruins my try for distance by mirroring me, so we're leaning side by side but facing opposite directions. His elbow's next to mine, so we have to turn our heads to look at each other, and when we do, our faces are way too close. This is some kind of body language bullshit, right? I've heard about stuff like this. He's trying to… to mind-fuck me. Be dominant or something. His lips are curled at the edges in this teasing, taunting smile, but it doesn't tug at a secret, electric part of me the way it did last night. It feels fake. Like a mask.

Not that I care.

"So," he says, "are you going to let me in?"

His silver-spoon accent seemed interesting before he ripped into me with it. Now it just grates on me, the same way the mystery of him grates on me. No-one shows up here by accident. I remember when I asked him, in my own roundabout way, why he'd come to Fernley. And how he didn't reply.

"If you're here for Henry," I ask, ignoring his question, "why are you staying above Mrs. Hartley's place?"

He arches an eyebrow. "Know where I'm staying, do you?"

I can't tell if he's really pointing out my stalkerish knowledge, which would be fair, or if he's dodging the question. I straighten up and fold my arms. "Fernley's a small place."

"I'm aware." He sounds so calm, controlled, lazily confident.

There's a joke dancing in his green eyes but I don't know what it is. There's also an almost-hidden shadow, one I recognise, one that drags me back years.

Just like that, I find myself faltering. *Feeling.* Lowering my voice and asking, like a knob, "Listen, are you—?"

He interrupts me, his voice suddenly a whip. "Ask me if I'm okay, and I'll put you on your arse."

I grit my teeth. That's the last bloody time I let my upbringing make me soft around him. If he wants to be strangers, fine, we're strangers. That's for the best, anyway. But before I can act on that, he speaks again.

"I'm here because the elderflower harvest interests me, and I intend to take part. I keep a travel journal, and I work for Montgomery Publishing, an independent non-fiction house." So he's going to write something about the farm? I don't know, because he didn't say it straight. "I had no idea Henry owned the place. We were at school together."

It's a reasonable—reasonable for posh gits, anyway—explanation, but something about his words seems hollow or shifty or ever so slightly wrong, and I could swear he's lying to me. Instead of nodding and accepting what he says, I'm eyeing him like I can see through his skin, like he might crumble under a hard look and confess to wicked crimes.

He arches a brow and asks, "Is there something on my face?"

I should mumble an excuse and turn away, but that burning coal in my chest shoves too much honesty out of my mouth. "Don't believe you."

I'm not even sure if I mean the words—until I see his reaction. He pales beneath the golden warmth of his skin, his lush mouth presses into a line, and his fingers tighten around the satchel on his shoulder. For a moment, the forest-green of his gaze becomes an icy threat. Then, blink and he's back: pretty, careless, unconcerned. "Why, Griffin," he murmurs, his eyes heavy-lidded like some kind of sleepy cat. "I'm insulted."

37

But his voice says he doesn't give a fuck what I think because someone like me could never bother someone like him.

I don't usually read into people's voices and expressions like this; I take words at face value, as if they were written on a stone slate, and I move on. I don't know what he's doing to me, but I don't like it—so I give him the coldest look I can manage. "Let's talk ground rules."

He leans closer, smiles wider, like this is an inside joke. He smells like crisp aftershave I can't afford, spearmint gum, and rained-on grass. "Rules, Griffin? Already? Do we have to?"

His voice is rich and deep and smooth. Last night, it stroked its way down my spine like a promise, but today it does nothing for me. The way he's acting reminds me of the boys I went to school with, the handsome, clever, confident ones who people fell all over—the ones who called my mum crazy and mocked my too-small clothes. Even now, his smiling eyes are slicing my scar tissue.

Unlike him, my words fall heavy and grey out of my mouth, like pebbles dropped into a pond. "Elderflower harvest's next week, and I won't have anyone fucking it up through sheer ignorance. This is a working farm; we don't have time for laziness or ego. Keep your head out of your arse, don't get in my way, don't bother my people, and we'll be right."

For some reason, Keynes responds to that clipped speech with a grin. His teeth are bright white and perfectly even, because of course they are. "If I agree to everything you just said," he laughs, "will you open the gate and let me in?"

Now I feel like a troll on a bridge demanding payment for passage. Fuck it; why not? I'll be a troll. I bet trolls get an unfair rep, anyway. I bet they're proper decent blokes trying to make a living, but handsome, entitled princes keep turning up to cause trouble, and...

And I've been silent for too long. I grunt, and Keynes smiles harder, his eyes crinkling at the corners. "I promise," he murmurs, "I'll follow the rules. I won't mess up your schedule. I might even make myself useful while I'm here; stranger things have happened." Then he twinkles at me. I don't even know what that means, but he does it; he fucking *twinkles* at me, and something tightens in my gut.

I don't want to, but I open the gate and let him in.

He flashes a satisfied smile at no-one in particular and saunters through the entrance to my livelihood, my pleasure, my only place in the world. And I just can't help myself. I catch his upper arm, not with the gentleness I tried for last night, but with a grip that shows him I'm dead serious. He looks at me sharply, and I see he gets the message, but I make it crystal clear. Regardless of what Henry said, I repeat, "Don't get in my way."

Keynes's unconcerned air disappears with a tight nod. "That works for me."

———

Olu

My first day on Fernley farm involves charming the staff and pretending to take Very Professional Notes, trying to ignore the brooding elephant in the room. This disappearance to Fernley is supposed to take me back to who I used to be, or at least act as an easy holiday while I grapple with all my awful new sensitivities. Instead I've managed to stumble across Henry Breton-Fowler, of all people—Christ, I hated him at school, and who knew his family owned a bloody cordial brand? As if I needed any more evidence that God isn't on my side. But even worse, there's this… this *awkwardness* with Griff. The bloody production manager, because of course he is. How very Olu of me to sour my working retreat before it even began.

At the end of the day, I wander along a near-deserted street washed in dying sunlight, the pavement dappled by shadows from the tall, blossoming trees that take up every spare inch of this village. The trill of my phone rises above the languid tweets of the birds. My sister is calling me, her timing predictably impeccable. When she was young, I used to tease her about having a sixth sense. These days, that same sixth sense is why I've been avoiding her more and more: time passes, my problems don't, everything feels suffocatingly worse, and Lizzie watches me a touch too closely.

But I can't truly ignore her, not for long, so I pick up the phone.

"Olu!" My sister's voice in my ear is a soothing balm. My nerves are frazzled from studiously avoiding a certain human mountain all day long—but I refuse to think about him. When I do, a disgusting urge to apologise rears its ugly head.

"Hello, my lovely Lizzie. How are you?"

"I'm very well, thank you. And you?"

"Never mind me," I say pleasantly, and it's not just avoidance. "We're talking about you. How goes the little mushroom?"

"The *foetus*," she says, "is doing very well."

"And how goes my little sister? Please, don't spare a detail."

"Olu," she sighs, but then she humours me and launches into a medical update that I mostly memorise. My recall is the only thing that got me through law school. I'll write it all down in my pregnancy journal later, and yes, I have a pregnancy journal, and no, I don't think I'm overdoing it. My sister is diabetic. I am keeping an eye on this. She has eyes of her own, and a paranoid brute of a husband who loves her to distraction, and an excellent midwife, but I'm keeping an eye on this.

Of course, right now, I'm doing so from a distance. Because I have abandoned her, running from my problems and leaving her behind, just as I've done so many times in the past. Add it to my list of sins.

A grey squirrel scurries down the trunk of a nearby oak, and I freeze, a reluctant smile curving my lips. I got one thing right, coming to Fernley: it is hard to remain miserable in this tooth-achingly wholesome environment.

"So, now that I've reported the colour of my snot," Lizzie says, irritated, "perhaps we might talk about you."

"So dramatic," I murmur, walking again when the squirrel disappears into the woods. My lodgings above Mrs. Hartley's garage are about ten minutes away by foot, much like everything in this village, and I'm almost halfway there. "I'm fine, sister dearest, as always."

"Hm." She is openly sceptical. Since I am her elder by quite a few years, and since I practically raised her—our parents certainly couldn't be trusted to do it—I shouldn't feel half as guilty as I do. Pseudo-parents hide things from their pseudo-children for the child's own good. Lizzie will learn this when she pops out her little miracle in five months' time.

"*Hm*, what?" I demand, in my most severe tones, which are severe indeed.

She doesn't sound remotely intimidated. "Just *Hm*. Where are you?"

"Away."

"Isaac misses you."

In the background, I hear a familiar rough and rumbling voice. "Do I fuck," says my sister's husband, but there's humour in his tone.

"I know he struggles to get on without me," I smile, "but he'll have to manage."

Isaac's voice again. "Tell him to come back to work."

"Isaac," Lizzie warns. "Olu doesn't work for you anymore."

But, as openings go, this one's too neat to pass up. "Actually," I interject, "I may have told someone today that I do."

I can practically hear my sister's silent surprise. When I found myself suddenly searching for a real job last year, my darling brother-in-law swept in and claimed he needed help with his new publishing company. I became a mostly useless in-house business and legal consultant. Though I tried my best to be worth it, the nepotism of it all pricked at my pride, so I quit. But when I bumped into Henry this morning…

"I found myself face to face with an old school friend," I explain, aiming for an airy laugh and missing by about five hundred miles. "He asked what I was doing here—"

"Where is here?"

"Oh, really, darling, it's nowhere. Some twee little countryside village. I wanted to…" When I say it out loud, it sounds ridiculous, which is why I couldn't say it to Henry. "I wanted to join in with an elderflower harvest, if you can believe."

There's a short pause before Lizzie says, "You're very odd sometimes, Olu. It's my favourite thing about you."

"I thought your favourite thing about me was my ability to mysteriously solve any and all problems," I say. It's a joke, of course. So why does my sister respond seriously, and why am I grateful?

"No," she says. "No. You can be undeniably useful, but I don't need to use you. I just love you." She stumbles over the last word, not because she doesn't feel it, but because we are who we are. When we were children, Lizzie and I, we didn't hear that word much.

And yet, I force my leaden tongue to say it back, since it's true. "I love you, too."

"So," she says brightly, moving on from the prickling discomfort that always comes with discussing feelings. I appreciate it. "You've gone to God knows where to pick elderflower and somehow bumped into an old friend. Continue."

"Well, it turns out he owns the farm that owns the elderflower. He asked what I was doing here, and I happened to have my journal, so I told him I was interested in the local history—"

"What's the local history?"

"Damned if I know. Anyway, I gave him my card so I'd seem a bit more authoritative and less like an unemployed wanderer who forces his presence on innocent fruit farmers. Only, the card's outdated, so… He decided that I'm a writer. Tell Isaac, if anyone asks him about my impending travel memoirs, to nod enigmatically."

Lizzie snorts. "I'm sure that can be arranged. And, really, Keynes, you *are* a writer."

"We'll agree to disagree."

"You're a pain, sometimes, brother-mine."

"As you never fail to remind me."

She laughs, but then her voice softens. "So… You're travelling again."

"Not really, darling." I keep my tone light. "Maybe I actually will take notes and give Isaac something to publish."

"Maybe you should. Your travel diaries have always been good." She actually sounds serious, which is disconcerting. My journals are just a thing I do, and she's the only one who reads them. No-one else is interested in pages of me swinging between acerbic sarcasm about the nature of man and genuine awe at the majesty of—*gag*—mother earth.

I turn a particular corner and amble into the garden of a pretty little three-storey house painted white. "Maybe," I say, all non-committal, which is code for *I would rather die than show my inner thoughts to the world.*

Lizzie knows the code because she used to use it too, before she fell in love with a poet and learned the power of emotion or some such rubbish. "Maybe," she echoes soothingly, promising it doesn't matter, that I don't have to. "Well, I have to go—I'm still holding evening pointe classes—but stay in touch."

"I'll call you tomorrow." It'll be no hardship. Lizzie's much easier to fool over the phone. "And remember, if you need anything, *anything* at all—"

"Yes, I will call you immediately. I know the rules. Goodbye," she says, and I slide my phone into my pocket as I approach the flat above Mrs. Hartley's garage. Before I can jog up the side stairs, though, I spy Mrs. Hartley herself, emptying something into a wheelie bin. And she spies me.

"Keynes," she says brightly. She's an achingly warm sort of woman, the kind I've never quite understood but always enjoyed. Over the past couple of days, I've heard her calling to her children, through the windows. Heard them calling back. They're wonderfully naughty, and they absolutely adore her.

I see why. With the fine lines on her fair skin, the silver in her hair, the comfort in her eyes, she must be about my age—but when I was a child, I dreamed of a mother just like her, one who would hug me and ask me questions and tell me I was clever or kind. Instead of the mother I got, the one who made me in her frostbitten image.

"I can't bear the child's snivelling. Take him away."

"Mrs. Hartley," I nod, offering my best smile in return for her genuine one. It's the least I can do.

"Call me Maria," she says, with the sort of instant intimacy that has nothing to do with charm and everything to do with easy self-possession. "We haven't had much of a chance to chat, since you arrived. How are you settling in?"

What she's saying is technically true, but then, I didn't think we needed to chat. Arrangements were made over the phone; I swapped money for keys; *fin.* "Very well, thank you," I say, feeling uncomfortable. Her eyes are a mellow, summer-sky sort of blue, but they suddenly seem very piercing. Like twin microscopes studying me in fine detail.

She comes toward me, smoothing down the skirt of her long, floral dress, and I have the oddest feeling that she's approaching me with the same caution she might a wounded animal. "I'm glad to hear it. I thought I'd mention—if you would ever like to nip down for a cup of tea, you need only to ask."

Oh, Christ. Understanding topples over me like a pile of bricks: she is one of those tender-hearted and selfless individuals who excel at identifying damaged souls. She has honed in on me and will not rest until she nurses me back to health. I barely resist the urge to roll my eyes. "I don't think that will be necessary."

"Tea is never necessary," she says, apparently undaunted, "but it's always a pleasure."

How much ruder, exactly, do I need to be? "I don't believe I'll have much time for social calls, while I'm here."

She cocks her head, and I see a flash of unexpected steel in her gaze. "Really? Because I noticed that you stayed in all weekend, lurking at the windows and doing an excellent impression of a lost and lonely man."

I'm so shocked that I forget to control my laughter. It spills out, refreshing as rainfall after a drought. She smiles, a little relieved and clearly smug. And, just like that, I like her. Hm. That's another thing that hasn't happened in a while, liking new people. Maybe I *shouldn't* avoid her. Maybe I *should* go down for tea.

I find myself asking, "What do you do?"

She blinks, as if surprised. "I'm a school teacher. Why?"

"Because I would've guessed as much."

"Ha! And you?"

"I'm a profligate rake. It's considered an outdated profession, but I'm rather good at it."

She blinks at me seriously, and for a moment I think that's all I'll get from her. But then laughter bursts from her closed mouth, as if she were trying awfully not to set it free but couldn't help herself. "Oh, God," she wheezes. "Really, I'm always in. Knock on the door any time."

Perhaps I shall.

4

GRIFF

By Keynes's third day on the farm, I can't decide what's worse; the way his presence fucks up my routine, or the way memories of him fuck up my thoughts. Whichever way you slice it, here are the facts: my work is the one place in this village where I'm actually respected, where I feel sort of free, but I'm stuck in my office like a rat in trap, doing whatever it takes to confuse my Keynes-addled mind into letting this obsession go. And when I say *whatever it takes,* I mean I'm checking spreadsheets. My eyes are blurry, my mind is numbed, my skin is itching for the fresh, warm air of the outdoors, and guess what? I'm still fucking thinking about him.

God only knows why. I don't even want to see him—but for all of yesterday and most of this morning, he was everywhere I turned. Bright and constant, flashing at me from the corner of my eye the way sunlight creeps into dark rooms when you're fighting a headache. I need mental black-out blinds strong enough to block Keynes, and the spreadsheet isn't cutting it. Neither is Rebecca's needling, which is how I know I'm seriously fucked.

Her teasing words are muted in the cool, empty office. "Are you gonna tell me why you're all mean-looking today? Or should... I... *guess?*" Rebecca has this thing about dramatic emphasis. She watches too many musicals.

I grunt.

"Guessing it is," she sing-songs. "I suggest your terrible mood has something to do with one Mr. Olusegun-Keynes. Am I wrong?"

Another grunt. It's afternoon, and we're alone. She's sat on the edge of my desk, pulling a loose thread in her cardi and being optimistic. Those are bad habits of hers. My bad habit is being a prick, and I'm doing it right now.

She sighs. "Come on, Griff. What did he *do?*"

Barely anything, really. That's what gets me the most: all he did was chuck a few sneering words my way, and I'm tied up in knots over it. I flick a dead-eyed look at her and say, "He's trouble." And a half.

"*He's trouble,*" Rebecca mocks, lowering her voice to imitate mine. "You sound like my dad." She can't say I sound like *my* dad, because I don't have one. And she can't say I sound like my mum, either, because Mum never said things like that. She had this whole bit about not judging people since she couldn't really know their hearts. Pity no-one ever gave her the same courtesy.

Bex is trying to cheer me up, but my gearstick's stuck on 'miserable', so it's not fucking working. In fact, she's just getting on my nerves, which almost never happens. I set my jaw and come up with a massive understatement: "He just rubs me up the wrong way."

She smiles. "But that's the mystery I'm trying to solve—I thought he wanted to rub you up the *right* way."

My glare could flatten cities, but it won't cow my best friend. Still, a man's got to try. "Don't you think it's weird that he's shown up out of nowhere, he's mates with Henry, but it was all some big accident? A coincidence?" I stab savagely at my

47

keyboard and the spreadsheet freaks out, colours changing and formulas fucking up. I've messed with something and now I'll have to fix it—unlikely—or email accounting for help. Because I'm actually too thick to understand shit like this, and I should stick to climbing trees and playing with dirt.

No, Griffin, I tell myself sharply. You have to be sharp, with thoughts like that, or they'll eat you alive. I've had them under control for a long time now—but *someone* set them free with a few razor-sharp words on Sunday night.

I scowl and continue my conspiracy theory out loud. "I don't think it's a coincidence at all. I think he came here on purpose, but him and Henry are hiding why. Like, maybe he's a… a consultant, and he's monitoring us all to see if we're shit at our jobs. Or maybe Henry's not in on it and Keynes is here to… to… doublecross him. It's some kind of rich people drama. Yeah." I nod, certain that one way or another, the man is here for evil reasons.

Then I look up to find Rebecca staring at me like I've grown a second head. "That was a lot of words for someone you keep telling me doesn't matter."

"He doesn't, so leave it."

"Also, have you been watching your Mum's old *Dynasty* tapes? Because, Jesus Christ, that was dramatic."

I don't know why, but *Dynasty's* the hit that makes me crumble. "He called me stupid, okay? That's it. I'm just pissed." I shouldn't be, though. I should be stone, oak, immovable earth. Earth doesn't care who thinks it's stupid. Why can't I be fucking earth?

"Ah, Griff." Rebecca abandons the thread in her cardigan and crawls across the desk, because she's small enough to do things like that. Rising on her knees, she puts her hands on my shoulders and says, "Smack him into the ground, babe."

Laughter is the last thing I expect, but here it is, bubbling up from my belly. She's magic. Of course, brilliant moments never last. This one is over before it really begins.

Someone clears their throat, and I shouldn't be able to identify a near-stranger by a low, rasping sound like that—but somehow, I do. It's crisp, purposeful, pointed. It's the subtle, slow and unconcerned *I'm here* signal of a bloke who probably thinks he owns the world. It's Keynes.

I jump, and Rebecca jerks away from me. He lounges in the doorway watching us lazily, like a lion stretched out in the sun. My face heats because Christ—what did he overhear? Like a pillar of salt, I'm utterly still while Rebecca slides off the desk. Keynes's steady gaze meets mine, but I can't read him for fuck. That shouldn't feel unusual—I can't read anyone, and they certainly can't read me. But with him, it's weird.

Maybe because I read him before. I remember his hands shaking, his chest shuddering, as he tried to convince me to devour him. I wasn't wrong. I know I wasn't wrong. And that sudden, absolute certainty cools the burning coal beneath my breastbone, just a little bit.

"I needed you—" he begins, then cuts himself off sharply. I know, the same way I know he was shaking, that he hates what he just said. After a neat little pause, he starts over. "I have a question, and apparently, you're the one to ask. About the elderflower harvest next week."

For once, I don't think before I speak. "Researching for your book, are you?"

"I'm sorry?"

Maybe I'm being ridiculous, but his surprise buoys my conspiracy theory, and I like my conspiracy theory. It gives me a reason to be wary of him beyond hurt pride. "I thought you were here to write a book."

"I never said that." The words are clipped, flat, final: a roundabout way of telling me to shut up. Now, shutting up is usually my favourite thing, but I prefer it to be a choice.

"Is a lie a thing we say," I ask, "or a thing we let people believe?"

Keynes stares at me for a moment, breathing slow but deep, as if to calm himself down. All I can hear are those steady inhale-exhales and the near-silent patter of light rain against the windows. Rebecca's blinking at me like *What the fuck are you doing?* Starting a fight, it looks like. My mum wouldn't approve, but she's not here, and I'm on the edge today. I think Keynes shoved me without even knowing.

I clearly can't shove him, though, because in the end, he doesn't snap back. Instead, he speaks to me with painful control. It's like he has a fist wrapped around his own throat. It's like he's so worried about his words running wild that he only lets them leak out inch by inch: "I'm sorry."

Once it's said, he looks as surprised as I feel. Judging by his expression, that flicker of slack-jawed astonishment I see before his mask returns, he didn't plan on saying that. I didn't plan on hearing it. Rebecca's gawking at us with zero shame, like we're one of her favourite films. An odd sort of silence settles like dust

Then Keynes disrupts it with a harried urgency that might, on a different man, be called babbling. "I apologise if I reacted poorly on Sunday night. That was... a private issue. You weren't at fault, and I shouldn't have made you feel as if you were. And I certainly didn't mean—or I should never have inferred—that you were stupid."

Well, fuck. There's my answer about how much he heard. A warm weirdness blossoms inside my chest, and it should be embarrassment, but it's not. It's really not.

Keynes isn't lounging against the door anymore. His spine is ramrod straight, his head is high, and his jaw is set, as if he's daring me to make something of this. His eyes burn into me with unbelievable focus, but I doubt it's because he finds me bloody hypnotic. No; I think he's trying to pretend Rebecca isn't here. I think he's awkward and mortified and worried about how much I told her. Silently, I try to let him know that I didn't share anything he might call... private.

But, before I can crack the mystery of telepathy, I hear the heave of the building's door and a shout. "Griff! *Griff!*" Booted footsteps, and then—"Oh, hello, Mr Keynes."

Vulnerability vanishes like it never existed. That gorgeous, golden head turns slowly to face someone in the corridor. He drawls, "Peter, please, we've talked about this. Just Keynes. I'm begging you."

I have a sinking feeling that, while I've been brooding and storming around the farm these past few days, Keynes has been flitting like a butterfly, charming the pants off of people who barely tolerate me. People like Pete Manning, who looked right through me until I was made production manager, whose little brother called me Frankenbastard at school. My teeth are on edge again, but this time I don't know who I'm irritated with.

"Keynes, then!" Pete says, sounding friendlier than I thought he was capable of. "I'm in a bit of a tizzy. You wouldn't believe what's happened. Here, I don't suppose Griff is in there?"

"He is," Keynes murmurs, and makes no move whatsoever to leave the doorway. "Are you quite alright, Peter? You're looking rather flushed."

Instead of issuing a brisk order to move, which would be his usual style, Pete all but giggles and says, "Well, that don't surprise me one bit. It's bedlam out there, it is!" If I didn't know better, the tone of my gruff, *married* harvester's voice might convince me he was flirting.

Rebecca shoots me a disbelieving look, like she thinks the same. I pinch the bridge of my nose and wonder if Henry's mysterious 'school chum' is the honest-to-God, actual devil. Charm and temptation in the flesh.

Except… I don't think the devil says sorry and means it.

I shake my head sharply to dislodge bullshit thoughts and call, "Pete. Problem?"

"Oh, ah!" He's remembered himself. His ginger head pops through the doorway, squeezing past Keynes's breadth. "Woodward's sheep are out again, whole flock, and they're at the west elderflower something awful."

"For fuck's sake," Rebecca mutters, which about sums up my reaction.

Shit, shit, shit.

Olu

Sheep, it seems, are a great enemy at Fernley Farm and not to be trifled with. Griffin practically tramples me on his way out the door, and the little woman, Rebecca, rushes after him with just as much urgency. Obviously, I follow them both.

We hurry across the courtyard, race through a small copse, and hear distant shouts growing louder over the patter of rain. A bramble scratches my right forearm, and it feels like the sting of coming across Griff and Rebecca. But I won't think about that—I don't want to think about that. I met Rebecca yesterday, though I recognised her from the pub, and she reminds me of my sister. Maybe that's why I'm fixated on the fact that she's Griffin's best friend. Knowing that Griff can be so close to someone, while I'm forced to keep everyone—keep *Lizzie*—at a distance so they can't see me falling apart... it burns. And the fact that Griff discussed me with Rebecca burns even more, in a different way. A way I'm in no mood to examine.

So I keep my eyes straight ahead and examine Griffin instead.

His size should make him slow, but, since he's fundamentally irritating, it doesn't. He sprints ahead of us like some kind of athlete. I watch the muscles in his back bunch through his T-shirt as the fabric grows steadily wetter and more transparent, this slight April shower having a catastrophic effect. Everything about him is so... big. Thick. Excessive. He is height and muscle layered with soft, simple *weight*, and looking at him makes me want to sink my teeth into something. Which is, of course, a disgraceful response; I should have enough dignity not to salivate over my enemies.

Then again, I haven't salivated over *anyone* for countless panicked months, so maybe I should let myself enjoy the sensation. Plus, it may be overzealous to think of Griff as my enemy—even if I've been doing so for the last three days. What can I say? I have a tendency toward melodrama when I'm stressed, and Griffin Everett causes me… considerable strain.

Apparently, I did the same for him. Shame is not an emotion I'm familiar with, but when I heard him talking about me the way I might talk about my father—well. An apology sort of threw itself from my mouth. Must be the fresh country air, softening me up.

Griff disappears from my line of sight, pushing through the trees. Next goes Rebecca, then Pete. I follow, bursting through crowded branches to break out of the copse, and find myself in a field of chaos.

This, I suppose, is an elderflower plantation. It's naturally fenced in on one side by giant, ancient oaks that disrupt the pale sunlight, casting an ethereal gloom over the very edges of the verdant space. The crops themselves are rows of sprawling bushes dotted by tiny, bright white flowers, and right now a few too many of those flowers are falling victim to slow sheep jaws.

Sheep, sheep, everywhere. And—is that a goat?

Sheep, as a species, have a fundamental flaw: I hate them. They lack charm, and they do not respond to charm. They are difficult to move and impossible to command. Currently, about two dozen of them wander around looking woolly and dirty, with their demonic eyes and their munching mouths. I spot Holly from HR trying to herd one elsewhere, her kitten heels digging into the grass. I suppose she wasn't expecting to leave her desk today, but apparently, all hands are on deck.

"Keynes," she calls, catching sight of me. "You're a big, strong man. Come and help me with this bloody sheep."

At the sound of my name, several other employees look up and smile at me, waving and shouting greetings. I spot Matt the accountant and Emily from admin and Mary-Margaret—yes, that is her name—who's always in the orchards. There's a strangled sound of disbelief from my left, and I turn to find Griffin staring at me as if he seriously suspects I'm the anti-Christ.

"What," he asks faintly, "have you done to my staff?"

I smirk. "I simply introduced myself. I can't help it if people like me."

He appears genuinely baffled, as if he's wondering how that could possibly be true. As if I'm so *unlikeable* it does not compute. I set my jaw and turn away. Clearly, he has atrocious taste in humans. Although, his taste didn't seem so atrocious when he was trying to taste *me*.

But I fucked that up, didn't I? And for the first time in a long time, knowing I'm a mess doesn't make me angry. It just makes me sad.

For Christ's sake, Olu, now isn't the time for emotional exploration. I have sheep to deal with. *Shudder.*

Griffin's already off, striding over to an anxious-looking, farmer-type man, snapping at him to "Control your bastard sheep, Woodward!" I watch him for a moment—all that massive, commanding bulk, the fearsome scowl, the rough, expressive hands that flex and tense at his sides.

Then I do as Holly asked and help with the damned sheep.

It's not easy work. The sheep man, it seems, has lost his sheep dog, and also the ability to maintain his fences, so all his stock ambled over here. He's rather useless at herding them back. This must have happened before, because Griff's outrage is resigned rather than astonished, and he goes about collecting stray animals with the air of a man who's done this one too many times. Unlike the rest of us mere mortals, he doesn't resort to coaxing, chasing, or even pushing. He picks the bleating balls of wool clean off the ground, and carries them a good hundred metres to a fence beyond the trees. Then he dumps his sheep, jogs back, and does it all again.

Before long, the sheep get wise and run faster when he comes near.

The air grows thick and heavy as we work, but I barely notice because the sun is still bright and the temperature is mild. So when the spattering of rain abruptly becomes an outright downpour, I'm shocked and disgusted by nature's mercuriality.

Peter tromps past me, grinning wide, his red hair plastered to his face. "April showers!" he shouts.

Thank you, Peter, I've heard of the term. I just don't bloody like them. But I keep going anyway. When I find myself next to Holly again, she gives me an assessing look and says, "I bet *you* could pick up a sheep." Like Griffin, she means.

My snort is loud and indignant enough to be heard over the rain. "Holly, darling, you don't understand. Sheep and I barely associate. We are not on speaking terms. This entire situation is pushing me over the edge as it is."

But she makes a valid point; I could probably pick up a sheep. I really don't want to, but I *could*. I've certainly been watching Griff closely enough to grasp the, er, mechanics, and my urge to help people with their problems has certainly been awoken by the chaos around me. Alright then; while Holly laughs at my look of disgust, I sneak up on a thoroughly distracted sheep and grasp its odd, sturdy-soft body. Like Griff does, I make sure to secure the head quickly—and as soon as I do, the creature's squirming lessens. But it's still heavy as fuck and bleating in my ear.

I'd drop this thing like a hot potato if I weren't concerned that would damage the creature… and if its presence in my arms weren't making Griffin Everett stop and stare at me. There's something rather satisfying about the slack-jawed expression on his face as he stands there, frantic staff and naughty sheep milling around him. He is a veritable column of surprise, and I do like surprising people—which must be why warmth floods my chest, easing the strain of the bloody sheep cradled in my arms. It's only when the ache in my biceps gets really intense that I realise I've been standing here like a sheep-toting lemon, staring at Griff while he stares at me, for far too long.

Breaking the connection feels like the icy shock of being slapped by rain. Ignoring that strange sensation, and my even stranger thoughts, I drag my burden over to the appropriate fence and dump it awkwardly in its own territory. My lower back has served me well for thirty-eight years, so I feel incredibly guilty when it twinges as I drop off the sheep. Why am I subjecting my poor body to this abuse? Oh, yes—because "hard work cures all ills," and I'm drowning in ills.

Interestingly enough, I do feel much better now that I've carried a farm animal. Sort of... real, earthy, human. Simple. Perhaps I'll snatch another. Griffin certainly isn't slacking. I can see him now, a few metres away; his shirt is so thoroughly soaked, it's like transparent tissue painted to his skin, displaying the flex of his muscles as he bends to grab a roaming fluff ball. He thinks he's got the creature, but at the last minute it rushes out of his grip and comes barrelling toward... me.

I really do hate sheep.

Griff stands, his gaze following the animal's path straight to me. His wet hair is shoved out of his face, and when I squint through the blur of rain, he looks something other than ugly. Maybe *rugged* is the word. As if he was raised by wolves on a mountain somewhere, and he kills his prey with his bare hands.

I choke off that line of thought and step back, neatly out of the sheep's way. Then I see Griff's eyes widen. Register my calves bumping into something hard. Lose my balance. Trip and fall.

Oh, for fuck's sake.

———

GRIFF

56

Even if Keynes hadn't apologised earlier—even if the sight of him still caused a burn of shame-edged anger in my chest—I don't think I'd enjoy watching him trip over one sheep while dodging another. It *is* kind of slapstick, but he hits the ground way too fucking hard.

On the slippery grass, with this low visibility and sheep running everywhere, he never stood a chance. The one lurking behind him reaches the back of his knees, so when he goes over, he lands badly. This green space vibrates with sheets of rain, but even so, I think I *hear* his fall. I'm sprinting for him before I realise I've moved, because I'm the resident first aider, and because, knowing my luck, he'll have snapped his fucking collar-bone or something, and...

And I'm not sure what else.

He's already sitting up by the time I crouch beside him, but I know he's hurt real bad. I didn't notice, before, how fluidly he moves—only how clumsy it made me feel in comparison. But now that smoothness is gone, and it's jarring to see him slouch like a normal person. There's mud smeared on his face and up his side, grass stains on the clothes he wears so well, and a wince freezing his handsome features. He raises a hand to touch his own ribs, then stops, flinching.

I don't know if he can move his arm. Automatically, I grab his elbow for support. "Pain?"

"Ribs, nothing major." His answer is clear and no-nonsense, even though his voice is tight. I hesitate for a minute because he's taking this seriously without a second thought. I suppose I expected angry, macho defiance, a rejection of my help and a denial of any injuries.

I move my hand to check his ribs, but at the first brush of contact he jerks away, his brown skin paling. "Don't."

I press my mouth into a disapproving line. "Let me have a look."

"No."

"Keynes—"

"I think it's just bruising," he says, dragging himself painfully to his feet. I can barely hear his words over the rain, they squeeze out so quietly. "I'll make sure later. If I'm wrong, and I've punctured a lung, I promise to call 999."

Now I'm pissed again, because who the fuck jokes about puncturing a lung? "I know you think you're the smartest man on the planet, but unless you're a bloody doctor, you need to respect my authority here."

He barks out a laugh, then screws up his face and releases a ragged groan of pain. My hands are humming with the need to reach for him. You know, to make sure he's okay. "Hate to piss all over your *authority*," he says with a weak, wicked smile, "but I fucked a doctor on and off through med school. I do believe that gives me the edge over first aid training—unless you're a nurse as well as a farmer?"

He's doing it again; shoving me, without hands this time. He wants me to tut and glare and turn away in disgust. Instead, I snap, "Do you think knowledge travels from body to body through come?"

Now *he* looks scandalised, which is sweeter than it should be. I've wiped the tiny, smug smile right off his face. He takes a breath, winces, and cuts it short. Croaks out a sharp, "Shut up."

I think I want to grin.

"Keynes! I saw you go over, my love. Are you alright?" Holly from HR has hurried over and a crowd of concerned staff members are bringing up the rear. That snuffs out the light in me, replacing it with a jealousy that swallows everything else. I watch, grim and speechless again, while everyone who knows and avoids me drowns Keynes in worry and affection. At times like this, the truth about me is as unavoidable as rain in England: I'm so difficult to care for that the people I've lived with all my life still hold me at a distance, but they fall all over this outsider with ease. Twenty-eight years versus, what, three fucking days? The numbers speak for themselves and they're damning.

I sigh and raise my voice over their questions. "Keynes, come with me. The rest of you, finish up here."

They nod solemnly because I'm the production manager. But they smile and wish Keynes well as I lead him away, because he's more than that.

5

GRIFF

Walking back with Keynes is proper slow, since he's wincing, and he won't lean on me. Rain is dripping from the tips of our eyelashes, and my patience is dissolving in the downpour like sugar. He's stubborn as the fucking sheep and twice as annoying.

He also looks damn good wet, though I wish I didn't notice. His hair seems darker, his shirt is see-through, his skin glistens in a way that makes me want to run my tongue over my teeth. I do, behind the safety of my closed mouth, and my thoughts spiral into patterns so fast and wild, I can barely see them anymore.

Giving orders is my only social strength—but by the time we reach the staff kitchen, I forget I'm even capable of that. I'm too busy worrying. Worrying about him, worrying about the farm's insurance if he tempts fate and really does puncture a lung, worrying about whether or not he'll let me touch him to check the injury, worrying about why I'm worrying so much. Thinking so much. Staring at him. I'm staring at him. I drag my eyes away and find the first aid kit in a cupboard.

The staff kitchen is spacious, dotted with a few rickety sets of tables and chairs. The counters and cupboards are made of stained, old wood, and chipped mugs dry on the rack by the sink. The room smells like bleach and burnt toast. I turn toward Keynes with my first aid kit menacingly in hand and falter when I find him watching me with way too much focus. Laser focus, genius-scientist-in-the-lab focus, the kind I never draw. Something strange buzzes over my skin like an electrical charge.

Then the kettle hums behind him, distracting me. He must've turned it on while I searched for the kit. The two of us are dripping rainwater onto the lino, and his lips are curved into that unkillable smile, the one that makes me uncomfortable because I don't know why I want to smile back.

"What?" I bark. I may be quiet, but that doesn't make me subtle.

He just arches a brow and murmurs, "You think rather ferociously."

I don't even know what that means. "Are you calling me thick again?"

"As if I'd waste my gracious apology so soon. It almost killed me." He straightens as the kettle sings. Grabs two floral mugs with his left arm, still keeping the right tucked close to his side.

"Stop," I say. "Let me have a look at you."

"Be a darling and fetch the milk."

I sigh and fetch the milk. God only knows why. I think he's hypnotised me.

We take our tea the same: splash of milk, no sugar. Don't know why I assumed all posh people took it different; Henry certainly does. But Keynes and I have near-identical cups, and we stand face to face as we sip from them. He's leaning against the kitchen counter, I'm blocking him in like a brick wall. The night we met slams violently against the closed door of my memories.

Close; we're too close. I should put down my tea and do my job, be brisk and managerial, make sure this strange, undefined guest hasn't been seriously injured on our land. I know that. But I don't do it.

My eyes stay locked on him, and my body stays locked in place. He's studying me with subtle warmth in his expression, welcoming creases bracketing his eyes, the rim of his mug pushed against his full lips. *Pressure.* The word whispers through me, spiralling from the centre of my chest, winding tendrils around my limbs. That mug must be hot against his tender mouth.

He notices me noticing, and his green gaze turns hooded.

My stomach turns to lead in response. "Let's get you out of that shirt," I mutter, looking away.

"Short and to the point. I approve. But it's not the most compelling offer I've ever received." His voice is so soft it merges with the tea's steam.

It's easy for me to ignore his innuendo. I just remind myself that some people flirt like it's a hobby or a hilarious joke—usually people who look good and charm easy and don't take guys like me seriously.

"Will you do it or not?" I demand.

"Not," Keynes says delightedly, like this is a kid's game, and smiles. It's so rare for him to smile at me, and he looks so beautiful, that I almost forget to be stern. Truthfully, I almost forget my fucking *name.*

But then I remind myself that I'm the responsible first aider here. Supposedly. "If you take that shirt off without my help, it'll hurt."

"I predict taking a shit will hurt for the next week or so, too, but I'll still be visiting the bathroom," he replies.

I just stare at him. My silence is monumental, which doesn't always come in handy, but I think it might right now. Rain bounces off the roof. The world is cool and shadowed, and Keynes is slowly relenting. I see it in the downward sweep of his lashes and the sharp, annoyed line of his jaw. He puts his mug by the sink with a clatter and faces the window, his back to me.

After a moment, he says tersely, "Fine."

Then he starts unbuttoning his shirt.

This really shouldn't feel like a strip tease, not when it's for first aid purposes. But I suppose my dick doesn't know that. It sees a masterpiece of a man undressing with subtle, deliberate movements, fixates on the shift of his shirt as each button is released, wonders what that sunshine skin looks like below the neck, and springs to life. My blood is hot, too hot, for one electric second. Then I force myself under control, because he needs my help, not my inappropriate attraction.

I hesitate, then reach out and ease Keynes's shirt sleeve down his right arm. My breathing is steady, and my heart's barely pounding at all. This is fine. He's wearing a vest beneath the shirt, and I focus on helping him drag it over his head, rather than the rasp of his exhales and the unsteady movement of his hands. He seems nervous. I have no idea why, or if I'm even reading him right, but it reminds me of the way he froze up on Sunday night, and I feel like a sick fuck for enjoying this. That kills off the last of my desire like nothing else.

But, if it hadn't, the sight of his ribs would've done the job too. "Why didn't you say something?" I scowl, my fingers hovering over his skin. I can't bring myself to touch. His right side is a mess of abrasions and a few mottled bruises. "*Nothing major,* you said. Doesn't this hurt like a motherfucker?"

"Yes, it does. But I'm not dying." His nervousness has faded, replaced by a wry smile. I think he'd laugh at me if it wouldn't hurt his ribs.

"Alright, tough guy. Move. I mean, excuse me."

He snorts, winces, steps aside.

I wash my hands in the sink and say, "Sit down."

"I don't think that's a good idea."

"Oh, it's not. We need to see how *bad* an idea it is, so's I can decide what to do."

He tuts and goes to sit. His breath hisses through his teeth on the way down, but he doesn't clutch himself or even whine about it, so I suppose he'll live. I grab the first aid kit and some painkillers, chucking the little box of pills onto the table. While Keynes pops the blister packs, my knees hit the lino beside his chair. We begin.

Antiseptic wipes, an icy sting that makes him stiffen; my clumsy hands, trying so hard to be gentle, and he doesn't complain. I expected him to complain. Or call me stupid, or flirt to make me sweat, then laugh when I drop things. Instead, he's a silent statue while I clean and bandage his grazes.

I ask him all the important questions. "Do you feel nauseous?"

"Only when exposed to poor hygiene or mayonnaise."

My jaw flexes. "Do you have any shooting pains in your stomach or shoulder?"

"Yes."

I look up sharply. "What?"

"My stomach. I haven't eaten since breakfast, and I could murder a baked potato."

For fuck's sake. I scowl and continue. "Do you feel any—?"

"Oh, don't waste your time. I raised a ballerina," he cuts in. "I know all about falls and bruises and potential complications. I am fine."

I rock back on my heels and blink up at him. With his effortlessly upright spine, despite his bandaged side, he looks a little bit royal. "You got a kid?" It occurs to me that I have no idea how old he is. Put a gun to my head, and I couldn't guess.

"My sister."

So he raised his sister. That's common enough round here, but not from people who speak like Keynes. It makes more sense than him having a child, though. He doesn't seem the family type; he seems the type who's left a string of broken hearts behind him during however many years he's been alive. The fact that I still can't guess those years is starting to bother me. There's fine lines around his eyes and bracketing his mouth, but since smiles are the main weapon in his charm offensive, he's probably had those since he was nine. There's a permanent freshness about him, but there's something heavy, too.

He says, "Why are you so quiet?" just as I blurt, "How old are you?" Then we both look at each other.

He speaks first, no surprise. "I'm thirty-eight, and you're very rude."

"I was curious. And I'm not being quiet. I just make sure of what I say, which is better than running your mouth all the time."

"You look very severe," he murmurs. "Are you trying to hint?" *Don't smile at me. Don't smile at me. Don't—*

He fucking does, and I'm hypnotised. This is how he wins, how he makes me all dizzy and soft: he smiles, for real, and for me.

He's dangerous.

He's also still shirtless, and now that his injury is bandaged, all I can see is... the rest. Brown skin, lean hips, tawny hair trailing down his taut belly. His chest is broad and defined, his nipples tight little discs. My mouth is dry as a desert. I need more tea.

Keynes cuts into my thoughts, taking me by surprise. "You're the only one who's ever noticed, you know."

I do know, without being told. I know exactly what he's talking about: shaking in the dark.

But he explains a bit more, with a self-conscious chuckle. "Well. The only one who ever noticed before I really lost my shit, anyway." There's a tension vibrating through him that matches his awkward laugh. One that says, *I know this seems serious, but I don't want it to be.*

So, even though I feel weirdly protective, like he's a sapling starved of light or a baby bird that fell from the nest—and even though I want to ask him what the fuck he thought he was doing, taking someone outside when he knew it would hurt—and even though I want to snap at him and scold him and then do something... else, something softer—I try my best to make a joke instead. "What do you do with the ones who don't catch on fast enough? Eat them alive?"

His laugh, this time, is real enough to hurt his ribs. I know because he winces as he says, "Something like that." Then, out of nowhere, Keynes gives me a touch made of words: "You look good down there." His voice is even deeper than usual, feeling like midsummer air, heavy and sweet. When I look up at him, his mouth is soft and open, and his gaze is hot on me. But there's a spark of surprise in his eyes, as if he's not sure where his own words came from.

"I look good everywhere," I joke, because I definitely don't, and then I wink. I *wink*. Who am I?

Apparently, someone Keynes likes, because he smiles again. "I think you might be right. I think you're a dark horse."

Am I having a fucking stroke, or did he just call me attractive? I honestly don't know, but when I wet my lips, his gaze dips to my tongue, and I heat up from the inside out. There's an almost violent wrench of *want* in me, of hunger, but I leash it with gritted teeth. This moment is fragile like apple blossom: petal by soft petal, we could easily collapse. I need to be careful with him.

When I speak, my voice is rough and raw. "What else do you think?"

Olu

A simple question, five words, but it feeds the little, leaping flame of my desire. What's come over me in this kitchen is the opposite of my usual, uncomfortable distance. I tell myself this firmly grounded feeling is down to the icy rain, or the intense ache in my side—anything but the sight of Griff on his knees before me with those dark, gentle eyes.

Then his big hands disappear behind his back, as if he's protecting me from touches I might not be able to handle, and my cautious flame grows. It would be so easy to put my hands on this man, the man who makes me feel things—real things. Not just lust, but all the emotions I've missed for months, the parts of myself that hovered out of reach.

Vanity, vicious anger, petty and childish teasing; they're arguably my worst qualities, but they're nowhere near as terrible as the cold nothingness, and Griff brought them back. Then there's the urge to gentleness, and the pride in hard work, and the temptation to touch—these are the things I used to like about myself, and today, they're back too. I'm almost giddy. I lean toward him until my lips graze his ear. His closeness races up my spine. He smells rain-wet and fresh, with a hint of something like berries, and for such a hard man, his skin looks ridiculously soft —like the vulnerable, inner curve of a petal. Like the silk of his hair.

He's holding his breath.

"I think," I whisper, "that something about you makes me 65% less violent, and that's well worth exploring."

He laughs, but the sound is shaky. Affected. Good.

"What about you, Griffin? What do you think?"

"I think…" His voice is scratchy, his hesitation filled with my assumptions. He'll say he thinks we should fuck right now. He'll say he wants to drag me onto the floor and cover my body with his until I beg. That's the sort of thing men always say to me, and I suppose I'm not entirely myself again, because the thought doesn't thrill me like it used to.

In fact, the longer he pauses, the faster my heart pounds. I tell myself it's just this precious, budding arousal, but the truth is, it's anxiety. *Anxiety*. That's a word I've never used for the stomach-roiling discomfort that chases me, but it… fits. Hm.

I'm swallowing hard and worrying about that when Griff finally speaks. "I think," he tells me slowly, "that I want to hold your hand."

My thoughts grind to a halt. My heart stutters in my chest. I stare at him, speechless, and he looks steadily back, those strong and stony features impassive. As if there's nothing remotely unusual about what he just said.

Something rises inside me like the sun, burning away every sickly, nervous fear that was trying to encroach. The voice in the back of my mind can't whisper that he's a stranger, that he can't be trusted, that he's trying to hurt me, when all he wants to do is hold my hand. So the voice fades.

I reach for him.

But then we hear the building's front door open, down the corridor. It's as if we've been trapped in a gleaming, iridescent bubble, lighter than air, and that noise pops it. Suddenly the air feels cold against my bare chest, and the feelings churning inside me are as much a vulnerability as they are a victory. I don't want anyone to see me like this.

Like what?

Wanting.

It strikes me like lightning that this is the foundation of my fears: I don't want to touch anyone, don't want to be with anyone, because even the men I sleep with can't be trusted to see me wanting.

But there's no time for me to think about that. I'm rigid and robotic as I jerk away from Griff—until he rises to his feet and picks up my vest, holding it out in a way that warms me through. I stand, and he slides the fabric over my head, quick but careful. As if he knows instinctively that the first priority is getting me dressed, because no-one can be permitted to see my nakedness or my injuries.

I let him see, though. And I wasn't afraid.

Once the vest is on, he grabs my shirt and helps me ease into it, though there's no time for the buttons; I can hear voices in the corridor. I move faster, gritting my teeth against the pain, and Griff glares as if he'd like to tell me off. I focus on the furrow of his heavy brow. I focus on the occasional graze of his fingertips over my skin. I focus on him.

Rebecca, Holly, and Pete walk in just as Griff adjusts my collar, their expressions caught between smiles and curiosity. I do believe they think they've stumbled on a scandal. Perhaps because we're standing so fucking close.

Griff steps back.

"Everything alright?" Rebecca asks, calmly enough, but there's a teasing glint in her eye.

She's likely directing that question at Griffin, but I don't think he'll relish dredging up an answer under so many avid eyes. It feels natural to slide into the gap for him, to distract the social attention that I've noticed, these past days, weighs on him heavily. As natural as the way he just dressed me without a word.

"You won't *believe* what this monster did to me," I say, light and airy and smiling. "He put a blue bandage on my ribs. *Blue*. Not a nice, subtle blue, either: it's a disgusting, E number blue. Completely clashes with my eyes. Sabotage, that's what I'd call it."

Everyone laughs. Nothing to see here. But when Griff walks by me a moment later, the back of his hand brushes mine.

6

———

OLU

I go to Maria's for tea that evening, and every time I smile at her, I mean it. She is sweet and slightly bossy and entirely wicked.

"What do you think of Fernley?" she asks me.

"There's barely anything to think of," I drawl, and she laughs.

A cup of tea later, she says, "When you go to the farm, do you see much of Griffin Everett?"

The more time I spend in this place, the clearer it becomes that Griff is the local anomaly. People at work who are all warmth with me give him wary looks that I know—I *know*—he's done nothing to earn. There are meaningful pauses and subtle sneers when his name comes up. So I stiffen at Maria's question and say cautiously, "I do. It's rather difficult to miss him."

She laughs again, but there's no malice there. "He's a sweetheart, isn't he?"

Relief. I'm deciding how to answer when the floorboards creak, and one of Maria's sleepy-eyed children appears in the doorway. "Mam. I'm thirsty."

Maria is distracted and my scrambled emotions are saved from exposure.

The evening rolls on easily, and the more we chuckle and chat together, the more I feel like myself. Like an undead thing coming slowly back to life. We call it a night, and as I climb the stairs up to my flat, I realise that for some months I have been lonely.

I suppose that's what comes of purposefully avoiding everyone you love. But I had to—*have* to—stay away from them, at least until I'm not so miserable, so distant, such a burden. Don't I?

I'm no longer sure. After getting ready for bed, I find the journal marked *F* and spill out my thoughts by the light of the moon. My eyes, quite frankly, are not what they once were, so this practice involves a lot of squinting and a sneaking suspicion that every sentence I scrawl has been written at a slant. Oh well. I have to put all these thoughts somewhere, and brooding in the dark makes me feel childishly like a real writer, like someone with actual talent and purpose rather than an excess of emotion and a pen, so I continue.

When I'm done, I put my journal aside and run my thumb over the splotches of ink on my fingertips. The night is quiet and patient, as if waiting for something. Maybe for me. I don't know where the impulse comes from, but suddenly I'm reaching for the empty leather duffel at the foot of my bed. There is a box of Amitriptyline at the bottom with my full name printed on the label, taking up a majestic amount of space. I focus on the familiar letters and tell myself, *These are mine. They're for me. Nothing wrong with that.* Then I count out five tiny pills, just as I'm supposed to, and swallow them with a glass of water.

I don't feel any different.

"Of course you don't feel any different," I mutter into the silence, rolling my eyes at myself. But it doesn't help. I'm on edge and uncertain now, waiting for some monumental shift in my mind that, logically, I know isn't going to come. I search for something else to think of, and my focus wanders, predictably, to Griff. I see him on his knees before me. I feel his knuckles grazing my ribs as he helps me put on my clothes, as he protects the proud, fragile parts of me without being asked. *He didn't even make me ask.* My body tightens in that hot, reckless way I no longer thought I was capable of.

Fuck. None of my thoughts are safe or simple tonight. And now I hear my father's voice, telling me I think too much, I feel too much, I should just be a *man*. Whatever the fuck that means.

I shove the voice away, get up, and throw on some clothes, hissing when I forget my ribs and move too fast—which Lizzie explicitly warned me not to do, during our call this afternoon. I creep out of the flat, careful to lock up well behind me. Then I go for a peaceful night time walk—the perfect antidote for a man whose confusion is a cage and whose unexpected need is a shock of white-hot, jittering heat that refuses to leave his body.

A man who's afraid the need will disappear eventually, replaced by disgust again.

Fernley is the pitch-black of true, empty night, silent except for atmospheric hoots and the rustles of bunnies frolicking in the bushes. Or whatever. Do bunnies frolic at night? Moles, then—I don't bloody know. I wander on to the main road, which runs parallel to the woods. The trees beside me are taller than five grown men or three Griffins, stacked one on top of the other. Perhaps they should intimidate me, but they feel oddly protective.

Then the night is shredded by the rusty, hacking roar of an engine pushed to its brink, punctuated by youthful, clearly drunken whoops and yells. Headlights flick into view, glowing bright white and moving closer at a disturbing speed. It all seems so out of place that I take a long moment to grasp what I'm witnessing: an old, green, box-shaped Punto with a monstrous exhaust, covered in obnoxious stickers and stuffed to the brim with grinning yobs, the Northern Countryside Edition.

I shudder as they race by me; surely Theo and I weren't that awful when we were young? Then I think back and remember tragic, mildly misogynistic poetry and all the rent money we wasted on speed. Hm. Perhaps we were. Still, at least we kept our foolishness indoors.

I'm still thinking boring, dated, *In my day* thoughts five minutes later, when the youths are long gone and I've continued my walk. I turn a corner and stumble into what might be a very solid child, or a rather strangely situated brick wall. "Oof," I grunt, all elegance and wit, as my knee connects with a concrete skull.

"Watch it," mutters a familiar voice. A voice that sends a ripple of awareness over my body, catching me off guard.

Surely not. Surely fucking not. I wrestle my reaction under control and croak, "Griff?"

"Keynes?" Because of course it's him. Not for the first time, I find myself thinking—ridiculously—that he should call me Olu.

I don't know why. Even Theo rarely calls me Olu.

A light appears out of nowhere, slicing through my thoughts. I wince, squint, and raise a hand to protect myself from the sudden brightness of a phone screen. There's Griff, behind the light, crouching at the edge of the pavement, looking dark and wild in the shadows. And next to him…

"Those lads clipped a fox," he says, nodding at the too-still heap of orange fur on the ground. It has a face neither feline nor canine, one that seems like it should be mischievous but is instead blank with shocked exhaustion. Only the creature's ribcage is moving, a slow, laborious shift with each breath. Those breaths disturb me.

I'm horrified in a way I can't explain. "Fuck." The word slips from my numb lips. I've never been big on animals—I simply wasn't raised that way—but this living being is hurting in front of me, and I… "What can we do?"

I can't quite make out Griffin's features, but the sudden jerk of his head suggests that he's surprised—which, in turn, makes me embarrassed. Irritated. I may not be Mr. Care and Concern, but for God's sake, surely I don't come off as a completely selfish monster.

Or maybe I do. Maybe I *am*. The jury, at present, is out.

Griff doesn't say anything to spike my sudden temper further, thank God. Just hands me his phone and says grimly, "Hold the light." I do as I'm told—I am capable of that, occasionally—while he begins to unbutton his shirt.

My mouth runs dry. I shift my weight to one leg. "Ah… hm… Griffin, what are you—?"

"Don't suppose you have your phone on you, too?" he asks, cutting through my stumbling with clinical precision.

"No. I just came out to… no."

"Alright." His shirt's off completely now. His chest is like a hunk of concrete, only softer, covered with crisp, dark hair. That hair arrows over the curve of his belly and disappears beneath the waistline of his jeans in a taunting path that I refuse to follow. He looks as if he might be part-bear. He looks as if he'd be rather comfortable to lie on.

And I'm clearly losing it, possibly experiencing some sort of sympathetic shock reaction that's tangling up all my thought processes. Who knew I was so sensitive to poor little injured foxes?

I drag my eyes off Griffin's body, watching his hands instead. With slow, easy caution, but not an ounce of fear, he covers the injured fox in his shirt, making a little nest around the creature. Then he holds out his hand and says, "Phone."

I pass it in silence, and he taps at the screen before bringing it to his ear. The light disappears. After a long moment, the person he called picks up.

"Yeah," Griff says. A pause. "Sorry. Yeah." A longer pause. Then, "Fox. East end of the main road."

I'm not sure why he bothered giving instructions. He could've just said, "Fernley," and whoever's flying to our rescue would've found us in 0.5 seconds flat.

"Yeah," Griff says again. "Bye." He ends the call, but the light doesn't come back.

"Who was that?" I ask, mostly to soften the silence.

"Mandy Benn. She's a nurse at the wildlife centre over in Rodham."

"Oh?"

"Lives five minutes away. Nowhere's open round here at this time, so she'll take the fox home and keep an eye until morning."

"I see." For once, I have run out of things to say. So, sue me. I'm tired, and oddly worried about this wounded outdoor creature. Plus, something about the texture of Griff's quiet makes it alright not to talk.

We wait in silence until a car, bigger and slower and quieter than the one that caused all this, arrives. Its headlights illuminate the scene, and the driver leaves them on as she gets out. Mandy Benn is a tall, stately woman with near-white hair and a grim face that softens when she smiles. But there's nothing soft about her when she lays eyes on the fox.

"Those fucking lads again," she snaps after Griff fills her in. "I'll be on at Chris about them in the morning, see if I'm not."

Griff just grunts.

"I don't know why he never listens when you tell him."

Griff says nothing.

"Well, I do," Mandy mutters, clearly furious as she expertly manoeuvres the fox into a little carrier. "Because he's a fucking twat, same as everyone 'round here, that's why. But let him ignore *me*," she huffs, rising slowly with the carrier, fox firmly ensconced.

Griff thanks her, she thanks him, then it's a storm of people thanking each other and me standing in the midst of it all, uncharacteristically statue-like. I don't know why I can't seem to speak. I can't stop thinking about the fox.

Mandy is gone before I know it, and then it's just Griff and I again, staring at the darkness in front of each other's faces. I wish I could see his eyes. It took me a while to notice, but they're quite... compelling. That's the only word for them. They grab you and hold you and fill you with the urge to work out what's behind those midnight mirrors.

But since I *can't* see his eyes, there's nothing to stop me from fixating on the fox. I remember the heavy rise and fall of its ribs, and feel a stab of pain in my own. I think I'm breathing too hard. I'm not sure why.

After a moment, Griffin says, "Come 'round mine for a cuppa."

So, I do.

———

GRIFF

Keynes, I've noticed, is never delicate—until he is. I wouldn't have guessed a hurt fox would mess him up like this, but here we are. I guess I don't know him very well.

I almost trip over my own feet when I realise how much I want to change that.

Clearing my throat, I unlock my back door and lead him through it, into the kitchen, searching for something to say. My mum used to get like this when animals were hurt—people too, but with Keynes, the issue seems to be animals. His silence and the sound of his ragged breathing is unsettling me. But I rarely knew what to say to my mother, when she was sad, and I don't know what to say to him either.

Luckily, when I switch on the kitchen light, he starts talking again.

"Good Lord." He folds his arms over his chest and looks around with shameless interest, chewing his bottom lip. "I won't bother to ask if you enjoy your job."

My cheeks heat a little at that, maybe because his voice—beneath the strain he's trying to hide—is almost teasing. I turn away from him, toward the kettle. "I like plants." It's an unnecessary statement. I don't usually share those, but something tells me Keynes doesn't usually hyperventilate, and he's done it twice around me, so…

So, I suppose this is how things go with us. Different than usual, I mean.

I hear him wandering around behind me and imagine what he's doing, what he'll look at first. The rubber trees growing either side of the door like sentries? Their leaves do need dusting. Or maybe he'll head to the ferns in hanging baskets I rigged up over the kitchen table. Don't ask. I have a feeling he'll like the bright, spiky petals of the bird of paradise on the counter, or the little chili and lemon trees lining the windowsill, but I'm standing next to those right now and something tells me he's trying for distance.

I let myself take one quick look over my shoulder as I fill the kettle. I was right. He's as far away from me as he can get, his hands hovering over the thick leaves of a rubber tree. "You can touch," I blurt, then look back to the sink.

There's a pause that feels years long before he murmurs, "Thank you. I don't want any tea."

I blink at the herbs in the window, thrown off. What the fuck am I supposed to do with him if he doesn't want tea? He's just exhausted my social knowhow with five words. Typical bloody Keynes.

"You grow your own herbs," he says. Four steps, I count them, and he's standing at the counter, a metre of space between us. I watch him from the corner of my eye. He's not impeccably dressed tonight: he's in a creased, white shirt that's buttoned up wrong (yes, I noticed, don't judge me), some grass-stained jeans I know he wore to work (I remember the way they fit his... well, never mind), and the kind of fancy shoes I'm pretty sure don't match the outfit. I'm suddenly desperate to know what made him leave the house looking like anything other than himself.

Instead of asking, I put the kettle down and answer his statement like it's a question. "Yeah. I grow everything I can."

"You cook?"

I shrug. "Don't want to die of starvation, do I?"

His lips quirk. He's not biting the bottom one anymore, and I'm glad to see it. "What a sensible attitude."

I'm fighting a smile now, too. "Surprised?"

"Oh, no. One thing I will say for you, Griff: you are eminently sensible."

I wonder at all the things he apparently won't say for me. If I were smarter with the way I speak, maybe I'd ask him. Maybe I'd coax more kind-of-compliments from his soft mouth. Another time, I might give it a try, but right now he still looks shaken under his smile. He's thinking so hard I can almost hear it, and breathing so hard that the movement of his chest reminds me of that poor fox.

I ask, "Doesn't that hurt?"

He follows my gaze, looking down at himself with the strangest expression. "I... yes." He seems almost lost.

"Can't stop?"

His eyes meet mine. I see winter firs and ruefulness. "Can't stop," he confirms softly, and I finally know what to do. It's what my mum would do for me—what she *did* do, when I needed it. When she could.

"Hang on." I grab two paring knives from the drawer, then find two hands of ginger in the fridge. "Here we go." I give one to him, along with a knife. Then I take one for myself and start peeling, focusing on the movement—not just for safety reasons, but because you don't stare at unnerved creatures while you're trying to coax them. You look away, act casual, give them space. My mother taught me that, too, during our midnight rambles under the moon.

After a long moment, Keynes says, "Don't we need chopping boards?"

I snort. "Look like I use chopping boards to you?"

He must study the scarred wooden surface of my kitchen counter. He sounds almost amused when he murmurs, "No, indeed." Another long moment, and then... then, though I refuse to look, I hear the slow, harsh sound of him peeling the root. I roll my lips inward to control the little smile that wants to sprout.

Minutes pass in solid, steady silence. He doesn't ask for help, and I don't think it's because he's proud. His hands are moving just as fast as mine, just as efficiently. I find myself asking the same question he did, curiosity nibbling at my insides like an excited puppy. "You cook?"

"I suppose you could call it a hobby," he says. He sounds better now. Calmer, more like himself.

And I'm so pleased by that, I lose my fucking marbles for a minute and tease, "You can cook for me, then."

The sound of his slicing knife stumbles, then restarts almost instantly. "I'm a guest in this humble village, Griffin. I rather think you should be cooking for me."

When I slide a sneaky look at him, his lips are curling at the corners. It's not his charming smile, not the one that stuns like a camera flash. It's a quiet, secret one that exists on its own, even when others aren't looking. There's a warmth in my chest, like I already turned this ginger into tea and downed it all.

I force myself to focus on peeling again. "Truth is, I'm an okay cook, but you're probably better."

"I'm glad to hear you recognise my general superiority."

I don't mean to let a laugh escape; I have this weird feeling, like if I'm going to express emotion, he's got to do it first. But my weird feeling doesn't matter because a chuckle bubbles up anyway. I barely even regret it.

"If you're not a chef," he says, "what do you do with all these spices?" The sound of his knife changes. He's chopping, now, which means he's beaten me at the peeling. He really does cook.

"I—" Telling him feels easier than it should, which is surprising. This is the sort of topic that usually makes me go silent, one I'm careful not to get anywhere near. Except I brought him home, and let him touch, and told him things, and here we are. I find myself clearing my throat and starting again. "I make drinks. Tea and cordial and…" *And that's it, genius.*

Keynes doesn't let my silence go on; he's right there, like he knows I'm done. "For yourself?" he asks. "Or for work?" He actually sounds interested. He's asking questions about me. I wonder what that means.

I don't dare believe I know.

To fight off ridiculous fantasies, I shoot a question back. "You're very interested in my work. Why are you here, again?"

He stops chopping abruptly. Says, slow and uncertain, "You… That is, I thought—"

"Fernley," I clarify. "Why are you in Fernley?" Because there was an odd, lost hesitance in his voice, like he thought I meant, *Why are you in my house?*

As if I'd ever ask him that, even as a joke. Keynes is here because he needs looking after, whether he wants it or not.

The chopping continues, like he's settled again. "You still believe I'm here for secret and nefarious purposes? You're a very suspicious man, Griff."

Now, that's the truth. "Just making sure."

He sighs. "I find this topic dull. Let's change it." But there's an edginess hiding beneath his disdain. Maybe it's because I'm right and he's a sleeper agent sent to smuggle secret codes in our bottles of elderflower bubbly, or maybe he's just irritated by my questions. He'd be well within his rights, but…

"I just don't believe in coincidences."

"Well," he says, "you should. The world is huge. The universe is huger. There are so many tiny, ridiculous, random events happening and independent choices being made each second, we couldn't possibly count them all. It makes statistical sense for coincidences to occur all the time."

I pause in my own chopping, the scent of ginger sharp. He's got me there. "But that doesn't explain why you act so shifty every time I mention it."

"Shifty?" he echoes, clearly outraged. "I am not, nor have I ever been, shifty."

"You seem pretty shifty to me." I look up at him and realise I'm enjoying himself. There's a gleam in his green eyes that makes me wonder if he is too.

"Shifty people," Keynes says seriously, "tend to be unattractive and underwhelming. Tell me, Griffin; am I—?"

"I find this topic dull," I say, and go back to chopping.

His laughter is low, rich music. When quiet comes again, it doesn't feel uncomfortable at all.

"So," he says after a while, "these recipes you devise…"

I grunt, comfortable enough not to bother with words.

"*Are* they for work?"

I grunt again, mostly to see if it annoys him. But Keynes, by some witchcraft, seems to know the difference between my *Yes* noise and my *No* noise.

"Really? All those ridiculous flavours that people lose their heads over—is that you?"

Typically, conversations like this make me feel awkward and embarrassed. But right now, the near-awe in his voice makes me feel slightly… proud? "They're not ridiculous," I mutter, my cheeks warm.

"Good Lord." The words are faint. "I do hope you're paid a mint for that." He sounds sceptical about whether I am. Probably because he's standing in my house right now, and it's—well.

This place, old and crumbly as it is, has always been the family home.

Not that there's any family left bar me. Not that it feels like home without my mother in it.

Her ashes don't count.

I grunt in response to his question, a *No* noise, just to test if he can really tell the difference or if last time was luck.

Apparently, he can tell. "Really, Griffin," he sighs, putting down his knife with a despairing clatter. "Please don't tell me you do it for free."

I shrug.

"I knew it. You're gleefully handing out valuable intellectual property. What on earth am I going to do with you?"

I don't even know what the fuck that means, so I just say, "It's fun."

"So is eviscerating people, but if I were asked to draw up a deliciously cruel contract, I'd still charge."

I blink at him. "Does that mean you're a lawyer?"

He waves a hand over his body. "Attractive, intelligent, too talkative by half and generally in control of any situation. Of *course* I'm a lawyer." He arches a brow like he's daring me to argue. It's painfully fucking hot.

Down, Griff. Chop your bloody ginger.

I obey my own common sense and say, "Thought you were a writer."

"If you think it isn't reasonable to be both, you don't know much about royalty percentages."

"If you're trying to tell me you're hard up," I snort, "I don't believe you."

"Are you changing the subject?"

Yes, but so is he. I'm clearly soft as shite, because I sigh and let him. "It doesn't matter. The recipes, I mean."

"Your mind, your work, your skill—don't matter?"

"I... what?"

Keynes's expression is severe, not in an insulting way but in a scolding parent kind of way. "That's what you just said to me, Griff. And, since you're strangely kind to me, I feel compelled to show you the same courtesy and point out that that's bullshit."

I don't know how to answer that. I couldn't manage even if you put a gun to my head, so I stare down at the scarred counter while his surprisingly gentle words tear up my mind like a tornado.

He must take pity on me, because he shakes his head and looks absently out of the window. "It's late, isn't it?"

"Are you leaving?" I sound like a disappointed kid.

I don't think he notices, though, because he asks stiffly, "Do you want me to?" Then, while I'm thinking about how to say *Hell no* without sounding like an obsessive serial killer, he clips out: "Yes. Yes, you must be tired."

I'm not. He's here. How could I be tired? But I don't know how to say that, so I blurt, "Why were you out so late, anyway?"

For a moment, I think he'll toss some meaningless answer at me and disappear. The idea of this strange night ending so abruptly squeezes something in my gut, and I make a decision—I don't want him to leave. He doesn't want to leave. If he tries, I'll convince him otherwise.

But in the end, I don't have to. He picks up his knife and faces the counter again, and the knot in my chest loosens as he goes back to mincing ginger. "I couldn't sleep." The words are tight, reluctant. "You?"

I'm pretty sure if I ask *why* he couldn't sleep, he might 'accidentally' stab me in the shoulder. So, I move on. "I was on my way home."

"From where?" It's sharp. Demanding. He clears his throat, and for a moment he sounds almost as awkward as me. "I mean… what is there to do in this place, so late?"

"I was with Rebecca." And her fella, Lewis, but for some reason I don't say that part.

"Oh. You two are close." Keynes sounds like he's talking to a pair of flies stuck together as they fuck. I'm not looking at him, but I imagine his lip curling with a hint of superior disgust. That's the sort of thing he does, when something bothers him.

"Yeah," I agree, "we are." There's a tense, impatient pause, like he's waiting for me to say more. I don't.

"You are gay, aren't you?" he asks suddenly, sounding vaguely irritated.

I find myself biting back a smile. "No."

"Ah." A short little sound, but it's bursting with… I don't know. Would it be sheer fantasy to call his flat, metallic tone *disappointment*?

I try and fail to slow down my heart, to snuff out the sparks glittering in my blood. "I do like men." Just in case he thinks I'm the type to want a guy in a dark alley and blank him the next day.

"Oh." Now I'm imagining I hear relief. "Are you bisexual?"

Hands, ginger, gleaming blade. "Something like that."

"Pansexual?"

Looking up, I tell him, "I am who I am. I want who I want. It doesn't matter what you call it. That's what my mum taught me."

When he just nods—no sceptical frown, no argument, no helpful explanation of why I really need to choose a label other than *definitely queer*—tension I didn't know I felt drains away. He's reduced his ginger to snowflakes, so he watches me while I finish mine.

After a moment, he asks almost carefully, "So. What's it like being just you in a place like this?"

"Fine, or shit. Depends."

He doesn't ask what the hell that means, probably because he knows. It's always fine or shit, isn't it? And it always depends.

Still, his silence feels spacious, like he's giving me room to keep going. And, for some reason, I do. "There was a boy at school," I say. "A year older than me. We had nothing in common, but we were together for a while. He left when he turned eighteen. Since then, five men from Fernley have come to me. I turned one down, because he was married at the time. The rest probably wake up cold in the middle of the night, worried I'll tell."

Keynes looks—what's the word?—appalled. I don't fully understand why until he murmurs, "I used to be like that."

"Like—?" But I get it before I finish: he used to be afraid. Somehow, I can't imagine that.

He must see that I'm about to ask questions, because he speaks abruptly. "Do you ever think of leaving?"

"Leaving?" I echo, my mind still on the hurt in his eyes when he said—

"Fernley. Do you ever think of leaving Fernley?"

"No." The word is too quick, too hard, too loud. I clear my throat and swallow the acid on my tongue. Then I say slowly, "No. No, I don't think of leaving. I don't suit change." It's taken me a lifetime to be myself here, in a place I've always known. How the fuck am I supposed to do it anywhere else? The thought makes all my old anxieties laugh out loud.

But the idea that I'll stay here forever makes me freeze up inside, harsh and hurting and empty. Time to think about something else.

I finally finish my ginger, fetch a little plastic bag to put our bounty in, and shove the package into the freezer. Keynes washes his hands, I do the same. I think I'm in some sort of trance, brought on by the late hour and his nearness and the cool, minty scent of him, and maybe by the things we've talked about. Maybe by the fact that I've talked at all, more than I ever do, and that it didn't feel like some big effort.

This is how he got me that first night, I remember. I approached him, but I didn't really want it, not until he flirted the conversation right out of me. How does he do that? I'm standing there, staring at him, wondering about it, when he bursts my bubble.

"You mentioned your mother, before," he says.

I did, didn't I? The realisation hits me like a ton of icy bricks, as if an igloo just collapsed on top of me. I didn't even notice at the time, the words slipping out in a way words never do, not for me—but now I go back mentally, and hear myself say it, and freeze inside. I mentioned her. Out loud.

To him.

Why the fuck did I do that? How did he make me do that? I didn't want to do that.

He asks me, "Are you close?"

I'm already shutting down. I think he sees it in my face, because his own expression becomes carefully blank and he takes a subtle step back—away from me. I let him. That way, there's a nice, impersonal distance between us when I tell him what everyone around here already knows. "She's dead."

7

Olu

Griff avoids me for the next couple of days—which seems rather unreasonable, but who am I to judge?

Well, I know who I am: I'm the poor, innocent fellow who was simply asking polite questions about another fellow's mother, and who is now being unfairly punished for it. Not that Griffin's avoidance is a punishment. I truly could not care less. I barely know the man, and no wonder, if he ices people out the moment they ask after his family. It's Friday afternoon now, and he's still treating me like a pariah. Everywhere I am, he suddenly is not. When I catch sight of him, he turns and goes elsewhere. He's made himself a permanent dot on my horizon.

This sort of thing is exactly why I shouldn't bother with people.

His vanishing act captures my attention only because fruit farms aren't particularly exciting, while his skill is comparatively fascinating. How is a man of such conspicuous size, a man with a gravitational pull like he's the moon to my *exceedingly* reluctant tide, so good at disappearing? It's as if he's been militarily trained. It's as if he's a phantom who can shift through walls. It's as if he and Rebecca, and maybe several other staff members, are muttering, "The peacock has landed!" into secret earpieces whenever I enter a room. I'd be impressed, if I weren't so furious with him.

Well, no. *Furious* is far too strong a word for a man I've only known a week. What I'm really furious about is the fact that he's made me feel guilty—again. It's an uncomfortable state of mind that I'm strongly allergic to. I wait impatiently for it to pass and curse his name all the while.

When I finally get within a hundred metres of Griff again, we're both outside and the air is cool. I'm heading from the admin office, where Emily has been feeding me Godiva chocolates, to the main office where Henry awaits. He wants a meeting, possibly about my brewing non-fiction epic on the fruit farms of Great Britain. Yes, I'm still doing this intrepid writer bit, and no, I'm not going to stop.

But before I can reach Henry, I spy Griff in the grassy courtyard created by the configuration of the office buildings. A smattering of farmer-type people, Pete included, are gathered before him, standing to attention as if he's their fearless leader. Griff's hands are folded behind his back, making his shoulders broader, and his booted feet are spread wide, drawing attention to his thighs.

Not *my* attention, but someone's, I'm sure.

"Volunteers will be here next week," he says. "We all know organisation is key. I don't want any fuck-ups. Listen close." When he speaks at length like this—well, at length for him—the gentle roll of his accent is easier to hear. It's soft and soothing, like those country mornings that come with crisp air and a shy, pale sun. Some people are very fond of those mornings, but I believe I'd rather sleep in.

He hasn't noticed me yet, so I slow my pace and hover, purely for the satisfaction of outwitting him. Well, maybe it's not just that. Experiencing his presence after such a drought brings its own sort of satisfaction, one I can't quite name. There's just something about Griffin Everett, I suppose, that encourages a grudging fascination.

It must be his sparkling wit and warm, open manner.

Or perhaps, a treacherous part of me admits, it's his way of tucking shirts around injured foxes, stuffing his kitchen with plants, and soothing shaken men with the rhythm of basic tasks as if there's nothing amiss. Perhaps.

I listen as Griffin outlines next week's extra responsibilities, clear and concise. He has a calm, commanding manner and a quiet, bone-deep confidence, as if he's actually a half-decent manager. The way people jump to obey him, I think they agree.

I could hover as the staff disperse, could force Griff to be around me, even though he clearly doesn't want to—but for some reason, I find myself ducking my head and striding away before he can set eyes on me. I have a meeting to attend. Wouldn't want to make Henry wait.

Henry's office, in the same building as Griff's but less well-used, has a golden plaque on the door that features his name and the fact that he is CEO. Employees probably need the reminder, since Henry seems to work an average of two hours a week, and, judging by the phone conversation floating through his door, suffers from a woeful lack of focus.

"Yes, darling, I will. In about five minutes, actually, so do stop nagging, Katherine. Yes. Mwah, mwah."

At least he sounds as if he's joking when he calls his wife a nag.

I wait, rather politely in my opinion—what has come over me lately?—until he finishes his fake kisses and puts down the phone. Then I give a brisk knock before barging in.

Henry's office is large, cluttered, and filled with photographs of him around Fernley Farm: his toothy grin, his cream-puff face, his tweed and Wellington boots. I falter, astonished, while at least ten Henrys stare down at me from the walls.

Then the man himself booms "Keynes, m'boy!", dragging my

attention to his true face. Lounging behind his massive desk in a plush leather armchair is Lord Henry Breton-Fowler, his visage a little more worn now than in the photographs. I decide—or hope —that his character's likely matured in line with his appearance, despite the self-centred shrine.

"Henry," I say, closing the door and taking a seat. "Lovely to see you. You wanted a word?"

"Yes, yes! Just a quick one." When we were at school, he used to irritate the teachers something awful with his foghorn of a voice. He hasn't changed. I do believe I feel a slight headache coming on. "About that dinner!" he goes on, speaking in exclamation marks as always. "Friday, m'boy! Kate has it all arranged."

I blink. Check my mental calendar once, twice, three times. "By Friday, Henry, do you mean today?"

"Oh—yes, yes! We'll expect you at seven."

I bet he bloody will. It's on the tip of my tongue to point out that a man such as I generally has Friday nights written off months in advance, but then I remember that, 1. That is currently a categorical lie and, 2. I'm loitering around Henry's farm on false pretences for the sake of my, ah, mental health, so I probably shouldn't aggravate him for my own amusement.

And, speaking of my mental health, or however one wishes to refer to it... unreasonable yet compelling men aside, it strikes me that I'm quite enjoying myself here in Fernley. Bumbling around this idyllic little farm with my journal in hand is wonderfully restful. In fact, it's been five days since I last wanted to commit murder. I, for one, call that progress, and my mood vastly improves at the realisation.

I find myself smiling at Henry as if we're true friends rather than men who went to an insular little school together long ago, having been born purely by accident into the same insular little world. "Seven it is, then," I say. I'm almost relishing the prospect of socialising, of sparkling in a sphere I've avoided since Jean-Pierre betrayed me and Lizzie tried to save me. I'm not the same man I used to be, but this I can—and *will*—do. Just like before. "I look forward to it."

But a quiet voice in the back of my mind, rough and blunt and slow, asks me if being who I once was is truly the best I can do.

When I stand up, the journal in my satchel feels oddly heavy.

———

GRIFF

"Demanding meetings with Henry? I don't know what's gotten into you, Griffin," Rebecca says wickedly, "but I like it." Her blonde eyebrows waggle. She looks ridiculous. Usually the sight makes me laugh, but I'm all tangled today, so it doesn't hit me the same.

She seems to sense that, the way we sense most things about each other. "I'll tell you what I don't like," she adds, a little bit breathless. We're walking to Henry's office, but I'm being a bastard about it—when I don't shorten my strides, she has to jog to keep up with me. It's supposed to be a hint. Surprise, surprise, she's not taking it. "I don't like how miserable you've been lately," she finishes.

I'm not miserable. I'm... thinking.

"You've got a face like a slapped arse," she goes on.

I say honestly, "That's just my face."

Her cackle scares off the starlings perched cheekily on the admin building's roof. Good. Those bloody starlings.

"This have anything to do with your golden boy?"

"He's not *my* anything, and he's ten years older than you."

Her grin widens, and she clicks her tongue. "That means he's ten years older than *you*!"

"So? No, don't tell me." Knowing her, it'll be something weird. "Don't tell him, either."

"Why?" she demands, only she sounds delighted. "Are you worried he won't like you anymore?"

I stop walking, my messy confusion rocketing into *bad mood* territory. My voice is low and tight, the headache I've had since Wednesday morning a sharp stab at my skull. "Age is the least of my worries when it comes to him, Rebecca. If he doesn't like me it'll be because I'm a rude fucker with no social skills who can't figure out the basics of... of polite death-talk." I don't even know what I'm saying right now, so I snap my mouth shut, turn, and start walking again.

Pause. Blessed silence. Then Rebecca follows, because of course she does. "What the bloody hell is death-talk?"

"It doesn't matter."

"You're proper weird sometimes, Griff, you know that?" But she sounds so honestly fond of me that I can't take offence. And even though I want to strangle someone—*anyone*, but preferably myself—the truth is, I like the sound of Rebecca's voice.

"Clearly, you've done something," she's saying, all studious like a woman on a TV documentary. Like she's got a degree in Griffin Everett's Bullshit. "You've done something, you're feeling guilty about it, and it's making you all awkward and angry the way it does."

Obviously, she's right—but what she doesn't realise is I've done something twice over. To Keynes, yeah, because I was so awful when I chucked him out the other night, I really was. But I also feel like I've done something to my mum, I suppose. When I realised I'd mentioned her, it felt like something bad, and that gutted me. My mum's not something bad. She was all the good in the world.

So, there's my mess. I can't exactly apologise to Mum for treating her memory like some terrible secret, since she's, you know, dead. And I don't know what to say to Keynes.

My mum took her own life, and it's kind of a touchy subject? I'm so used to everyone pissing all over her memory, I never bring her up?

I sigh and tell Rebecca, "I don't want to talk about this."

"Shocking!" she gasps.

Once she gets arsey, I know it's time to change the subject. "Whatever. Tonight, yeah? You and me again."

"Ooh, yes please." She wrinkles her nose. "But yours instead of mine, I think. Lewis is being a dick. Or maybe it's me. I'm not sure."

"We'll talk about it."

"Hm," she says. "So we can talk about *my* issues, but yours are a no-go?"

I pretend to think for a second. "Yeah. Spot on."

She elbows me in the ribs, then turns the elbow into a one-armed hug. We're in front of my office building, also known as Henry's office building, and I'm not sweating but it feels like I should be. That's how nervous I am.

"Are you going to tell me what this mysterious meeting is about?" Bex asks.

"No." That way, if I fail, it won't be too terrible.

"Well, whatever it is," she says, "you've got this."

I hug her back, careful not to whack her over the head with the folder I'm carrying. Yes, I have a folder. I've been busy, these last two days. After I got rid of Keynes in the early hours of Thursday morning, then hyperventilated a bit, I decided I needed something else to think about. So I thought about…

Well, I thought about what he'd said before. *"Your mind, your work, your skill—don't matter?"*

He sounded so incredulous. Of course he did. Because, I tell myself firmly, my skill and work do matter. They *do*. Which is the argument I'm about to put to Henry.

I tell Rebecca goodbye and make my way to his office. I'm hovering awkwardly outside, checking my watch and wondering if I should knock, when the closed door opens. Sound stumbles out, loud and a bit too enthusiastic—like laughing along at an old man's jokes even though you don't understand them. Then the door opens wider, and I see Henry. And Keynes.

I haven't been this close to him since the fox and the ginger and the panicked mistake I made. Now his laughter quiets and his smile fades when he sets eyes on me, and something in my chest twists. Painfully. Can he read my mind if I stare at him hard enough? Can he see the knot inside my head and understand? Is there a way to show him I'm, you know, sorry?

Yeah, there's a way, genius. Talk.

"Griffin!" Henry says, spreading his hands wide, and my nerves swallow me up again. I'll find Keynes later, fix things later; the next thirty minutes of my life will be difficult enough without splitting my mind in half.

"Hi," I nod.

"Come in, come in!"

I try to smile at Keynes as we pass each other, but I'm pretty sure it looks more like a grimace. His gaze is cool, wintry, shark-like. Or maybe that's just paranoia on my part. Before Henry shuts the door again, Keynes says to him, all warm and close, "I'll see you at dinner, then, old friend."

Dinner. I've never had dinner with Henry, haven't even set foot on his land. When Bex and I were kids, there was this rumour that it was legal for his dad to shoot trespassers, or that it wasn't but no-one would care because they were cousins of the queen. Something like that. I don't *want* to have dinner with Henry, of course—something about him makes me uncomfortable—but it's a reminder of how different Keynes and I are. How low-down I am in the social order of things. Which is not something I usually care about—but it's also not a reminder I need moments before asking my boss to pay me more.

I take a breath and try to push everything out of my mind except what I came here to do. But the thought of Keynes sticks like a burr anyway.

"So!" Henry slaps his thighs before he sits down. "What can I do for you, Griffin?"

I sit too, wincing when my chair creaks, and pull myself together. This is work, after all, just work, and I'm good at that.

Calm finally floods me like cool water. I open my folder, take out the pages, and begin. "Thanks for meeting with me."

"Of course, of course," he says, all generous, like it wasn't sheer luck I pinned him down so soon. Henry only takes meetings when he's already planning to be at work. He's given me a half hour slot because he likes to go home early.

It strikes me suddenly that I do most of his job for him. Me and Holly and Bex, we run this place between us, one way or another.

"I'm here to discuss my recipes." I planned that sentence in bed last night. I planned a few sentences, actually, and they haven't all fallen out of my head, so this is going well. "I've noticed that my… my intellectual property has had a positive effect on the business." I show him a graph—don't ask me how I made it because I don't fucking know, luck and fairy dust—displaying the increase in profits since I took over Fernley Cordial's flavours. The profit streams directly connected to my recipes are bright green, so he can't miss my point.

Carefully, I continue. "I've been thinking that perhaps, from now on, I could be compensated for—"

"Compensated?" The word huffs out of Henry with breathless amusement. I've been staring somewhere behind his left ear for most of this discussion, but now I look sharply at his face. He's pinker than usual, his cheeks creased, his eyes bright like he's trying not to laugh at me. His lips roll in, and he tries to look solemn, like he's humouring a kid too stupid to notice the cracks in his serious mask. "Ah, Griffin."

I scowl. "What?"

He sighs, shakes his head kindly, and taps my graph. "I think you've made some mistakes with your data. There are countless other factors involved—but then, you must know that. Surely—" His words bubble with laughter, and he has to start again. "Surely you don't believe that our recent upward trajectory has anything to do with a few flavour ideas you've dreamt up in your kitchen?"

He's laughing properly by the end of the sentence, as loud and obnoxious as everything else he does.

I stare stonily at him while panic eats away at my determination. Of course I don't think I'm responsible for everything—we've had great yields, and it's Rebecca's marketing that's really done the trick, I know that. I do. But... I studied the data, didn't I? Yes, I did. Of course, data isn't my strong-suit... I rifle through the papers for a few more details, but my hands feel slow and clumsy.

"Griffin," Henry sighs, with a hint of well-hidden pity. But not quite hidden enough, I guess, because it creeps over my skin. His blue eyes flash sympathy at me as he says, "I'm afraid— It's just that—"

I'm not going to make him say it. "Yeah, no, right." I gather all my papers, trying to slide them back into the folder, but they won't fit. Patience fading, I shove them in, creasing and bending the edges, snapping the folder shut. "Sorry. I'll—"

"Don't rush off. Is there anything else you wanted to discuss?"

"No," I say shortly, and leave. Now feels like the perfect time to disappear into one of the orchards, climb a tree, and never come down again—or maybe to set my stupid fucking folder on fire. Only I can't storm off to do either of those things because, after shutting Henry's door, I find Keynes leaning against the opposite wall.

I can't help it. Humiliation burning through my brain, I snap, "What?" As in, what is he doing here, what did he hear—Christ, I hope he didn't hear—and what the fuck was he playing at, telling me I should ask for... for *anything*? What, what, what?

He arches one tawny eyebrow. The way I run hot for him, the way my body reacts to that tiny fucking movement, pisses me off even more. "Big meeting?" he asks calmly, his gaze flicking down to my folder.

My fist tightens around the plastic. "No."

He doesn't push, which isn't like him. Or maybe it is—I don't fucking know him, and he doesn't know me, and I need to stop thinking like we're anything other than weird acquaintances who can't escape each other. At least he'll be leaving soon.

I hope he's leaving soon.

He folds his arms across his broad chest, his forearms all lean muscle and raised veins and fine, golden hair. I think I want to punch him. "You," he drawls, "have been avoiding me."

I definitely want to punch him. Even though he's absolutely right, and before this meeting, I was hoping to apologise. "Nope," I say flatly.

"Yep." He pops the *P*, and now I'm staring at his mouth. All I want is to go and lick my wounds alone and forget this entire day ever happened—but here I am instead, staring at his mouth. Fuck, I wish he'd go away.

Which is why I turn on my heel and stalk off, muttering, "Take the hint, then."

He follows anyway, with long, unconcerned strides that really get on my fucking nerves. "Why don't you spell it out for me? I wouldn't want to misunderstand."

I think the last fifteen minutes have proven I'm shit at spelling things out, even to myself. I ignore him, shoving into my office, leaving the lights off and opening the blinds. I want washed-out half-light right now, not fluorescent brightness.

He leans in the doorway while I throw myself into my desk chair. "I hope you're not planning on working like this," he says.

"What?"

"In the dark. You'll strain your eyes."

For some reason, that's the comment that makes me snap. Or maybe it's the look on his face: careful warmth, tentative humour, like he's testing to see if we can slide back into the way we were. Well, we fucking can't, because he and I are so different that he demands shit in return for his *intellectual property* and goes to dinners and laughs with whoever the hell he wants, while I get laughed *at*. And deserve it.

I surge to my feet, my pulse a war drum in my ears. "Just fuck off, okay? Fuck. Off. I'm avoiding you because I don't want to fucking see you, do you get that?" My chest's heaving, and I feel slightly sick. I'm lying to him. I'm lying to him, and I'm making everything worse, and suddenly the acidic adrenaline in my blood is draining away until I feel half-empty.

Oh—and Keynes isn't leaning against my doorframe anymore. He's arrowing toward me, every line of his body hard, his gaze cold as if we're strangers again. When there's nothing between us but my desk, he tilts his head and looks at me like a wolf eyeing its prey.

"Do you know what I think about you?" he asks. His voice is soft, quiet, vicious. It tugs at the tangle in my mind. My thoughts unravel rapidly, until I'm almost dizzy from seeing clearly all at once. I'm being a shit. If my mum were here, she'd give me one of her disappointed looks and say something like, *Lashing out only spreads poison, Griffin*, and then she'd make me go and sit with the earth or something.

"I'm sorry," I say, the words almost instinctive. As soon as they're out, they feel right. They feel true. I *am* sorry, and the last of my resentment leaks away.

But Keynes is still cold, cold, cold in front of me, like an iron blade dipped in frost. He narrows his eyes and murmurs, "I don't give a shit about *sorry*, Griff. Do you know. What I think. About you?"

The way he pronounces each word like a weapon is the final clue: I just hurt Keynes. And now he's going to rip me to shreds.

"Don't," I say, not because I don't deserve it, but because we'll be enemies again. I know we will. I can see it in his face.

His lips curve in the coldest smile I've ever seen. "I think you're an overemotional child who's far more effort than he's worth."

When I say, "I think you're right," his expression falters for a minute, and I see his hurt. Then it flickers away like a hologram.

"Of course I'm right," he snaps, as if he's not sure what I'm up to, but he knows he doesn't like it. Thing is, he hasn't walked away yet, has he? He hasn't stormed off and left me to stew in my own awfulness, so maybe I still have a chance to fix this. The hope wraps itself around me like armour, making me brave.

"I was pissed," I admit, "with myself. And embarrassed. And jealous of you, obviously."

He's so surprised at that, he stops leaning over the desk like some kind of mafia enforcer and straightens up.

I keep going. "So I took all my shit out on you, which I shouldn't have done. I'm supposed to be apologising to you right now. That was the plan."

His mouth tightens, like he doesn't believe me, which twists something in my gut. I didn't realise until this moment how much I really, really, really fucking *like* Keynes. I'm not sure how it happened, but it feels impossible to undo. My hope is tinged with a bit of desperation now, making me reckless. Walking around the desk, I reach for him slowly, and he doesn't jerk away. Instead, he watches me take his hand with disgusted interest on his face, like I'm some foreign amoeba and he can't wait to see what I do next. His masks are really good. I wonder how he got like this.

Probably had something to do with people like me, throwing his tentative, bossy attempts at kindness in his face.

His hand is solid and real in mine. I lace our fingers together and the graze of our palms sends a spark of something good through my chest. His winter fir eyes are so cold, it's like snow lining the trees on Christmas morning—but they warm up for a moment, a second, and I catch it.

"So, if you could accept this apology," I say, "I would really like to start the next one."

He huffs out a sudden breath that I think might be an acci-dental laugh. He doesn't lean toward me, doesn't smile, doesn't stop glaring like he's plotting my death—but I'm 99% certain he just laughed for me. Progress.

"I'm sorry," I say again.

"Fuck off," he tells me.

"I promise not to work in the dark."

"I don't give a shit. If I'm being really honest, I hope your eyeballs fall out of your head and roll into a gutter."

Now I'm trying not to laugh.

"Don't fucking laugh," he snaps.

I clear my throat. "Sorry. Listen… You were right, before. I have been avoiding you, but it wasn't your fault—of course it wasn't your fault. It was just that I don't talk about my mum, ever, so when I mentioned her with you, and it wasn't a big deal —when I barely even noticed—it scared me. You scared me." I squeeze his hand like I can push the truth into him through the places where we touch. Judging by his face, which is maybe 2 degrees less frozen than it was a minute ago, this is working. So I squeeze harder, talk faster, forget to worry about my words or to feel self-conscious. "I didn't know how to fix it or how to explain what needed fixing—what the *it* was, exactly—so I pretended it wasn't happening. I pretended you weren't happening, but you are. You're happening. To me."

That doesn't make any fucking sense, but it's too late. I said it.

Only, it doesn't work. Long moments tick by, and then he pulls his hand from mine, and I realise I left this conversation too late. He needed an explanation yesterday morning, or even this morning, before I made everything worse. But I left it too late.

"Hm," he says.

I wet my lips nervously. I'm nothing but nerves today. "That it?"

He shrugs and walks away.

8

Oʟᴜ

At a little past seven in the evening, I find myself loitering in the Breton-Fowler family manor alongside a handful of people I would rather not be sharing oxygen with. Sometime in between accepting this invitation and actually arriving, I have lost every fuck I ever had to give.

And when I say *some time*, I mean, *immediately after Griffin Everett pushed me away again.* If that sounds hideously emotional and a little melodramatic, I don't give a damn. I have lost all my fucks, if you recall. Which is why I don't care that he apologised, either. I don't have the energy for all these feelings he causes. It's disgusting. So I've decided to use my alien nature to my advantage and forget all about him.

There are six of us at the party, including our illustrious hosts, and we all share the same razor-sharp way of speaking, our accents rooted in class rather than home. We laugh the same way too: airy and studied and careful not to flash genuine amusement. Not to flash genuine *anything*, in fact—intimacy of any sort is gauche at best, dangerous at its very worst. We know this, because we were disciplined by nannies of similar origin, and raised within the same cutthroat shark-tank of a society. What a dinner party we make.

And how strange it is that I can hear the world outside—the world that Griff belongs to, where *Sorry* is simply a word one says after making a mistake—beating down the door.

I banish the image of his tortured expression and focus on my surroundings. On my present, my past, and my forever, on the evidence of who I am. The room we stand in with flutes of over-priced champagne suits my mood beautifully: it's so eerily empty, all clean, magnolia marble and absolutely no furniture, that it feels a little bit haunted. I assume this style of décor—if a complete and no doubt expensive lack of anything can be called *décor*—is the latest thing in interior design. And I assume that Henry's wife, Kate, is behind it, since she's wearing a floor-length sheath dress in eggshell silk and no jewellery beyond her engagement and wedding rings.

Then Kate claps her hands and says something I can't quite hear over the rush of anxious blood in my ears, and we are herded into another room like sheep. Sheep remind me of Griffin, and suddenly I feel raw, exposed, and separated from the world around me as if I'm underwater. Not in the usual, distant way. In an entirely new and disgraceful way that appears to be made completely of emotion.

Focus.

This new room, the dining room, is not modern at all. It's pure Henry, cluttered and creaking under the weight of generations of familial self-importance. The dining table is far too large for us all—far too large for anyone, in fact. The carpet would be too busy, even if it weren't covered haphazardly by several different rugs, all of which I'm sure are Aubusson and all of which are hideous. Candlelight glitters, because men of Henry's ilk pine for ye olden days, when they were legally allowed to beat their serfs and people like me were rarely permitted to taint the purity of their class—or indeed, their race.

Oops. Not supposed to think about that sort of thing in this sort of situation. Makes it rather difficult to smile.

I tell myself I'm doing Henry a disservice, reading too much into his horrible décor, and drag myself forcibly from the depths of my irritation. When I re-enter the world, the soup course has been served and a debate about the (un)suitability of the Duchess of Sussex has commenced. Clearly, I chose a terrible moment to resurface, so I go under again. My smiles and nods are polite and unhearing.

When I venture out of my mental shell around the third course, I find, with relief, that the topic has shifted to more local matters. Henry is shooting me strange looks every so often, probably because he remembers very well that I am a leader of conversations, not a grim and silent cipher who eats his food mechanically. I suppose I had better buck up.

When a woman to my right, one with a bloody feather in her hair, of all things, mentions the local scenery, I leap in. "It is gorgeous here, isn't it? Henry's farm, in particular, holds some beautiful sights."

Henry visibly expands, like one of those birds who puff up when they wish to mate. "You're too kind, Keynes, m'boy. Here, now, did I tell you all that Keynes is a writer and traveller extra-ordinaire? Something of an explorer, really, and he's graced our tiny village with his presence." He and Kate share a calculated look of humble pleasure before he continues with a gloating edge. "Now, he's keeping his cards very close to his chest, but I do happen to know that he's attached to an esteemed publishing house."

All attention turns to me. The guests who previously wrote me off as dull and pitiful now appear interested. I am no longer the gentleman who's been so silent as to seem impolite; I am a writer, a creative, and therefore clearly shy and/or tortured. Once they enter my confidence, I can make a protagonist out of them, and not just on the page.

I wonder how many people treat ostracised, circumspect Griff like that—how many see in him a mystery rather than a man, an opportunity to insert themselves into some dramatic, meaningful tale, as if he is a character rather than a human being.

Actually, I don't wonder that at all, because Griff isn't on my mind.

Trying my best to look coy, I murmur, "I couldn't possibly say a word about my magnum opus."

"Aha!" Henry bellows. "So there's an opus!"

I smile to myself and concentrate on my food. Apparently, this is the fish course. What have I been putting in my mouth for the past hour without even noticing? For the first time in a while, I find myself questioning if my ability to go so far inside my own head is necessarily a good thing. I know where it comes from, or rather *when*. I hear the echo of my father's razor-sharp insults every time I do it.

I tried it in bed, once, after Jean-Pierre, but it didn't work: the disgust still came along, ruining my pleasure, making me push my partner for the night away. I was furious at the time, but suddenly, I'm grateful. Perhaps being present is something I should value more, no matter what inconvenient emotions it might bring. After all, this week in Fernley has proven that when it's good, it's good.

"Of course, there's all sorts of *drama* in a place like this," Kate is saying. Apparently, they're still talking about my non-existent book. As if drama is the sort of thing I put in my travel journals. Drama's universal; I look for the unique. Like the way the air tastes in this village, filtered by a thousand lives, ancient and impossibly fresh all at once.

But I won't bother to explain that, because I don't think anyone at this table would care to hear. I simply let the conversation wash over me.

"Drama indeed," Henry says gleefully. "Why, even at the farm."

"That Everett fellow alone—"

I look up sharply. So sharply that just the movement makes Kate zero in on me, her interest piqued as if she smells my blood in the water.

She doesn't stop speaking, though. After that infinitesimal pause, she continues, far more slyly than before. "That Everett fellow alone," she says, "could be the hero of some novel or other."

"I don't write novels," I reply, but my voice is too quiet. It lacks conviction because the fact is, I don't write anything.

"This is good, Olu," my brother-in-law tells me, an old journal in his hands. *"Proper good, I mean. Have you ever thought—?"*

"No."

"Perhaps not Griffin," Henry corrects his wife. "The mother, however—"

"—Oh, gosh, yes, the mother." Kate's avid gaze hits me like a pair of snide, blue spotlights. A bead of sweat creeps down my spine. I can feel my own pulse thrashing at my throat, so violent it almost hurts. I know what she's going to say, or rather, how she's going to say it, before she even forms the words. "Keynes, darling, have you heard about our tragic *Ms*. Everett?"

I swallow hard. My voice is anything but smooth when I say, "No."

There's a murmur of faux-shock around the table, a thrum of smug pleasure. Now they have the opportunity to tell me something ugly, something they absolutely shouldn't.

I'm unnerved, but I can't let them see that. So I continue slowly, my attention on my sea bass as if I really couldn't care less. "I can't imagine it's anything I'd like to hear. Now, Henry's fascinating business—"

"Oh, no, Keynes," Henry booms happily, "this is much more interesting than work."

"But the lady in question has passed away, hasn't she?" My veneer is cracking now. "Perhaps we shouldn't—"

"Passed away?" Kate snorts indelicately. "That's one way of—"

105

I hear the jarring scrape of a chair being shoved back, its feet screaming against the marble floor. Then I blink down at the shocked faces around the table and realise that I am responsible for the sound. I bolted upright as if my arse had been electrocuted, and now all these eyes are on me, demanding to know why.

For a moment, the last scraps of my societal training hold fast. The urge to laugh airily and patch over every awful crack in this room has me in its clawed and icy fist. My mother's fist, I think, but the slight prick of fear comes from my father, as does the ghost of his cane against my palms. I rub my hands against my thighs and let it go.

"I do not want to hear about Ms. Everett," I tell the room, "because Ms. Everett is not my business or yours." My voice is different. A little hoarse, shaking with a rather vulgar excess of emotion. I am not unaffected, I am not distant and sparkling, I am not even sheer, safe ice. I suppose I'm human right now. I'm human out loud, in public, and I wonder why I've never done it before.

Henry frowns up at me, curling his pink mouth into something ugly. "Keynes," he snaps, ruffled by the fact that I'm making a scene, clearly baffled that I'm doing it over Griff. Or rather, over Griff's mother, whose story I'm certain is not entertainment fodder for stuck-up strangers at a dinner party.

No-one's story is.

"Do sit down, old boy," Henry tells me. It has the cadence of an order. I've never responded well to those.

"Henry," I say, suddenly furious, and my next words are going to be *Shove it up your arse*. But then I remember that the harvest begins on Monday, and I probably won't be welcome if I insult the farm's owner so very grievously. I need to be welcome, you see. I need to be there. Because I need an excuse, for the rest of my time in this village, to work beside Griff.

So I swallow my rage and finish, "Henry, please excuse me. I'm not feeling quite the thing."

The tension in the room eases a fraction. I force a wooden apology from my lips, directed at Kate even though she doesn't deserve it, and then I thank them for their hospitality. I seem polite, if reserved and slightly off, but since I have an excuse—since I'm clearly unwell—no-one minds. Henry even looks a little relieved, now that he has a reason for my strange behaviour tonight.

And I haven't exactly told a lie. I feel quite sick.

Emotions thrash around in my belly like the tentacles of some great fairy tale beast, fighting for dominance, for attention, but most of all fighting to break free. I don't know how I ever ignored them before. I feel as if I've been rolled up tight in layers of plastic, the world insulated from the violence of my feelings, but now they all want out. Am I exhausted or alarmed or relieved that they're strong enough to bother me at all?

As the housekeeper leads me through Henry's strange home, with its too-empty rooms and its too-full ones, I roll the problem around in my head and decide the answer is relief. Because I do believe this mess is what it means to be human, and isn't that what I'm supposed to want?

Outside, the evening is grey and gentle, the air crisp and clean with fresh-fallen rain. The deep breath I take feels like my first ever. I walk down the drive and know exactly where I'm heading.

―――――

GRIFF

If anyone from Fernley ever came to my house, they'd knock at the back door. Most folks round here won't answer the front, and my garden gate's always shut, anyway, so it's obvious the back door is the way to go. It's just—no-one ever *does* come to my house.

Well, except Rebecca, but she's already here.

So when a fist pounds at the wood, she eyes me over the rim of her wine glass, which has been permanently fused to her mouth all night. And I say, agreeing with her silent suggestion, "Lewis has come to throw you over his shoulder."

She gives the wine a breather and mutters, "Let him bloody try."

I'm still ferreting out the details of what's going on between them, but they've been together since we were all at sixth form. They do this about three times a year. I'm not worried. I'm also not expecting to open my back door and find, instead of Lewis's pale blonde head, the most beautiful man in the world.

Keynes. It's Keynes, and I just about shit myself in shock. He looks like himself on speed, eyes huge and stormy like a black-green ocean, his jaw clean-shaven and sharp enough to cut, his fancy suit pale pink with a mint pocket square. He's undone so many buttons his shirt's practically open, and I barely stop myself from staring at the bronze coils of hair on his chest. Don't think he'd appreciate that. But what I can't stop is the way I feel, the wild and rootless hope that springs to life in me whenever he's near, no matter how badly we keep fucking this up. I don't even know what *this* is. I just know it feels like the start of something good and I want it.

Before I can pull the scrambled sections of my mind together, before I can decide how to do or say something perfect, he speaks.

His words are jumbled and hot and frantic in a way they've never been, and I see in those different, darker eyes something achingly honest. "I'm sorry. What I mean is, I'm sorry I hurt you when I asked about her. I didn't know it *would* hurt, but that doesn't make me any less sorry. I don't want to cause you pain, Griff. That is the last thing I have ever wanted to do. You don't deserve…" He looks down at his spread-open hands, but his gaze is different, as if he's seeing something else. His fingers flex, then curl into fists. "You don't deserve the shitty people in this shitty place. No, it's a beautiful place, when I'm with—" His mouth presses shut. He shakes his head. All I can hear is the harsh rhythm of his breath—his ribs must kill right now, which twinges at something in my chest, God I wish he'd bloody look after himself—and then he says, "You're a good person, Griff."

He turns and walks away.

I watch him stride off like there's a fire under his arse, and I wish I had words. Wonderful words like his, words that say a thousand things all at once. But I don't.

Until I do.

"Hey," I call.

He freezes in place and stays like that for a long, tense moment. Then, slowly, he looks over his shoulder at me. And he always seems so golden and so handsome, but right now, despite his barely-lined face... fuck, he looks old.

I tell him a truth I don't think many people know. "You're a good person, too. You get that, right?"

He stares at me for what seems like a century.

"I want to talk some more," I tell him, "but I can't right now. Can I see you tomorrow? If I go to the flat, will you be there?"

"Yes," he says slowly, like he's not quite sure what's happening.

"Good," I say. "Good. Then I'll come. Okay?"

He stares at me some more. "If I thought I deserved it," he says, "I'd probably kiss you."

I stand frozen while he walks away. The cool air kisses my cheeks while his words kiss *me*—the way he doesn't think he should. *If I thought I deserved it,* he said. What the fuck does that mean? As if anyone needs to deserve me. As if he wouldn't make the list, if deserving did come into it. Doesn't he know no-one's ever made me feel so many things at once in my whole life? Doesn't he know I haven't really believed in anyone's kindness since my mother left, that only his really sinks in? Doesn't he know I've spoken to him more in a week—a fucking week—this is so ridiculous I almost laugh out loud—than I've spoken to most people in this village over the last twenty-eight years?

How can he talk about deserving, when I've got this gut-deep suspicion that what we really deserve is each other? And I don't mean because we're a pair of brooding arseholes.

Or, you know, maybe I do.

"You," Rebecca says from behind me, "have been keeping secrets."

I go back inside and sit at the kitchen table. Then I steal her wine and toss it back.

She watches me, surprised, because I don't usually drink; alcohol is a depressant. But the wine feels hot and full in my belly, and now I'm imagining the reluctant curve of Keynes's grin if he saw me, and the way he'd murmur, "Look out, world," or some sarcastic shit like that.

I'm smiling at nothing. Bex looks worried. I clear my throat and shove the last of my giddy feelings away, because I have a mission tonight, one nothing can interrupt. "Don't worry about me. Talk."

"Griff—"

"Talk." I've given her two hours of aimless moaning, letting her avoid the hard shit because she needed to, but it's time to figure this out. "You. Lewis. What's up?"

She huffs because she knows this tone, steals her wine glass back, and gets up to grab another of the bottles she keeps here. With her back to me, she says, "It didn't need to be an argument. I think I'm the one who made it an argument."

I know why she thinks that—because Lewis is so laidback he might be asleep, while Bex pushes and pushes and pushes. But sometimes an issue needs pushing, and that's what she's best at, and I'm sure it's one of the reasons Lewis loves her. I mean, it better be. He best love everything about her, or I'll be having words.

Finally she faces me, her glass full to the brim again, and leans against the counter, sipping and glaring at nothing. She looks like a character off *Desperate Housewives*.

"Come on, Bunny," I nudge.

The childhood nickname makes her pull a face, but it works. She blurts out, "Lewis wants to leave."

I frown.

"Fernley," she explains. "He wants to leave Fernley. He's been going on about it for a while now, and then the other day I found him looking at jobs in York. Not just for himself, either. He was looking at marketing positions!"

Ah. I nod and swallow all the negatives crowding my mouth. I want to strangle Lewis, and then I want to lock Rebecca in the cupboard under the stairs. I want everything to stay the way it is. I want her to stay with me. But I also want her to be happy, so I say, "You do like York."

Her jaw drops. "I know I like York, Griffin! As a holiday!"

That's true, but... "You saw your dream house in York." She came home and told me all about it. Honeysuckle winding up to the top floor windows, three storeys and red bricks and all that lark. I still remember the colour in her cheeks and the awe in her voice.

"I know that," she snaps, "but I can't leave Fernley."

She sounds like me. "Why not? Your parents already moved to—"

"I can't leave *you*!"

That takes me a minute to process. "Why?"

Her wine glass hits the counter with a *clink*. She barely seems to notice, storming over to me. Her little hand shoves my shoulder. "What would we do without each other?" she demands.

But I think she means, what would I do without her.

"Bex..." My mouth opens, closes, as a thousand realisations bloom in my brain all at once. I feel impossibly soft and incredibly annoyed. "Have you stayed here this long because of me?"

"Not *because* of you," she scowls, her arms folded. Then, quick and quiet, she adds, "But maybe, yeah, a bit because of you."

I give her a stern look. "Do you want to live in York?"

"I want to be with *you*."

"I hope you didn't say that to Lewis. He's going to think you're knocking me off."

She bursts into hysterical laughter at the thought of cheating on Lewis with me, which is what I was hoping for. Only, she laughs a bit too long. "Hey," I say, fighting a smile. "It's not that funny. I'm—" I break off, surprising myself into silence. I was going to say, *I'm not a bad-looking bloke.* Except, I don't think I've ever thought that about myself before. Weird.

Rebecca doesn't notice, too busy wiping tears from the corners of her eyes. I'm not really offended. The laughter is just because she loves Lewis. She really, really loves Lewis. He moved here when we were seventeen, and she set eyes on him in assembly and leaned over to me and whispered, "Oh, that's *all* mine." Turned out, she wasn't wrong.

He makes her smile, which is why I tolerate him. And if leaving Fernley will make her smile, I'll tolerate that too.

So I put my hands on her shoulders and give her my best *I'm not fucking around* face, which has been known to make people run away in terror.

Rebecca rolls her eyes and sticks out her tongue.

I ignore her. "I'd be fine without you, you know."

She looks sceptical.

"I'd be less happy," I admit. "I'd be uncomfortable. But maybe that's a good thing." My mum would say: *We'll never know how big we could grow if we stunt ourselves.* People are like plants. You gotta give us what we need, cross your fingers, and see what happens. I won't be the reason Rebecca withers.

She rolls her lips in like she does when she's trying not to cry. "But you'd be so far away!"

"There's these things called phones. Also, cars."

She sobs, a burst of sound cut off real quick. "You hate phones!"

"I wouldn't hate them if you were on the other end, you donkey." I pull her in for a hug. "Our lives have been the same for a long, long time."

She sniffles. "Are you saying we're boring bitches?"

"I'm saying there's nothing you can't do, so do it. I dare you."

She's still sniffing as she pulls back, but there's a flash of mischief in her watery blue eyes. I've laid down the challenge and now she'll pick it up. She never could resist a dare. In this moment, I know Rebecca's gone.

Not completely, I tell myself. This is like moving a plant to a different side of the garden so it'll get more sun. She'll do better, and that's what matters, even if I have to walk—or drive, in this case—a bit further to see her bloom.

And how will I bloom, left here in the dark? I push that thought right out of my head. It's pointless in ways I can't even explain.

She dabs at her watery eyes and gives me a smile that's part rueful and part grateful. We don't say things like *thank you* to each other, not when we really mean it, because of what Rebecca calls her allergy to mush. But I see it all over her face. And I hear it in her teasing voice when she says, "You need adventures, too. Maybe you could ask Keynes about that. Hasn't he travelled a lot?"

As if Keynes would take my lumbering country arse anywhere. I can see it now: him leaning against some bar in the Maldives, or wherever it is rich people go, me hovering behind him like an irritable kid, cramping his style and growling at anyone who looks at him too long.

I expected that image to make me feel awkward, to remind me of all my worst parts, but instead my lips twitch. All I see is him rolling his eyes at me and making snotty comments that we both laugh at.

All I say to Rebecca is, "Uh-huh."

"Of course," she smirks, "it might be difficult to ask him anything while he's kissing—"

I put my hand over her mouth. "Nope. Not going there. Back to you."

She snorts. Then she cries some more. By the time she goes home to Lewis, well after midnight, she's ready to end their fight, and I'm...

I'm ready to get used to the idea of change. I hope.

No; I know. I'll do it for Bex.

9

OLU

On Friday night, after making a fool of myself in Griffin's garden, I debate going all the way home to see my sister. I spend Saturday morning writing a list of pros and cons in my journal. Each side has one entry.

Pros: Seeing Lizzie. Avoiding Griff's visit today.

Cons: Lizzie seeing me. Missing Griff's visit today.

I'm painfully conscious of the feelings rioting in my chest like the daisies on Griffin's lawn; a pretty profusion of weeds. They shouldn't be there, but they are, and I don't have the heart to remove them—though common sense says I should rip out this infatuation by the root before it spreads.

Instead, I take the journal marked *F* and write about us. About the fact that we've known each other for a week, and I've spent most of that time being the best bastard I can be. I scribble to myself that connections don't develop so quickly, and they certainly don't grow in the arctic drought that is me in a bad mood. Then I remember that I've decided not to be in a bad mood anymore—not with Griffin, which should be easy, since hurting him makes me flinch every time. And not with myself, which will be harder, because hurting me has become a habit.

I write that down, too.

By 11a.m., Griff still hasn't come over, which is fine. I wasn't expecting him to come, anyway. People, especially the people I know, say things like that all the time: *I'll come to see you! I'll visit! We should meet for coffee!* But it's just good manners. Either they don't come, or they show up, shag you, and leave. I don't think Griff's the type to show up and shag me, which means he's just not coming. Okay. Well. Good; this puts me in the perfect position to see Elizabeth.

I call her first, just to make sure she's in.

"What do mean you're—Isaac, get off—what do you mean you're coming down? Are you done with your holiday?"

That's what Lizzie calls it when I go off the rails: a holiday. "No, darling. I've another two weeks here." That number is chosen at random, but I like the sound of it. I lean against the little kitchenette counter, which gleams because I woke up early and scrubbed it. What can I say? I'm awfully conscientious, just in general.

"Why are you coming all the way down, if only to go back— Isaac Montgomery, behave yourself!"

I don't particularly want to know what Lizzie's husband is doing. I'm going to pretend that she is still twelve years old and unmarried, and also that he doesn't exist.

"You're not trying to sneakily check on me, are you, Olu?" she asks. "Because I promise, I'm fine. The mushroom is terribly well-behaved, which means he doesn't take after his father or his uncle. Thank God."

"Very witty, Liz. No, I simply thought I'd—"

There is a knock at my door.

"Never mind," I say. "You're right. It's a very long journey."

"Well, even so, of course I'd be thrilled to have you."

"No," I say firmly. "We must think of the fossil fuels, my darling. We must think of the earth. I'll call you tomorrow."

Griffin looks very well, standing at the top of the stairs that lead to my flat. When I open the door, the sun is shining around his dark, messy hair like an angel's halo.

"Hi," he says.

The memory of my speech last night returns to mortify me. The grossly adoring things I said hover between us, heating my cheeks. I tell him waspishly, "You're wearing odd socks."

It's a weak effort. He doesn't look offended; he doesn't even look down to check. "Thanks for noticing," he says, and then he pushes gently at my shoulder until I step back. Invites himself in, bold as you please, and shuts the door. Looks around. "Never been in here before."

"Oh. So you don't make a habit of seducing all visitors to Fernley?"

He pauses his examination of the screen that hides my bed, flashing a tiny, teasing smile. "Seducing you, am I?"

I open my mouth, then snap it shut. Awful man. "What do you want?"

"All sorts." Before I can get a handle on that quiet, casual response, he tells me, "Mandy called. The fox is going to be fine."

"Oh." I am ridiculously glad. It's only a bloody fox, for heaven's sake, and nature is all about life and death and what have you. Yet I want to grin like a child. In fact, if I were alone, I might give in to that impulse. But since I'm *not* alone, I nod and say shortly, "Glad to hear it. I suppose I'd better make tea."

"Cheers. Are you tired?" he asks, moving to sit on the tiny loveseat that separates the kitchenette from the living space. He has a knowing look in his eye, but I'm not sure if it's because he can tell I'm pleased for the fox or because he can sense my strange, edgy mood. Neither option is acceptable, whatever the case.

"Are you saying I look like I slept in a ditch?" I'm hoping he'll stutter in response or something equally delicious.

He doesn't. "I'm saying you're not as scary as usual today."

"You barge into my flat, squash my"—*Maria's*—"sofa cushions, and now you gravely insult my character. I should invite you outside."

"I thought you wanted to kiss me?" he smiles.

I find myself gaping like a fish. I think I'm blushing. No, let me be honest—I am most definitely blushing, and it burns. "I— you—who *are* you?"

His smile becomes a grin. But he must be able to tell that I'm panicking, just slightly, because he looks around and asks, "What do you do in here? For fun, I mean."

I switch on the kettle and tell the truth. "I write."

"You really are a writer," he says, and I wish *that* were true. Lizzie claims it is, that the act itself is enough, and sometimes I almost believe her. Occasionally, I visit somewhere new and write a line that perfectly captures every facet of the jewel that life can be. Then I find myself wishing for a breathless, silly moment that I could show the world these journals—but that moment always passes. Because those lines can't be as good as I think they are, and I don't need anyone else to tell me so.

"Yes," I lie to Griff. "I'm a writer."

He gives me a strange look, as if he heard my falseness, which is impossible. I was in the closet for thirty-seven years. Put me on stage and I'll hold my own beside Dame Judi.

"What are you thinking about?" he asks me, like we're children at a sleepover.

I pluck a random bit of honesty from the back of my brain. "Elizabeth. My sister."

"Tell me about her, then."

I face the kettle and fetch the mugs, the teabags, the milk. I remember how he takes it, because he takes it just like me. For a while, the only sound is the whistle of the kettle, then the clink of my stirring spoon against ceramic. He doesn't try to speak. But when I bring the tea over and sit beside him, I do.

"She's wonderfully bossy and frighteningly competent. She runs a dance school."

He takes the tea and nods. "Because she was a ballerina."

I don't know why I'm pleased that he remembers. "She's retired. And now she's having a baby."

"You're smiling."

I bite my lip, then take a too-hot sip of tea. "Am I?" I ask innocently.

"You happy to be an uncle?"

"I do believe it's what I was born for." It's not. I want to be a father, but I'm too old and too cold and who would ever have a baby with me anyway? A glutton for punishment, that's who. But the thought isn't a whip the way it has been in the past. For some reason, it just makes me chuckle ruefully into my tea.

"Lizzie's married to an awful man," I say. "He's terrifyingly huge, and he never speaks."

A wry laugh. I'm used to cold sarcasm, but Griff's is warm. "Sounds like a piece of work."

"Actually, I'm strangely fond of him." At that moment, I shift in my seat. My knee brushes Griff's, and I jerk back, my heart pounding with something that isn't panic. Touching him sends odd sparks through my body, crackling up my thigh and across my nerve-endings until I feel like velvet brushed by a bare palm.

His smile fades as he looks at me, worry in his eyes. "You know I only came to talk, right? Not to do anything that makes you…"

That makes you a mess, is what he's trying to say. "I know," I tell him briskly, suddenly uncomfortable—not because I'm upset, but because I'm… not. Touching him doesn't make me nauseous. It hasn't since he held my hand and told me he was sorry, and I'm not sure how to deal with that realisation. I should probably be jumping for joy and then jumping *him.*

But for some utterly incomprehensible reason, I don't want to. In fact, what I really want is to hold his hand again.

We sit in silence for a moment before I think, *Fuck it.* "You know, we'd be far more comfortable sitting on the bed." It's true; we are both entirely too big to fit on this loveseat. "But, just to be clear, this is not me being coy or playing hard to get. Nor will I be overcome with arousal once we're on a mattress. You are completely safe from ravishment this afternoon." But not safe from my sudden hunger for closeness, it seems.

"Thank you," he says gravely. "I was worried about my virtue."

Soon, we're lying side by side, sunlight and birdsong washing over us from the open window, and I have made a liar of myself. Because, all of a sudden, I *am* overcome with arousal—but it's not the way I remember it, like a mosquito bite in need of scratching. No; I sink into wanting Griff the way people sink into hot baths after a long day, and it's… glorious. I'm not even worried that the feeling will turn on its head, that I'll be punished by the revulsion again, like I have been before, because this need feels different. This need tastes like Griff, not like the random-man-at-a-bar he was last week. It's rich earth and cool rain and careful, creeping roots.

I think it might be safe. I think he might be safe.

Griff talks in his low, slow voice, all gravel and thoughtful gaps, about the orchids he's growing at home. I talk about my last visit to Alsace, where an acquaintance runs a wine hotel—tentatively, at first, because I don't usually mention the travelling that took up most of my life. It's barely ever relevant, and I didn't do it for fun; I ran away from home, and I took a path across almost every continent to do it. Plus, not everyone's interested in travel stories.

But, for someone who claims he's never thought of leaving Fernley, Griffin is.

At some point, I make us both a stir fry. He tells me I'm a good cook and asks for seconds, which I, of course, don't care about, because I do not require external validation. But, hours and hours later, I make him dinner too. Might as well.

When he finally admits that he should probably leave, it's dark outside. Summer dark; rich and fragrant and clearly later than it should be. We've been holed up in this tiny space for far too long, and I'm not even the slightest bit bored of him. I have a sudden urge to tell him I hate him, but I manage to wrestle it into submission and say something true instead.

"I had a nice day."

He's grinning on my doorstep, hands in his pockets, as if he'll never leave. I wish he wouldn't. "So did I. Can—wait, no." He frowns slightly. "I was going to ask if I could see you tomorrow, but I already promised Rebecca I'd help her with… something."

The image of my hands shoving Rebecca into a conveniently located ditch is there, then gone. "That's okay," I say, because I am a normal and reasonable man. "I'll see you on Monday."

"Yeah," he smiles. "Monday."

But the night vibrates around him, and he doesn't leave. Instead, he watches me in the barely-there glow that leaks through my door. I watch him right back, and the lust that's danced gently around me all day seems suddenly heavy—like summer heat or a beloved body creating a dip in my mattress.

Not that I've ever had a beloved body in my bed. I don't know why I'd think such a thing. Just like I don't know why I blurt out, "You held my hand. The other day, that is."

"Yeah," Griff says softly.

"Why?" It's a ridiculous question. I know *why*; he did it because he was apologising, because he wanted to get through to me or to stop me from running away.

Except, that's not what he says. No, what he whispers into the quiet is, "Because I wanted to."

I release a breath so heavy, the bruises on my ribs ache.

Then he says, "Want me to do it again?"

I don't know how to answer such a question. But the man I've become today, trapped in a bubble with Griff, apparently does—because that man murmurs, "Perhaps I wouldn't mind."

Griffin laughs, his smile ripping through me with all the devastation of a hurricane. Then he reaches out and catches my hand in his, and says, "Like this?"

I feel his calloused palm against mine, and something stirs in my belly; something fucking wonderful and achingly intense. God. *God.* I've been lying next to him all day, watching his fine mouth move, trying not to focus on the breadth of his body, the shape of his thighs under his jeans—and I did so well. I suffocated the confusing need in my blood until I almost forgot it was there. But in this moment, his smile and his eyes and his fucking hands all make me feel like an animal.

I hold on tight and drag him toward me, so hard he stumbles a little. Then we're pressed bodily together on my front doorstep. Griff puts a hand on my shoulder to steady himself, and I grab his hip. The shadows between us are impenetrable, but I know he's staring at me. Wondering what the fuck I'm doing. Thinking he doesn't understand me, no-one could, and I'm a mess, and will I make up my fucking mind—

His hand cradles my jaw, and the touch is so gentle it shocks all my sharp thoughts away.

"Keynes," he murmurs, and just like the first night I met him, I feel his breath against my cheek. But this time, nothing in me shudders with disgust.

This time, everything in me *wants.*

"Tell me you're okay," he whispers.

I can't speak. I can't do anything but stand there and feel him —so real, so close, so *Griff.* The heavy planes of his body make my cock swell against my thigh. The urge to roll my hips against his is so irresistible, I almost do it. Refraining takes everything I have. I'm biting my tongue to stop this, tasting my own blood.

"Keynes," he says, his voice a growl now, one that rumbles through my veins. "Talk to me."

"Fine," I manage. "I'm fine." I'm not, though; I'm teetering on the edge of possibility, my voice a tortured rasp. My fingers are tangled in his shirt, holding tight as if the fabric is my control. And Griff—he's still, so still that I know he heard the desire in my voice.

I don't think he knows what to do about it. But I do.

"Monday," I say for what feels like the thousandth time. "I'll see you on Monday."

There's a slight pause before he agrees. "Okay."

"Goodbye."

Slowly, slowly, he lets go of me. Eases away, leaving me weak with the need I denied. It's not that I don't want to rip his clothes off; it's that I'm suspicious of the urge. How do I know this isn't a fluke?

I had no idea I could care enough to be so cautious, before now.

"Look after yourself," he tells me, and makes his way down the stairs.

When he's gone, I strip myself naked and lie on the bed, press my face into the pillow he used all day and smell him: spice and faint citrus. Then I squeeze my aching cock with the hand that held his, and I do exactly as he told me. I look after myself.

The next day, Sunday, drags something awful. By the time evening rolls around, I have thought of Griffin countless times and fucked my own hand twice. I have cursed myself at least once an hour for not making him stay last night. I have promised myself that the next time he touches me, as long as I still want it, I will eat him alive. And I'm certain that he *will* touch me again.

I don't know why I'm certain, but I am.

Glittering energy cascades through my blood, and I find myself in the strange position of wanting to share my constant smiles with someone, so I go downstairs to see if Maria is free.

She answers the door with a smirk and says, "Did my eyes deceive me, yesterday—"

I sigh. "Maria."

"Or did I spy our lovely Griffin—"

"*Maria.*"

"Skulking out of the flat at an unholy hour, looking rather pleased with himself?"

"Maria!" But I'm grinning.

She slaps my shoulder with a tea towel and says, "It's only been a bloody week. A week, and there's romance!"

"It's not romance."

"Get inside, you slut, and tell me all about it."

"There's nothing to tell," I protest, but by the time my arse meets her kitchen chair I'm already babbling, "*He liked my cooking,*" like a fool.

I am a happy fool.

GRIFF

On Monday morning, the sun rises like it's shy. When I don't see Keynes roaming around the farm, I begin to wonder if maybe he's shy, too. All morning, the need to see him again rolls over my skin like thunder, but the longer he stays away, the more it occurs to me that he might not feel the same.

I assumed that he sent me away on Saturday night because he wasn't ready, not because he didn't want me. I decided that we'd had the most amazing fucking day of my life, and that something was growing between us, as gorgeous and temperamental as my indoor azaleas. But with every minute that passes, I'm starting to doubt myself. What if he's prickly and distant again, overcompensating for Saturday's ease? What if I'm reading too deep into everything that happened, misreading the way his pulse beat at his throat, misunderstanding the cadence of his breaths when we touched in the dark? It's possible. After all, he's not in Fernley to stay. My life is a holiday to him; I doubt he's getting attached. The thought has fangs that won't let go.

My job today is simple, but I pour all my focus into it. I'm handing out collection bags to the support staff, telling them how to distribute the plastic sacks between groups of volunteers. Once that's dealt with, I make sure everyone left behind in the offices knows exactly what to do and where to direct people. Then I head to my section, concentrating on work instead of worries.

Everyone assigned to the main plantation arrows after me, like a group of baby ducks. There's a mix of villagers and strangers from the closest small town, here for fun or to earn some spare change. More than a few have children, giggling and chattering about the fact they'll be hunting flowers all day. I know Emily has given all parents a strict talking to and their own special plant identification sheets, because some flora can be eaten by cheeky little adventurers, but others definitely cannot.

As if to prove my point, a tall, tattooed guy calls to his son, "Josh. Josh, kiddo. Don't eat that."

I look behind me to make sure Josh isn't poisoning himself. No; apparently this kid just enjoys chewing on grass. The group chuckles together as we trudge toward the plantation—not via the shortcut through the woods, but along the official, grassy path.

"Josh," the man tries again, more firmly now. But a quick glance over my shoulder shows me one grinning boy with a mouthful of grass and no remorse, swapping looks with a girl who might be his sister.

Then the pretty black woman holding the man's hand shakes out her long, white dress and calls, "Joshua."

Grass falls out of that tiny mouth as if the kid tasted a worm.

I laugh quietly to myself and keep walking. The amusement lasts for thirty busy minutes as I get first timers settled into the task and greet the regulars who come to help us out every harvest. But once that's done, my empty mind slides right back to the topic of Keynes. The longer I shove elderflower heads into a bin bag without his drawling company by my side, the longer I curse myself for not seeing him yesterday, after I was done with

Rebecca. She told me to play it cool, and that knocking on his door at 8 p.m. would be the opposite of cool, but now I think I should've ignored her. Keynes is cool enough for the both of us; my job is to keep him warm. I should've stormed down regardless, and if he clammed up and refused to let me in, I should've camped out by Mrs. Hartley's garage—her kids are barely scared of me, anyway—and held my position until I caught those winter fir eyes with mine.

But he would've let me in, wouldn't he? Saturday was good, wasn't it? Yeah, it was good, and I have no reason to worry like this. Me and him, we're... *something*, now. There's a current between us I've never felt before, and I know exactly what my mum would say about it: *There are things you have to reach for with both hands, and fuck the doubts.* I'm mumbling under my breath, telling myself to relax, when a shadow spills over me.

"Have I ever told you," Keynes asks, "that you think rather ferociously?"

My heart throws a fit. I squint up from my position at the base of an elderflower bush, and there he is. He's blocking out the pale, nervous sun, his lips tilting at one corner, his hands in the pockets of his jeans.

"Yeah," I say. "You've told me that." I think I might remember everything he's ever said to me. The last time those words came out of his mouth, I assumed he was calling me stupid. Rising slowly to my feet, I ask him, "What does it mean?"

There's a short silence, the happy shouts of countless kids a faint drumbeat in the background. I watch Keynes swallow, his gaze drifting over me from head to toe before he meets my eyes again. And the spark of electricity I see in his expression tells me: Saturday wasn't one-sided. Saturday wasn't imagined. Saturday was real.

I somehow manage not to pass out with relief.

"It means," he says finally, "that you're intense."

This, coming from a man who got me monumentally hard just by standing close to me in the dark. I think he's trying to sound neutral with me today, but instinct tells me he absolutely isn't. Some devil possesses me, and I raise my eyebrows. "Intense. Do you like that?"

His smile is a surprise and a relief, teasing with an edge that I'm willing to swear is flirtatious. "Don't talk dirty to me at work, Griffin. There are children present."

Definitely flirtatious. Fucking bingo. I laugh, and everything between us is easy. Natural. Good. He winks at me and crouches down, shaking out a screwed-up ball of plastic from his pocket: he has a bin bag, too. He's here, and he's picking elderflower next to me, or he will be if I get my arse into gear and get to work.

Shoving down all the giddy fizziness in my chest, I kneel beside him and go back to picking. "You want me to show you what makes this elderflower?" I ask. "So you know when we go into the wild sections?"

He flicks a faintly interested look at me as he snags a head of blooms. "We're going into the wild sections?"

"I spend some time on all the land we own today, everywhere pickers might be sent. Just to make sure it's running smoothly."

"And I'm coming with you?"

The way he says it, light but satisfied, makes me realise what I assumed. "Well," I hedge, then cut myself off. *Grab with both hands.* "Yes. You're coming with me."

"My, my, Mr. Everett. Look how firm we've gotten."

"Shut up."

He smirks. "Thank you for the offer, but I don't need a masterclass on elderflower. Pete explained this to me on my first day."

I raise my eyebrows, let myself look at him. It's like sneaking a sip of ambrosia. "Yeah?"

"Oh, yes." He plucks a head and taps me on the nose with it, his voice crisp but not clipped, cool but not distant. Like he's a teacher. Or an especially good student. "The flowers grow on bushes that may become big enough to resemble trees, but they never have a trunk. Blooms burst from their stems in a spray and are pale yellow or pure cream in colour. The leaves have serrated edges and are commonly found in groups of five. Not to be confused with cow parsley, which is whiter and tends not to have the accompanying leaves, or prycantha, which are paler, larger, and packed more closely together." He finishes his speech and puts his elderflower in the bag.

I swallow. Hard. I knew I loved plants, but Jesus Christ, hearing him reel off information like that was hot. For a moment, all I can do is stare down at my hands and imagine them on him, making him moan plant specifications in my ear.

Eventually, I manage to say, "You have a good memory."

"You should teach me things, too, so I can remember them for you."

I look up sharply to find him focused on the bush, a sly little smile curving his mouth. That smile says he noticed the heat in my skin and the speed of my breaths. He knows that speech got to me. Which is kind of embarrassing, kind of useful. If he knows, maybe he'll do it again.

"I'll teach you whatever you want," I say, my voice low.

"Promises, promises."

If we keep talking like this, and he keeps smiling like that, I'm going to jump him in front of everyone. I don't even think he'd mind. But I have a feeling the woman in the white dress will stomp me into the ground if I traumatise her kids, so I better change the subject.

"You were late." It's a clumsy shift in topic, I know, but I'm curious. I just hope he doesn't realise *how* curious and decide I'm a weirdo clinger.

"Overslept," he tells me with a little huff of laughter. "Maria and I got carried away last night."

"Ah," I nod. That's not exactly what I expected to hear, but from the look on his face, I think they're friends. And I like that idea a lot.

While we work, we talk the way we did on Saturday: easy and eager, which I usually don't have the energy for. But Keynes *is* energy, and he makes conversation even simpler than Rebecca does. Our chatter doesn't feel like a weight or a landmine. It feels like being caught in the current of a lazy, winding stream, floating along under the sun, turning this way and that with every thoughtless word. It feels like nothing is—has ever been—could ever be—wrong.

I barely notice the slow path of the sun across the sky; it's only when my bag bulges half full that I realise the time.

"We should move on," I tell him, and he nods seriously and steps back, ready to follow. Because he takes *me* seriously—at work, anyway. I've noticed that. When it comes to my job, he doesn't tease or toy with me like I know he wants to. He just listens.

Except, of course, for the time when he talked back—when he told me that my work, my time, my skill, was important. Something soft and bruised inside me flinches at the memory, because according to Henry, he was wrong about that. But maybe Keynes really believed it. In fact, I know he did.

So, after we wave goodbye to those still picking here, I lead him to the shortcut through the copse, and I find myself mumbling: "Henry said no. About the recipes and that."

Keynes looks at me as we break through the first row of trees. "No? Just… no?"

I grunt and keep walking, satisfied when my booted foot snaps a twig in two.

"Wait." A hand on my arm, getting hotter and hotter with each moment the touch continues. So hot that by the time I turn to face him, I feel as if he's burning through my clothes. I actually sneak a look down, just to check he isn't, and then I'm frozen, locked in place by what I see: that elegant, long-fingered hand splayed over my biceps, digging in just a little like he won't let me get away. Something thrills through me, right down the middle, until my skin seems to crackle and my blood rushes in stormy waves.

I let my eyes wander over his hand, his thick wrist, the crisp golden hairs on his forearms. The mint green of his shirt's rolled-up sleeves, and his broad shoulders. His hard jaw and soft, open mouth. His eyes.

"Stop that," he murmurs, almost breathless.

"Stop what?" I don't wait for an answer, since I already know. It's a heady, drunken feeling, this knowing. "How are your ribs?" I raise a slow hand toward his side, and when he doesn't flinch or stiffen or go cold in front of me, I touch him. Press my palm against his body and wait patiently for an answer. That's me: patient.

I'll be so fucking patient for you.

"They're fine," he says softly. I can hear cheerful shouts in the distance, cooing wood pigeons above us, possibility between us.

I slide my hand down, from his ribs to his hips, and he doesn't stop me. Still, I have to ask, "Is this okay?"

"Yes." Immediate.

"Tell me how it feels." I'm worried he'll say *Fine* or *I can handle it* or something else that shows he's still shaking on the inside.

Instead, he whispers, "Good. It feels really fucking good."

Those words, the hint of wonder in his voice as he says them, knock the breath clean out of me. I'm still trying to recover when he changes the subject even more clumsily than I would.

"What did Henry say?" he blurts, sounding a little drunk. His perfectly-formed words are all wonky right now, his pretty face something other than serene. But he's not afraid. So I keep my hand in place, don't take it further, don't take it away. And the hand he put on my arm a minute ago? That's not moving either. He's burning me down to the bone. They'll find the scar of him on my remains.

But he asked me a question, and I want to answer. Problem is, even the memory of Henry's laughter seems gentle now, fuzzy and distant through the hazy screen of this moment. "He said…" I take a breath, focus on my thoughts instead of Keynes's mouth—and realise that Henry didn't say much at all. "I'm not sure what he said," I finish with a frown. For some reason, I don't worry about Keynes hearing that and deciding I'm stupid. He's good at some things, I'm good at others. People are not one of my things. He knows it, and he doesn't care, just like I don't care that, according to Pete, Keynes tried to eat catnip last week because he thought it was wild mint.

"I see." The words are sharp and almost deadly. He goes from handsome to shark-like and back again, a flicker of an expression, there and gone. "Let me guess: he acted incredulous that you'd dare to ask and laughed you out of his office."

I nod. "I don't think he even looked at my spreadsheets, not really."

Keynes's gaze has been narrowed on something in the distance, like he was trying to blow up a tree behind me with nothing but his mind. Now his expression softens and he focuses on me, laugh lines cradling his eyes. "You made spreadsheets?"

"I made all sorts. I wasn't going in there to talk out my arse. I had numbers."

"You're very good at your job, aren't you, Griffin?"

I shrug, suddenly feeling warm. "Well, thanks."

"And *his* job, really," Keynes adds, all thoughtful. "The lazy little shit."

I'm shocked and secretly happy, because I never thought… The thing is, Keynes and Henry…

Let me start again.

The way I see it, Keynes and Henry are the same. I mean, not in looks or dress sense or general goodness, but, you know—they're the same. They speak the same and went to the same ridiculous schools, and I bet Keynes's family lives in the same sort of massive old house Henry's family always has. So even though Henry's a prick and Keynes isn't, I suppose it never occurred to me that Keynes would agree. That he'd look at a man who's just like himself, and look at me, and say, *I choose you.*

In any way. Ever.

But I think he just did. And now he's blabbering about ways to make Henry listen to me, moving on from that moment as if it meant nothing.

I wish I could act natural and do the same, but I can't. I can't. I'm full of him, that's how it feels, and as I watch him rant in my defence, the sensation only gets worse. Suddenly I'm grabbed by this demanding, gut-clenching *need*, as real as the air in my lungs. My skin is flushed with it, my blood is hot with it, my teeth ache with it, and my dick, which has been hyperactive since I met Keynes, is waking up to say hello.

I tell it to settle down, first of all, and then I tighten my hand on Keynes's hip. Just the tiniest bit, just to catch his attention—but his breath hitches in his throat, and his words cut out in the middle. Then those winter fir eyes drill into me, and they're not saying *Stop.*

But still, I have to check. "Tell me if I'm doing something—"

"Keep going." The words are steel and silk all at once. "Keep going, Griff."

Yes, Sir. Since he's still holding my arm, and since I don't want to grab him or drag him or do anything that might make him panic, I limit myself to taking a step backward. One step, hoping he'll follow. He does. I take another, and another, the two of us connected by touch and a deeper, invisible thread that started out so fine but grows stronger every day.

When my back finally bumps into the nearest tree, he crowds me, his hands gripping my biceps. "Yes," he breathes.

The word puffs hot against my jaw, dragging me back to Saturday night. I want him so fucking badly it's starting to give me a headache. I can feel the ghost of his body against mine, the promise of it. If he moved an inch, just an inch, we'd be pressed together from chest to ankle. I want that. I want to rock my dick against his belly as I harden, I want to feel his ribs expanding with every breath. I want that fucking mouth. But Keynes hesitates, his eyes drinking in my face as time stretches. Some small part of me worries about what he sees, because Lord knows I don't look the way he does. A bigger part of me remembers the moment he said: *"If I thought I deserved it, I'd kiss you right now."*

Slowly, my heart pounding right through my chest, I move my hands to cradle Keynes's face. Sweep my thumbs over those sharp cheekbones, feeling the rasp of stubble he forgot to shave. My head falls forward until my brow bumps his.

I whisper, "You deserve it. Everything you want, you deserve it."

More thunderous beats of my heart. One. Two. Three. He's still.

Then he moves like a storm. His hands shackle my wrists, but he doesn't pull me away. He uses the connection to drag himself closer, so close all I can see or feel or breathe is him, so close he could crawl inside me. I wish he would. The hard length of his dick presses against my own, and I could collapse on the spot, as if this hunger has turned every bone in my body to liquid. Then his mouth takes mine, and the rest of me is liquid too.

His kiss is desperate.

Soft, full lips, a sweetly demanding tongue, a needy insistence that sets me on fire. He grabs me and wants me and owns me and needs me, and I let myself fall into him, get lost in him, cling to him, and kiss him back with breathless disbelief. This man is mine. All mine. The way he makes me feel, he couldn't be anything else.

Keynes breaks the kiss, presses his hot mouth to my jaw and then my throat—like he gives a shit about me, like he wants to make me a horny, reckless mess. He already has, but the feel of his teeth grazing my skin, his tongue flicking over the dizzying bite, makes my erection almost painful. I rock my hips hard against him, and he grunts. My cock throbs. I feel my own pre-come on my lower belly, where the tip peeks out of my briefs. Fuck.

He pulls back suddenly. Looks me in the eye. "I've been thinking about this all weekend."

"Since Saturday?"

"Listen to me," he says. "All weekend."

I am fucking volcanic right now.

He kisses my throat again, and my head falls back to rest against the tree. Above me, the forest's sparse canopy lets in streams of sunlight, and it looks like something holy. *This* is holy. Keynes slips a hand under my shirt, finds the head of my erection and pauses, looking surprised. I have one second to hope it's not too much for him, that this won't make him stop—then the heel of his hand presses hard against my dick, and my whole body jerks, and thoughts fly right out of my head.

"Jesus fucking Christ," I groan, thrusting against him, helpless and mindless and hungry. I cup his nape with one hand, pushing until he looks at me. His pupils are blown, his mouth wet and swollen, his breaths coming rough and uneven. He meets my eyes and swipes his thumb over the head of my dick. The noise I make isn't human.

Keynes raises his hand and sucks my pre-come off his thumb.

Oh, holy fucking hell. Need for him takes over me, humming through my blood like whiskey. I hold his jaw in my hands, coax his mouth open like he's been misbehaving—he *has* been misbehaving—sweep my tongue inside and taste myself on him. He moans, palms my dick through my jeans, squeezes.

Perfect. So fucking perfect, but— "I want to make you come." Want to do this for him, not the other way around.

"Do you?" he asks faintly, and I have no idea why he looks so fucking surprised.

"Of course I do," I say. "If you want me to. I'm about to come all over myself, so it's only fair." That's nothing but the truth, and it turns out Keynes likes the truth, because something about him seems to melt.

He drags his teeth over his bottom lip and groans. Then he says the most hilarious and adorable thing to ever leave his mouth. "I don't want to make a mess."

When I laugh, he glares—but his death-stare isn't as effective when he's rocking his swollen cock against my hip.

"I'll clean you up," I promise him. "But only if you want me to. It's okay if you don't. I'm just saying, if you do—"

"*Yes*," he growls.

I drop to my knees.

Then he blurts, "Wait," and my heart stutters. Is he okay? Did I push him too fast?

But he sinks to his knees as well, and kisses me again. Hard, deep, possessive—or maybe that's just wishful thinking. I don't care. His tongue battles mine, his teeth catch my bottom lip, and a groan rolls through his chest. He pulls away, panting harder than ever, and says, "I want to, but you'll get into trouble. If anyone—"

"Shit, yeah." A fraction of the blood filling my cock returns to my brain, and I remember that I'm at work and strangers are roaming Fernley Farm's land today. They aren't supposed to pass through here, but people do things they shouldn't all the time.

For example, right now I'm grabbing the swell of Keynes's arse and practically bending him in half as I kiss him again.

When the kiss breaks, he's laughing, and so am I. He is the purest thing I've ever seen in my life, smiling with kiss-swollen lips like a filthy angel, bumping his forehead against mine in a way that screams trust, closeness, a thousand things I never thought I would get from him. But now that I have them, even in the tiniest doses, I'm high. Being with him is like watching seeds slowly germinate, fresh green shoots fighting their way free of the earth. I think he might be sun and air and water. I think I might be hooked on the feeling of having him.

Which could be a serious problem.

I'm breathing hard, still smiling silly, but my thoughts turn cool and concerned in an instant, like spring showers washing away the heat. I lean back on my hands and feel the dirt and debris of the forest floor against my palms, letting it ground me. Sometimes, when she was quiet and pale and exhausted, my mum would lead me along Fernley's stream and tell me, or maybe herself: *If you're lost, go outside. Everything's easier under the sky.*

That must be how Keynes and I are doing this right now, how we're making each other feel so good without reservations. Because we're under the sky.

"Come on," I say, heaving myself up and holding out a hand to him. When he takes it, accepting my help without a moment's thought, something soft rises in my chest. I pull him up, keeping hold of his hand as we wander through the trees. The connection makes me feel even taller than usual. I am a forest giant.

"Griff?" he says.

"Yeah?"

"My name is Olu."

I roll him around on my tongue. He tastes like peach nectar.

———

OLU

Griff says it over and over throughout the day: my real, my private, my vulnerable name. *I think we should start over there, Olu. You're filling up fast, Olu—look, I got you a spare bag. Olu, could you show this lady to the next field?* Every time, he looks at me like he knows me. Every time, I wonder if maybe he does—if maybe he snuck in, under my armour, past every icy defence, and embedded himself into some vital part of me. I don't know if the idea is blissful or terrifying, but I do know every time those dark eyes caress me, and that fine mouth shapes my name, I shiver. And I remember how it felt, to want somebody for the first time in forever.

No, not somebody. *Griff*. It's Griff who makes me feel like myself, Griff who makes everything safe, Griff who's taking me apart piece by dizzying piece. No-one else. I can still taste that drop of his come on my tongue, sharp and salty, and I want more. I think of him on his knees for me, and the way my body felt— electrified, clean, *mine*—and then I have to think of something else before I disgrace myself.

Since my feelings toward him are rioting out of control incredibly quickly, I decide it's time to get to know him better. The more I know, life has taught me, the less I'll like him. And considering how much I *want* him, and how reckless it makes me, liking Griff as little as I can seems a sensible precaution.

So, while he makes me feel exposed and delicate with nothing but gentle looks and cheerful company, I try to peel him like fruit. Starting with Henry.

"What are you going to do about the recipes?" I ask.

"I don't know, Olu. Thank you, Sir, thank you very much." He nods at an elderly man who's leaving the fields with a bin bag of elderflower.

"But what do you want to do?" I prod.

"I don't *know*, Olu." Griff sounds exasperated and I don't blame him—my questions have been never-ending—but he has a soft little smile on his face and a fond sort of light in his eyes, and he won't stop saying my name.

"Well, you can't let Henry get away with using you." This is meant to be reconnaissance in my mission not to get too attached, but I am starting to suspect myself of ulterior motives. It feels disturbingly like I care about this, about *Griff*, although I cannot fathom why. I've liked lots of men, kissed lots of men, found myself tempted by a forest blowjob with lots of men, but I don't recall ever giving a shit about their daily lives, achievements or disappointments. I can't even remember what Jean-Pierre's job was.

Oh, no, I do recall; he never had a job.

Either way, the issue at hand is this: I want to shove my foot up Henry's arse for the way he manipulated Griffin. I can almost *see* how it all occurred, can imagine Henry's easy laughter and fake pity and the disbelieving tone he'd use, a thousand tiny things all designed to add up to, *Why are you even here? You don't matter. Not a bit.*

Bullshit. Bull. Shit. Griffin matters more than anything.

To the success of Fernley Farm, I mean. He is a very good production manager.

"I'm not sure what to do," Griff says, reaching up like the Big Friendly Giant to harvest the very top of the tallest bush in this field. "What *can* I do?" It should sound like a hopeless lament, but it doesn't. And when I look at him, at his raised eyebrows and calm interest, I realise he's not cursing society or capitalism or what have you. He's asking.

He's asking *me*.

For advice.

Twinkling, starlight pleasure hits me, scattered and shy in the dark of my past. I clear my throat and focus on what Griffin's asking. I want to answer well for him. I want to help.

"Lots of people do what Henry's doing," I begin. "They count on their staff not knowing enough to realise that they're being mistreated. Or on the fact that most people can't afford legal disputes, especially not with the kind of team I know Henry's family uses. He's in control of a huge part of your life, so he's effectively trapped you. This isn't my area of expertise, and I have laughably little experience, so don't take anything I say as legal advice—"

"I thought you were a lawyer?"

"I qualified. Sometimes I draw up contracts for friends or family, usually when they need them for underhanded purposes."

139

He gives me a baffled look, his brows drawing together. "Underhanded purposes?"

"For example, my best friend Theo once asked me to draw up a contract for a woman he was trying to sleep with."

"Uh…" Griff is frowning even harder. It's a good look on him. Recently, everything seems like a good look on him.

"It's a long story," I say, "and it makes Theo sound like an absolute twat, but he's married to the woman now, so…"

Griff huffs out a laugh and shakes his head. "So, you make good contracts, is what I'm hearing."

"No, I think the marriage is more to do with him being attractive and successful and a rather nice fellow."

He grunts. It's his *Uh-huh* grunt, a short, sharp noise that manages to sound openly mocking.

"The point here is," I say severely, steering us back on track, "that I can't offer you legal advice."

"So you really are a writer? You don't work as a solicitor at all?"

I falter, mostly because I keep forgetting that I'm here under false pretences. "I've never worked as a solicitor."

There. I told him the complete truth. And continued to imply a lie.

I feel guilty. Why do I feel so guilty?

"But I've never been published, either," I add. More truth. More implications. Manipulation, really, that's what this is, which makes me no better than Henry. "I just work for a publisher." I don't mention my brother-in-law, or how that position came about, or that it's now technically over.

I am sick of my own lying mouth. I change the subject.

"My advice, as a *friend*, would be to stop offering Henry recipes. Hoard them for yourself, and let's see how the brand fares without new seasonal flavours from you. Because from what I saw while haunting the admin and marketing teams last week, Fernley Farm's success really kicked in when you started putting out new, seasonal flavours—and those do come from you, don't they?"

"Yes," he admits.

Such a simple, quiet word to confirm what he's done. It seems to me that Griff's talent and leadership are largely responsible for Fernley Farm's status as some sort of soft drink rising star, but everyone around here treats him like an irritant at best. I'm so bothered by that, I have to take a deep, green-scented breath to calm down.

After a moment, I attempt humour. "Of course, you should feel free to share the recipes with other people. Such as me."

Griff gives me an amused, sideways look, still picking the highest flowers. "Hang on—is this that, uh, industrial espionage? Are you here to get my recipes for yourself?" He's smiling, shaking his head, and I know that was a joke. But does he realise he can't seem to accept my reason for being here? Does he even notice that he's secretly, subconsciously convinced I'm bull-shitting?

How does he know? How can he tell I'm not me all the way through?

I shove the worries and confusion away. "Maria may have given me some chilli and cranberry cordial last night," I say, "and I *may* have pledged my undying love to it."

He laughs. I drink down the sight greedily: the smile, the eyes, the way his tanned skin shines under the sunlight. I want to run my hands over the roughness of his beard and into the thick mess of his hair. I want to plaster myself against him once more and feel the exhilaration of being fearless and mindless and head over heels in lust, no caveats. I want to gorge.

"You can try more, if you want," he says. "More of my recipes."

And more of you? I hope so. "I'd like that."

"Come over after work?"

I breathe deep, my ribs twinging slightly, my body flooding with the sharp, bright scent of him.

His flush deepens, and he adds, "That's if you don't mind. I have to stay later, so you'd have to wait. And—"

I cut him off, and say again, "I'd like that."

He smiles at me, really smiles, sweeter and more open than I've ever seen before. His incisors are unusually sharp, his inky eyes are cradled by fine lines, his crooked nose is charming. This is Griff warm and approving—of *me*. It's a striking chime of a moment; it's brand new. He is shining like the sun, and I think... I think he might be handsome. Oh, God, yes, he is. Without any warning at all, he is.

I narrowly resist the urge to kick him and tell him to stop. My heart is pounding against my ribs, which are still feeling delicate. He really ought to have some consideration for my condition.

God in heaven, hear my prayers. I am in serious trouble.

11

OLU

Griff does indeed have to stay later, but that's okay. I perch on Fernley Farm's gate, the same gate he once scolded me over. That's what he was doing, that first morning; trying to intimidate me with dark looks and harsh words that I've since learned don't suit him. At the time, I was mildly unsettled and reluctantly intrigued. Now I recall the scene with something like arousal. I remember the things I used to want in bed and wonder if I'll be able to want them again. Then I remember the way Griff touched me earlier, his mouth a brand even as he gave *me* the dominant position, and I start to think that eventually, I could.

But I've spent enough time mooning over the man for one day. My journal is in my hands because writing kills time, and because helping a little fruit farm harvest their elderflower in a tiny village was just as much of an event as I hoped it would be. More, in fact. My hand is cramped from everything I've written so far, and images slide through my head, begging to be captured, to be funnelled into words so I'll never forget. I've tried my best, but it's hard to put down on paper how it feels to be alive.

That's always been my struggle, the reason why I've never

bothered to share my writing: I can't possibly capture how it feels to be alive. Therefore, everything I write is shit. Or something.

I roll my lips inward because if I don't, I might laugh at myself. Snapping the journal shut, I slide it into my satchel, closing the bag securely because I think it might rain soon and 'waterproof' only goes so far. The sky is a sad, city velvet, and the air already smells like wet earth: rich and fresh, laced with the threat of a storm. But I don't worry about any of that, because I see my giant coming for me.

"Ready?" he calls across the near-deserted courtyard, as if I might in fact be extremely busy right now. You know, sitting here on a gate, staring into thin air.

"I'm ready," I say, and hop to my feet. We open the gate and slip out, wandering down the lane—close, shoulder to shoulder, matching steps. We're silent. I don't look at him, an odd sort of coyness winding around me like a cat winds between legs. But I can feel him looking at me, just like I feel the brush of his hand against mine. Accidental, I think, until it happens again and again. I'm not sure if he's doing it or if I am. Just like I'm not sure who holds whose hand first; I only know that by the time we leave Fernley Farm's lane and turn into the village's main street, we're connected like a pair of high school sweethearts. I should be horrified, but I am incredibly satisfied instead. All this fresh country air is turning my mind. My sister won't know what to do with me when I go home.

The thought shudders through me like a gong, weighty and ominous. *When I go home.* For a moment, I almost forgot this place wasn't my forever.

The rain begins, but it limits itself to a scattered, pathetic plod. "Like it here?" Griffin asks, his low, rough voice out of place in the countryside peace. He should belong here, really, but sometimes—for reasons I can't describe—he simply doesn't. I think he knows it, too. I think that's why his self-consciousness seems as big as he is.

"The village is lovely," I admit.

He grunts.

I hesitate, then try something. "Have you ever left?"

There's a moment of silence before he answers. It isn't heavy silence, isn't difficult, but it's *something*. I just can't put my finger on what. Finally, he says, "Nowhere to go."

I tell myself the words hit hard because he sounds like me. Because, for years of my life, I felt like I had nowhere to go, either. The only difference is, instead of staying in one place, I ran across the world looking for home.

"I've been to fifty-two different countries," I tell him, my sad attempt at lightening the mood.

He whistles low, and I feel a little bit too pleased. "Bet you're bored here, then."

I *should* be bored here—soothingly bored, yes, but still bored. Instead, I'm alive, electricity humming over my skin even now. It takes effort to reply calmly, hiding all my fizz. "I must admit, a few trees and a single pub aren't exactly the height of excitement."

Griff doesn't answer, and I wonder if he has been awed into silence by my sophistication. Then he says solemnly, "Don't forget about the sheep," and I promptly piss myself laughing.

Something between us dissolves. My chuckles fade. We grin at each other, and my hand squeezes his, and this—*this* feels right. Better than control. Yes.

"Want to go through the woods?" he asks, nodding at the trees behind us. "It's a shortcut."

But he sounds like a mischievous little boy. I arch an eyebrow. "*Is* it?"

"It's a longcut," he says, as if that makes any sense whatsoever.

I'm grinning again.

The trees are tall and slender and straight as arrows, the canopy is sparse, and the sky is dark with thick, grey clouds. I pat my satchel as we hop over logs and push aside branches, reassuring myself it's firmly closed. Griff catches the action and gives me a strange look.

"How did you start writing, anyway?"

I confess before I can think better of it: "My first university application, I wanted to study literature. I'd filled out all the papers. I showed my father and he… he wasn't happy with that." I frown, because this was supposed to be a funny story, but I think I'd forgotten how bad things were. How horrified he was, how cruel he was. It's coming back to me now, as if I've broken the damn on a river full of vomit. "He wasn't happy with much, really. Especially not with things he found womanish, since women are inferior creatures, and so on. In the end, I read law, and writing became a hobby."

"Hmm," Griff says quietly. "Take it you aren't close."

"My sister and I cut all ties with our so-called family last year."

"Yeah?"

I nod. "It's funny—the whole thing came about because someone outed me—or was trying to out me. But now I wonder why I didn't come out years ago. I suppose I was afraid."

"Are you still afraid?"

"Of different things." My voice is soft, almost fragile. I clear my throat and force a smile, looking pointedly at our joined hands. He'll hold on to me anywhere, it seems, even in this tiny, backward village where people stare and whisper. "You don't seem afraid of anything."

"I'm afraid of lots of things," he says promptly. "Mum used to tell me fear will stunt you. Like growing a sunflower inside a cupboard. So I try to take my sunflower outside, even when it kills me."

"My, my," I murmur. "You're deep and meaningful today."

He snorts and elbows me. But he flashes me a grateful little smile too, and I think he realises what I'm doing: making light so he won't dwell on the fact that he's talking about his mother again, since the last time spooked him. So, in the spirit of distraction, I elbow him back. Just a little nudge. He laughs.

And then the storm begins.

There really is no build-up—or if there was, I didn't notice, which doesn't seem like me. One moment the rain is mildly refreshing; the next, the sky has snapped and spilled an ocean. We blink at each other, and then at the heavens, in surprise. When a fat raindrop bursts directly in my eye, I decide to behave sensibly and start jogging through the trees.

Griffin chuckles behind me. "You're running from the rain?"

"If you want to get soaked," I call over my shoulder, "be my guest."

He's following, his longer legs swallowing up ground easily. When we're level, his massive shoulder bumps mine. "You really are a city boy," he says, "globetrotter or no."

"*Globetrotter?*" I repeat, nudging him back. But perhaps, in my efforts to prove I'm not intimidated by his size, I overdo it. He veers to the right with a laughing yelp of surprise.

"That's what I said," he insists, and the nudging continues. Except now we're sort of like boulders smashing into each other. I bounce off a nearby tree and come back at him with even more force; he skids through the muddy grass, then shoves me properly. I wasn't expecting that, so I actually slip and go over. Apparently, there is something in Fernley's fresh air that ruins my notoriously cat-like balance.

I land on my arse and slap a hand over my ribs, partly because falling jarred them and partly because I'm laughing non-stop and it hurts.

"Shit," Griff says, and kneels down beside me, his denim-covered knees sinking into the earth. I can barely see or hear him over the rain; it's falling in sheets, now, sluicing through the air and sticking my shirt to my skin.

"I'm fine," I gasp between chuckles and groans.

"I'm sorry," he says and helps me up.

It's not discomfort that zips through me when our hands meet, and it's certainly not revulsion. No, this feeling is prickling and fidgety, a hot, swollen sensation that sweeps over me like this storm. It surrounds and consumes. When Griff drags me from the ground and onto my feet, his grip is firm, as if he'd fight before he'd let go. His other hand goes to my ribs, cradling them as if he can reduce the ache, his fingers filling the empty spaces between my bones. We're face to face, hip to hip, and our palms still kiss. Water drips from the tip of his crooked nose, his midnight hair plastered to his forehead. For a moment, his eyes aren't mirrors hiding worlds; they're windows I could climb right through, if I just had the nerve.

Breathless, I trace out a silent wish. *Put your mouth on me.*

Either he reads lips or minds, because he does it.

Griff's skin is cold, but his soft sigh is fire breathed right down my throat. His taste is all fresh rain and tenderness. One slick glide of rain-wet lips, then another, no tongue and no demands—just closeness, so sweet I can't bear it. I could melt for him. I'm dizzy. I'm breathless. I'm flooded with need and something even more fragile yet infinitely stronger. I want him under me, over me, in me.

With me.

Lightning splits the evening open, and we flinch apart. "Come here," he says, and drags me in another direction, to the right. A few metres, and we break out of the trees and on to Fernley's main road again, safer from the lightning, but not from the rain, of course. The thunder chases us as we run hand in hand, and by the time he ushers me, dripping wet, into his kitchen, I can barely catch my breath from laughing.

GRIFF

"We need to get you dry," I say, because focusing on details makes ignoring the ache in my dick easier.

"Do we?" Olu murmurs. Not like he's winding me up; more like he's not listening. He wanders through the kitchen ahead of me, the blue-grey light that spills through the windows shadowing more than it hides. But I can see enough to recognise what he's doing. It's just like that first day at work: he's got his back to me, and he's unbuttoning his shirt.

Only, everything's different now.

My mouth is dry, my voice is hoarse, my thoughts are wobbling around. "What are you...?" For some reason, I can't finish my sentence.

He turns around, the shirt spread open. It slides off his shoulders. There's a slight, wet *slap* when it hits the floor, but I barely hear that over the rush of blood in my ears. "Can't get dry in wet clothes," he says reasonably.

"Oh. Yeah."

Olu steps toward me. "So take off your clothes, Griff."

I would, I swear I would. But I'm worried I'll turn into a ravenous animal, the way I did earlier, and forget my own name.

Then again—would it be so bad, forgetting my name for him?

I fumble with one of my buttons, then lose patience and drag my shirt over my head. Blink in the semi-dark, and realise he's watching me with something like hunger on his face. Is that right? That can't be right.

Then he says, "You are magnificent," and I hear it throbbing through his voice as well.

A tension in my shoulders, one I barely knew was there, loosens. I admit, "I'm not like you. You don't look real."

"But I am."

"Believe me. I know." My words are heavy with the weight of my want. My feelings for Olu are verging on addiction already, but there are thick, mile-deep roots growing beneath that hunger. Earthing us. With a few steps, I close the distance between us—because distance should never be between us—and cradle his jaw in my hand. "You're very real. You're a stubborn, sarcastic, snotty little fuck with a serious ego."

His smile is slow and sexy as hell, his hands coming to rest on my chest. Just that light touch has me breathing funny, my cock straining against the zipper of my jeans until it hurts. "Is this supposed to be a seduction?" he asks. "Because if so, I think you're doing it wrong."

"I don't think you want seduction. I think you want someone to know you," I say honestly, "and this is all about what you want, Olu."

The smile fades, and his eyes lock on mine as if he's hypnotised. "What if I need to tie you to a bed and play with you until I'm not shy anymore?"

I huff out a laugh at the idea he's shy, but my answer is deadly serious. "Like I said. This is all about what you want."

Olu bites his lip, rolls his teeth over it, sets it free. His hands trail down my chest and over my stomach in a featherlight touch that makes me shiver and burn all at once. Then he undoes my jeans, nice and easy, and looks me in the eye. "You mentioned warming up."

"I did," I pant. "We will." *Touch me.*

"What did you have in mind?"

"Shower. Hot shower." *Touch me.*

His hands push my jeans down to mid-thigh, then my briefs. Somehow, he does it all without even grazing my dick, which should be impossible when I'm so swollen and desperate I feel like there's a fucking baseball bat between my legs. But he manages because he's magic.

Thwack. My length smacks hard against my belly, and he looks down for the first time. Makes a low, approving noise. "I've been meaning to ask for a while, Griffin, but are you, by chance, half giant?"

"Touch me." Shit. Think I said that out loud.

He ignores me, still staring. I look down too, just to see what he's seeing, and the sight of my own body is almost obscene—maybe because I can hear my thoughts, too, so I know exactly what's got me in this state. If I thought he could handle it, I'd have him on the floor right now, would lick him and spread him open and fuck into him hard. My cock twitches and a fat bead of pre-come drips from the tip, spilling down the almost-purple shaft. That can't be healthy. I need to come. Preferably all over him.

But Olu's not done with his inspection. He sinks to his knees, and I have to bite my fist—otherwise the sight of him, his face so close to my aching balls, would make me growl like an animal.

He's talking all cool and distant, trying to look unaffected, but I see the heat in his eyes and the tension in his body and the bulge in his jeans. He swirls a single fingertip in my pre-come, and I see actual stars, pops of light obscuring my vision. My breathing sounds like thunder, even to me. Then that finger, slick with all my need, trails down the length of my shaft. He leans in close, so close I feel the faint rasp of his barely-there stubble. Olu—*Olu*—has his fucking face pressed against my balls while he paints pre-come patterns over my cock. I don't know what my heart's doing in my chest right now, but it's not regular enough to be called *beating*.

"How do you fit this inside anyone?" he asks. "Actually, *do* you fit this inside anyone? I really shouldn't assume." Then he looks up at me.

Jesus, I wish he hadn't looked at me.

Sensation shoots through my body like the lightning flashing outside. My stomach tightens, my spine tingles, and I come in a violent rush of relief and embarrassment. I catch it all in my hand because I don't know what I'd do if I came on Olu's face. Actually, the problem is, I don't know what *he'd* do—I still don't know how much he's okay with, and the last thing I want is to fuck this up for him.

As my breathing slows and a blush spreads over my body, he gets to his feet. I watch him closely to see if he's distant now, if he's distracted and shaking, if me and my teenage lack of control messed up. But he looks fine. Actually, he looks really fucking happy, and also like he's going to tease me about this for a year. His smirk is huge, his eyes are dancing in the dark, and he palms his own erection lazily as if he's satisfied.

"Well," he drawls in that way he has. "I wasn't expecting that."

Now I know Olu's fine, I have more room to be embarrassed. "Been a while," I laugh awkwardly, and turn to the sink. I'm not lying; it's been a while since I did anything sexual with another human being. But it hasn't been a while since I last came, not at all, so I'm not sure why I blew like that.

Actually, yeah, I am.

I wash my hands, and he comes up behind me. I feel his warmth before I feel his touch. He's burning like a little fire, and when he grabs my shoulders and kisses the back of my neck, he sets me alight, too. My dick perks up immediately, and I wonder if it's been possessed by the ghost of its younger self.

"Griff," Olu mouths against my skin, "let's warm up."

I swallow hard. "Whatever you want."

"Let's take a shower."

———

OLU

This shouldn't be as easy as it feels. But when Griff shoves his jeans all the way off and faces me, completely naked, I'm not disgusted or suspicious or even bored. I'm not any of the things I've been for so long with other men. He takes my hand and leads me up his rickety stairs, and I follow him to the bathroom like some docile little lamb.

When he kisses me, I smile against his mouth. "I can't believe you came just like that."

"Yeah, well." He rolls his eyes, possibly at himself, and taps the button of my jeans. "Take these off."

I undo the button. Of course, my mouth's still moving. "I mean, I know I'm unbelievably gorgeous and incredibly sexy, but—"

"Maybe it wasn't you. Maybe I'm just a horny fuck who never lasts."

"Lasts?" I snort. "You weren't even *doing* anything."

"No, but you were." Griff sounds gloomy and fond all at once.

"If I sucked you off, would your head explode?"

"Probably."

The word is all unconcerned acceptance and unreserved desire, an admission that I'm his weak spot and he's fine with it. Something inside me pops like a firework, perhaps because I haven't even *tried* to charm this man. Not really. I haven't been glittering and perfect with him. I've just been… Olu. Rather shit, honestly. A trier, occasionally. And still, Griff wants me like this, as if it's obvious, as if it's inevitable.

Pushing out a breath, I fight the painful pulse of arousal through my cock and try not to lose control. Leaning my bare back against the cold bathroom tiles helps. In a moment of clarity, I listen closely for the nervous whisper of distaste that ruins all my touches before they can begin. That whisper is nowhere to be found.

I'm so beautifully alone with Griff.

He unzips my jeans, since I haven't done it yet, and pushes them slowly down. At one point, when he bends, we are exactly eye to eye, and there's something tender in his darkness.

"Is there anything I definitely shouldn't do?" he asks, and I know why he's asking.

"No."

"Are you sure?"

"No-one's ever touched me in a way I didn't want." I think it

153

might have crossed his mind, and I don't want him to worry more than he obviously is.

He exhales and nods, but the news doesn't erase the protectiveness in him, the way he curves his big body around mine and undresses me with slow, steady care. I know he likes the way I look, but when I'm naked in front of him, his eyes don't devour me the way other men's have. His regard is different, somehow. It's demanding, with an edge of barely restrained want, but there's a gentleness that says he'd rather die than rush me.

The back of his hand glides over the faded bruise at my ribs, down my abdomen, over my hip. Then he runs a finger from the base of my cock to the glistening tip, the reverse of what I did to him in the kitchen. Perhaps I understand his reaction now, because I release a strangled moan that might be his name. It certainly doesn't sound like any noise I've ever made before.

Griff's expression is almost wicked, definitely mischievous, incredibly satisfied. "Come on. Let's get warm." He switches on the shower, turns up the heat, pulls me in.

The stall is a narrow cubicle of glass, but there's space for us to stand apart. We don't. I face the hot spray, he moves behind me and wraps one thick arm around my body. I can feel the curve of his belly, the crisp softness of hair on his barrel chest. Then there's the thick pressure of his cock spreading my arse, the tip leaking against my lower back. I want to taste it. I want to taste him. Instead, he's tasting me.

He sucks the dip where my neck meets my shoulder, runs the tip of his tongue up my throat in a move so delicate I can barely believe it's him. He whispers in my ear, "Olu, I want you."

My words are meant to be a tease, but they come out as a gasp. "Would you let me fuck you?"

"I—" His hesitation is barely there, but it *is* there. "Don't know. Never done that before," he says. "But we could try."

"No, Griff, I only asked in case you *wanted*—"

"I might want," he interrupts. "I told you, I don't know. What about you?"

In the past I was happy on either side of the equation, but everything about me feels unknown these days. "We'll see," I say eventually.

"It doesn't matter. Come here. I need you."

I turn in his arms and take his mouth, his lovely, tender mouth, and kiss him hard like the filthy creature he's making me into. Our cocks slide between us, wet and rigid and so sensitive that each clumsy thrust sends an aching shiver through my body. Then Griff reaches for something, soap I realise, and slicks up his hand and grasps us both at once. I feel like I've been electrocuted. I grab his shoulders, needing his strength to hold me up because it's been so fucking long since this was good. And right now, it's good. Good like I never thought it could be. Perfect.

His hold is firm, his strokes long and slow, my spine burning with heat and my mouth a breathless, shameless, gasping thing. "Fuck," I pant, my hips jerking as I stab up into his hand. I don't think I've ever been like this. I should probably control myself, but I just can't, and I don't think he wants me to. He works us both with one hand, his other cradling my head as he nuzzles my neck. His beard scrapes my skin, a sweet burn that I hope leaves a mark.

Then he murmurs in that low, rust-and-stone voice, "That's it, sweetheart."

Oh, Jesus Christ. My body flexes like a fist. I want him harder, faster, more insistent, every-fucking-where, and I'm too far gone to care how wrecked I sound when I moan his name. "Griff. More. More."

"Yeah, babe." His arm is an iron bar crushing me to him, his hand tightens until it almost hurts, and that's exactly what I want. He sinks his teeth into my neck, hard, and I come all over us with a broken shout. Each hot spurt against my skin feels like a bolt of lightning. My legs shake, I'm holding on to Griff again, and in this moment, I would rather die than let go.

This, I suppose, is vulnerability. I should be panicking.

But how can I, when he grips my hips as if to hold us tight together, to keep us trapped in this moment? How can I, when he whispers such sweet things in my ear, things I didn't know he was capable of expressing?

"You're beautiful," he tells me, but this isn't like the other times. This is different because his eyes are closed, his face is buried against my neck, our bodies are pressed together. He can't see me at all, but he keeps saying, "You're beautiful. You're so beautiful, Olu."

———

GRIFF

We dry off in silence, but it's the good kind; the kind I feel at home in. Olu seems so talkative all the time, so constantly *on*, but when I go quiet, he never looks at me like I'm an alien. He doesn't try to talk my mouth open. He doesn't leave me be, either. He just is, and I just am, and we just are.

I'm hard again, obviously. I could spend forever watching him fall apart the way he does. It's like all his control is a huge, icy wall, but it's so badly built that when I yank a single brick, he crumbles. Big time. Olu coming hard for me might have been the best sight of my fucking life. I don't want to be done with him, not tonight.

But I also think that what we just did was… a lot, so I take my urge to kiss him again, and I crush it. I think he could do with something different right now, and I want to be the one to give it to him.

"Do you like musicals?" I ask.

He flicks a baffled look at me. "No. Where did I leave my clothes?"

"Take some of mine." I grab a T-shirt from the dresser and throw it at him. "Yours are still wet."

He catches the T-shirt and stands there, buck naked and unfairly gorgeous, staring at the grey cotton like it might bite him.

I can't help myself; I laugh. "What, are you allergic to normal clothes?"

"What is that supposed to mean?" he demands, his scowl sudden and sweet and familiar.

"Normal clothes. Instead of pastel suits that cost a bomb, or designer jeans, or—"

"My jeans are *not* designer. They're Levi."

"How much were they?"

"I don't know—ninety pounds. Griff, why are you laughing?"

"Put the T-shirt on," I say in between chuckles. "And these." A pair of my sweats smack him in the chest. "I promise they won't make you poor by association."

"You prick." He makes it sound like an endearment. He's smiling at me like the sun. "I don't care how much your clothes cost, Griffin."

"And I don't care that yours are ridiculously expensive."

"They're not—ugh, fine."

He looks good in my clothes. I'm not sure if it's because he always looks good or because I want to be all over him in every way possible. He's tightened the waistband of the sweats as far as they'll go, since he's built like a panther or some shit and I'm more like… let's say a bear. The T-shirt doesn't exactly hang off him, but you can tell it's mine. You can tell he's mine.

He'd probably be horrified if he knew how possessive my thoughts are getting, but that's okay. I know how to keep my mouth shut.

When he speaks again, it's abrupt and quick, like he's been holding the words in. "I'm surprised you'd give me your clothes."

"Why?"

"Because." He shrugs and rubs a hand over his jaw. "I don't know. I don't give people my clothes."

"People?"

"People I fuck."

Well, that's what I get for thinking all this soft shit. I nod as if I'm not flinching at the idea that I'm part of a generic group named *People Olu Fucks*. I don't know why. It's not like either of us ever said this was anything else.

My brain tries to tell me I'm an idiot. I tell it we don't think things like that anymore, and if it's not going to be a positive part of the team, it can piss off.

The silence between Olu and I changes as I shove on the last of my clothes. It's not so easy anymore. Now it's just heavy—or maybe it only feels that way to me. When I'm dressed, we stand and stare at each other like strangers instead of... instead of whatever we were ten minutes ago.

I guess this is how things work, when they happen fast. They unhappen fast as well.

After a moment or so of maybe-awkwardness, Olu claps his hands and says, "Well, then," which is the universal phrase for *I want to leave and don't know how to put it politely.* I may not be an expert in people, but I know that much.

It's not like I can stop him, so I rub my hands against my thighs and nod. "Yeah."

"Quite," he says.

I don't know what the fuck that means, so I grunt.

"Mm," is his response.

Now I think we've slipped into a foreign language. If you asked me to describe myself in three words, my first choice would probably be *patient*, but I think I've had a personality transplant because suddenly I don't know what that feels like anymore. "So are you leaving or not?" I blurt out.

At the same time, Olu says, "Why did you ask me about musicals?"

We stare at each other some more.

Then his expression ices over like a February morning. "Yes. Yes, I'm leaving."

"No, Olu, I don't want you to—"

"I did tell Maria I'd—"

"I thought *you* wanted to go, so—"

"You don't want me to?"

"Wait, you told Mrs. Hartley what?"

Silence. More staring. I want to carve out my own fucking eyeballs, at this point. Only, then I wouldn't be able to look at him, so maybe I'll leave my eyes alone.

"I told Maria," he says finally, "that I'd see her tonight, after her eldest goes to bed."

For some reason, I demand, "What, are you fucking her, too?"

Olu raises his eyebrows and blinks very slowly. I think that might be Morse code for *Don't be an imbecile.*

I mutter under my breath, "Sorry, Mrs. Hartley."

"Did you just say sorry to *Maria*? She's not even *here*. And, for Christ's sake, Griffin, I'm *gay*."

I think we're having an argument. "Are we having an argument?"

"No, you're just being an—" He breaks off, snapping his mouth shut. Then he says, "You're just being difficult."

I have the oddest feeling that he was going to call me an idiot. But then he remembered what I said to Rebecca last week, about feeling stupid. And then he stopped himself.

All of a sudden, everything about the last five minutes feels incredibly silly.

I misunderstand people all the time, and I'm shit at fixing it, but this time I really fucking want to. So I start with the simplest, truest part: "Sorry. I'm being a dick."

"I agree," he says immediately.

I should probably be pissed again, but I find myself laughing instead. When we first met, Olu had this magical ability to stick at the back of my skull and make me vicious with the need to get him out. Now he's still stuck in my head, but I want him there, and all his predatory roars sound like kitten hisses to me.

Maybe something's changed for him too—no, I know it has—because instead of dead-eyeing me the way he used to, he bites his lip, then laughs along with me. "Fine," he says, rolling his eyes. "We're both being dicks. Happy?"

"Yep."

He snorts.

"Look," I say, choosing my words carefully. "You—you said that thing, about people you sleep with, and I got weird because I like you. But I don't want you to go. Unless you need to."

Olu crosses his arms and shoots quick, considering looks at me, like a bird deciding if it wants to eat from someone's hand. "It's not even seven yet. I have hours."

"Okay," I say softly.

"Okay." Then he adds, "About what I said before—I just meant, no-one's ever given *me* their clothes. I was surprised."

That news changes how I think about what he said. Instead of hearing, *You're one of many*, I hear, *I've always been one of many*.

"Well," I tell him, "I like you."

"I believe you've said that already." A pause. "Perhaps I like you too."

It feels like there's a star inside my chest.

"But not enough to watch a musical," he continues. "Ridiculous things. People don't just burst into song, Griff."

"I know that. It's not real."

"Well, obviously it's not real. Imagine if people went through life singing about their feelings every fifteen minutes. Arrests would have to be made."

In the end, we watch *I, Tonya*. Olu tells me that, in some ways, she reminds him of his sister. I heat up two frozen pizzas, and he says next time, he's cooking.

That night, in bed, I murmur to myself, "Next time." Then I grin in the dark.

GRIFF

"…But Lewis reckons the ivy is a reason *not* to move there. He says the upkeep will be a pain, and anyway, it's ugly. He thinks *ivy* is *ugly*! Can you believe that?"

"No," I murmur, stuffing another spray of elderflower into my bag. I wonder if Olu will come over again tonight. I have a feeling he might.

"And when I said I'd pay for the ivy maintenance as a compromise, he said that *wasn't* a compromise. So I Googled the definition of compromise, and he said I was being petty! Can you believe *that*?"

I grunt a negative and part the bush I'm working on to reach another spray. Olu is sitting somewhere behind me, and I want to turn and look, but I can't. I've been staring at him a lot today, and every time he catches me, he runs his tongue over his teeth and gives me this look that makes me want to blush. But I'm at work. I can't run around blushing at work. So I won't look anymore.

"Then," Rebecca says, "I went to his parents' house and shagged his dad. Pretty sure I won that round, don't you think?"

"Yep." Blissful silence follows. I snag another hard-to-reach handful of flowers, put them in my bag, then pause. Frown. "Wait, what? Rebecca—"

When I turn, she's standing beside me with her hands on her hips, the office camera hanging around her neck and her expression... well, *unimpressed* is one word for it. "Griffin Everett," she says, all stern and annoyed, "I've never seen you so distracted in my life."

My cheeks heat. "Aren't you supposed to be taking photos of all the smiling volunteers or something?"

"Light's bad." She waves her hand as if to swipe away the beaming sunshine. "What's up with you?"

I try to resist, but I can't help it. As soon as Rebecca's words leave her mouth, my eyes fly like magnets to the sight I've been avoiding: Olu, sitting with his back against the trunk of an oak at the edge of the field, writing ferociously in his journal.

Just like he has been for, oh, the past two hours or so.

What the bloody hell is he writing? And how can he concentrate so brutally well while I'm a mess over here? The man is so controlled it's almost supernatural. It's also really hot.

"Ah," Bex says smugly. Shit. She's followed my gaze and figured out—well, probably everything, because of course she has. I wait for the trademark Rebecca Baird inquisition to begin, but all she does is turn back to me and say, "So, he does write."

"Of course he does. He's a writer."

"Uh... yeah. I know. But last time I checked, you were convinced that was some kind of long con."

I shake my head and start plucking elderflower again. "Doesn't matter what I thought before or what anyone else thinks. He's whatever he wants to be." It's only when Rebecca stares at me, all big eyes and raised eyebrows, that I realise I spoke a bit too passionately.

"Oookay then," she smirks. "So, I take it you're fucking him now?"

My face bursts into flame. There are fire-breathing dragons living in my cheeks. "Jesus, Bex."

"Aha! I knew it!"

"Be *quiet.*"

"It was only a matter of time." She claps her hands with a witchy little cackle that's part giddy and part evil. "I demand you publicly give me full credit for all of this at your wedding."

My embarrassment twists and shifts. It's not pink and spluttering anymore; it's a quiet, grey disappointment that I've been trying to ignore. "I don't know what you're on about."

"You *know,*" she grins, and smacks me on the shoulder. "Because I was the one who told you to—"

"No. No, I mean—this, me and him, it's not a wedding situation. It's not anything like that. Okay?"

"We've talked about this, Griffin. You have to fight your natural pessimism. Never say never."

"*He'd* say never. He's leaving." At the end of next week, in fact —and I hate that I'm even thinking about it. I already know it's going to fuck me up when he disappears.

But right now, he's here. Right now, everything's great. So I'm fine, right? Right. Or I was, until Rebecca brought up bloody reality. Now I'm panicking a little bit, because my skin is too tight, my heart is too big, my sneaky hopes have grown out of control like ivy, and I have no idea how to start cutting them back. I should've reminded myself, before I started all this, that getting attached would be a bad idea.

But I have this thing where I tend not to think ahead. Mum always said, *Live now, Griff, not in the past or future. It's no use being a phantom citizen of the present.*

"You're upset, aren't you?" Rebecca winces.

"No." My voice is firm. "It is what it is."

"Maybe he'll extend his stay. Maybe you could do long distance, or—"

"We're not together, Rebecca."

"Then what are you?"

"I don't know. He's all… sophisticated. He probably does stuff like this all the time, everywhere he goes." But the words don't sound right coming out of my mouth, not when I think about Olu as he really is. I shake my head. "It doesn't matter. I don't want to talk about it; I just want to do it."

"That's how you get your heart broken, Griffin."

"This isn't helpful, Rebecca."

"Oh." She perks up. "Did you want advice, then?"

"No."

"Here's what I think: this could all be very simple."

I sigh, stand, and pick up my bag. "Did you hear me say *No*?"

"Step one of Operation Griff and Keynes five-ever"—she holds out her palm for the five— "is deciding that, you know, you want him five-ever."

I start walking to a different section of the field, carefully not looking at Olu, and Rebecca falls into step beside me. "I can't decide that, because I barely know him." Sensible. I'm being sensible. "But let's say I did eventually want him for, uh, a bit. Or whatever. What's step two?"

"Well, that's easy. Step two is taking him."

Taking him. Right. I swallow. "What's step one-point-five?"

"Sorry," she trills. "There's no one-point-five."

"Step three?"

She makes a sound like a negative buzzer on a game show.

"So I just… take him? How the fuck am I supposed to do that?"

She shrugs. "Convince him to stay."

I stare at her, completely lost. Convince him to stay? I've never been enough to convince anyone of anything. Not ever. Not fucking *ever*. "This is stupid. It's just a… holiday… thing."

"Fling," she corrects. "But it doesn't have to be! You know how fast I decided on Lewis. And now look!"

"That was luck," I tell her.

"It was *instinct.*"

I have a feeling that's what my mum would say. Then I shake my head to dislodge the thought. My mum can't say anything because she's not here.

"Mark my words, Griffin Everett." Rebecca is poking me in the ribs for emphasis. I think she'd poke me on the nose if she could reach. "You're head over heels for that man. He's your destiny. In ten years' time, you'll be married with a bunch of posh little babies."

Who do you call when you're seriously concerned that your best friend is doing drugs?

———

OLU

Last night with Griff was lovely. In fact, almost everything with Griff is lovely—which means he will horribly disappoint and/or reject me very soon. I should already be pulling away from him in preparation. Instead, after a day spent simultaneously avoiding him and orbiting him like some pathetic satellite, I find myself leaving Fernley Farm by his side. Our steps are meandering, and our silence is… awkward.

The awkwardness is my fault, and I can feel Griff wondering where it's come from. I will never be able to tell him the truth, since the truth is this: I have accidentally developed an emotional attachment to him, and it's making me panic. Even burying myself in my journal didn't help; I tried to faithfully record every detail of this village, but when I read the words back, Griffin was everywhere. My travel journal now reads like some ridiculous love story. He is stamped all over me.

Searching for a way to break the quiet, I clear my throat and murmur, "Busy day." Obviously, I immediately want to shoot myself. I have never said anything so bland and useless in my life.

"Yeah," Griff says, "busy. Seemed like you wrote a lot."

Oh, just what I wanted to discuss: my massive, awful lies. I hum in agreement, press my lips together, and look away.

There are other people wandering Fernley's main street, people with dogs on leads and children on little bicycles. Some of them nod at us in greeting; most don't. No-one smiles. Instead, Griff gets constant, wary looks, as if he's a suspected serial killer. People really do treat him like shit in this place, and it occurs to me, suddenly, that he shouldn't be here.

So where should he be? Somewhere with me? Ha. *Grow up, Olumide.*

"Are you alright?" Griff asks me suddenly.

Oh, Christ. He's noticed. Well, of course he's noticed—I appear to have lost all the social charm and finesse I ever possessed. "I'm fine," I say firmly, giving my own thigh a little pinch through my jeans. I have been taking my antidepressants for a week, and I decide to blame my moment of uselessness on them. It's the sort of nonsensical connection my father would make, shortly before ranting about how depression isn't real, and medication of any kind is for the weak—but I'm not him, so I'm still going to take the fucking pills.

I just reserve the right to act suspicious and blame all of my failures on them.

Changing the subject in case Griff decides to dig any deeper, I ask brightly, "How's Rebecca?"

He slides me a confused, frowning sort of look—probably because he saw me chatting with the woman in question for a good half-hour this afternoon. "She's good. Her and Lewis are looking for places to move. Houses to buy. In York."

She told me as much herself. At the time, I thought, *I wonder how Griff feels about her leaving*—but I don't dare ask him, because I'm leaving too. Not that he'll care; he'll be worrying about Rebecca, for one thing, and he barely knows me, for another. I'm not sure why I keep thinking about this. It's ridiculous. I'm ridiculous.

Then Griff's footsteps slow, and I look up and realise why. We're almost at the turning where our paths home separate. Right to Maria's, left to Griffin's. He doesn't know which direction I'm going to take, because we haven't discussed it, and I don't know which direction I'm *supposed* to take, because we haven't discussed it. I've been a painful companion today, so I'm sure he's silently praying that I'll turn right and leave him to a peaceful evening. But when I think about actually doing that, it feels…wrong.

I should simply ask him what he wants, or tell him what I want—but did I mention that I'm feeling terribly nervous, today? Worst-case scenarios are rushing through my head so fast, I'm almost dizzy. What if I try to come home with him and he's disgusted by my presumption? What if he laughs and explains that I was a shit lay, there was no chemistry, and watching *I, Tonya* with me was awful because I wouldn't shut up while the film was on, and he's sorry, he thought I knew?

I mean, that doesn't really sound like Griff, but it *could* happen.

Then there's the opposite possibility: what if I mention going home, and he feels rejected? What if he thinks I got what I wanted last night, and I used him, and he decides to hate my guts? The idea makes me feel sick, and the calming breaths I take to stave off this panic aren't working. They're too fucking fresh and clean. I hate the fucking country. Where is my lovely, horrible pollution?

"Olu?" The sound drags me out of my head, and I look up to find Griff frowning at me. He seems concerned, probably because I'm bent double in the street, gasping like a fish. Shit. When did that happen?

"I need a cigarette," I manage.

"No, you don't," he says firmly, and then he *kneels in front of me* —in the *street!*—so we're eye level. "Jesus, tell me you don't smoke. No wonder you're always wheezing."

Now I'm glaring daggers, mortally wounded. "I do *not* wheeze." I give a little shudder. "Nor do I smoke, unfortunately. I quit." Worst decision I've ever made. I straighten up, and he stands easily, as if nothing strange happened.

"Good," he says. "You're already older than me. We don't need to add emphysema into the mix."

"What on earth does that mean?" I'm so outraged, I almost fail to notice that I've stopped hyperventilating. Stopped thinking in circles. Stopped hating myself, for now, which feels like being freed from the crushing weight of an anvil.

I've been thinking, lately, that I'd like to stop hating myself forever. I would like to try, anyway. But you know what they say: baby steps.

Beneath his beard, Griff's face is bright pink. "Uh… I meant that…"

I wait stonily, pretending I don't want to kiss his lovely, blushing cheeks.

"You might die first," he mutters.

Die first? He's speaking as if we'll know each other after next week—but that's not how things work when I run away. I disappear to places, and then I go home again and leave them behind. Leave some version of myself behind. That's how it's always been, and that's how it has to be.

Or is that just another way of hating myself? The question strikes me as too much too soon, so I shove it away and pretend it never crossed my mind—which is easy, when I have Griff to distract me. He's avoiding my eyes and walking briskly, the back of his neck burning bright red beneath his tan. I want to tackle him to the ground and press my cheek against that blush. I want to fall asleep on top of him like he's a mattress.

"How old are you anyway?" I ask instead, which is a far more reasonable course of action and might distract him from his embarrassment.

He blinks, then shoots me a look that's almost… shy? "Twenty-eight."

I narrowly avoid choking to death on my own shock. "Twenty-eight?" I shriek, and a woman walking two border terriers gives me a scandalised look. One does not shriek on Fernley's main road; only tractors are permitted to make noise here.

"Yeah," Griff mumbles.

"You didn't think to mention the fact that you're *ten years younger than me*?!"

"Didn't ask, did you?"

Good Christ. "I thought you were my age!"

"Cheers."

"I just meant—you're very serious, Griff. Why *are* you so serious? What's the matter with you? You should be off doing stupid, twenty-eight-year-old things." Then again, sleeping with me might qualify.

He shrugs his massive shoulders, squinting up at the still-bright sky. "I've always been like this." The words are quiet.

And we've reached the turning point.

We stop, as if by some mutual, silent agreement, and the air around us turns sticky with awkwardness. I open my mouth, close it, open it again. Lord knows Griffin won't say anything.

Except, just as I force out the words, "Should I—?" he blurts, "Do you—?"

We stare at each other like puppies who've just scared themselves with their own barks. Then he huffs out a little laugh, shaking his head, and his smile strikes me like lightning. Suddenly, I don't care about showing my hand or being rejected; all I care about is seeing Griff laugh again. A voice in my head snaps that my feelings make me weak, but I smother that voice with a pillow and order a Burberry suit for its funeral.

Then I say to Griff, "Let's go somewhere fun."

He raises his eyebrows. "City's an hour away."

"That's not what I meant."

"No?"

"I want to see bona fide country fun."

He snorts.

"Let's call it anthropological research."

"You're a dick."

We're both grinning as he takes my hand and leads me into the forest.

———

OLU

An hour later, I know far more than I ever expected about a game called Poohsticks. Also, I'm halfway up a tree.

Looking for Poohsticks, you understand.

"We can get them off the ground," Griff shouts up, but I shake my head and haul myself higher.

"I'd said I'd climb a tree," I pant. "And you *laughed*."

I can see his grin from here, white teeth shining against all that thick, dark facial hair. "You just don't seem like the tree-climbing type."

"Well, look at me now," I cry, swinging off a branch like a child. My reward is the hilarious sight of Griffin Everett absolutely shitting himself.

"Stop that," he barks. "You'll fall."

"Catch me, then," I say, and move on to the next branch.

"Olu, I'm serious. If you break your fucking neck, I'll be fuming."

I laugh for what feels like a century. Then I climb and climb and remember something I used to like about myself. No—something I still like about myself, even if it's a characteristic I occasionally use to escape: I am adventurous. I've been beating myself over the head with that fact for so long, but now, as I look out over the forest and glimpse the little houses of Fernley beyond, I remember that it's a positive.

When I finally come down, Griff mutters, "You didn't even get any sticks." His arms are folded, his scowl ferocious, his eyes avoiding mine. But there's the tiniest curve to his mouth that makes me grin.

"Maybe I was making a point." To him, or to myself, or both. I slide my hands over his broad shoulders, lean into his body, and kiss his cheek. "Don't be grumpy."

He grunts.

I kiss his ear. His jaw. The corner of his mouth. Then he turns all at once and grabs me—one hand cradling my head, the other splayed against my lower back in a hold he probably doesn't mean to be so possessive.

Except, who am I kidding? He definitely does. Just like he means it when he kisses me so hard I almost collapse. It's a laughing, breathless sort of kiss, but it says *ownership* all the same. Every touch of his tongue stamps his name all over me, and I like it. I like it so much I twist my fingers in the fabric of his shirt, stepping back and pulling him with me—until I'm pressed up against the tree I just climbed, caught between my rock and a hard place.

Then we kiss some more.

When we slowly, gently, come to a stop, he looks at me with cautious eyes and says, "Is this okay?"

"This," I tell him softly, "is perfect." Even though a week ago I would have been panicking, even though I should be panicking now. I can't, not with him, not when he's made a rose of my heart: it's still thorny, but around him it's also fragrant and lovely and *full*.

I can feel his hard cock against my abdomen, but he still kisses my forehead and rumbles, "Let's take a break." Then he moves away, giving me space even as he holds my hand.

Sometimes I'm so angry with him. How dare he make me feel like he adores me?

"Back to the stream?" he asks, and I nod, swallowing a pain I don't understand. We take a few steps through the trees and return to the stream he led me to in the first place. This is where we've been for the past hour, until I got grand ideas about climbing trees. The stream is shallow, rushing over pebbles and babbling like a brook in a children's story. I see tiny fish wriggling in the water and stalks of long, yellow grass floating lazily on the surface. There's a rickety, wooden bridge above the deepest section, which is where Griff leads me, picking up twigs on the way.

I take one, and we stand face to face on the bridge, arms held out over the water. "Ready?"

"Ready." We drop them. Then we rush to the bridge's other railing and stick our heads over the side.

"That's my stick," I crow with zero sophistication, pointing at the twig in the lead. I have grass stains on my jeans, bark grazes on my palms, and my shirt sleeves are rolled up to a disgraceful height. I am thoroughly enjoying myself.

"That's mine. You're full of shit," Griff says fondly, and looks at me like I'm a precious stone.

"Can you prove that in a court of law?"

"I can prove it with my bloody eyes, you toff."

"Language, sir. I will eject you if necessary."

"Eject me from what?" he laughs, and slides an arm over my shoulders, kissing my temple. I'm still trying to decide how I feel about such casual sweetness—*giddy is* not *the correct answer, Olu*—when he speaks again, his tone sober. "My mum used to bring me here."

Carefully, I look up at him, and the expression on his face breaks my heart. It's not grim, resigned grief. It's pure longing. He stares down at the water as if he might see his mother's face, and he is full of nothing but longing.

I know I should keep my mouth shut, keep my distance, but all I want to keep is *him*. "Would you tell me about her?"

Softly, he says, "Okay."

We leave the bridge and sit in the dirt as the sun sinks low over the trees. Griff's shoulder touches mine, or maybe I'm touching his, and then we're leaning on each other.

"Her name was Gemma. She was my only family and I... I really loved her." He swallows, then says with the air of a man trying to shock away sadness, "Also, she was a witch."

Surprise makes me splutter. "I beg your pardon?"

"You know," he grins. "Phases of the moon. Candles and herbs and all that stuff. I fucking loved it. She used to take me out with her at night to watch the stars. We'd go to the forest and feed all the animals we could find because she said we were the earth's caretakers. And they were never scared of her. She taught me how to make things grow and how to be silent."

"Your two favourite things," I say dryly, and he shoves my shoulder with his, but he's laughing.

"We were always on our own." His smile fades. "Her family, they all died."

I stare. "That sounds ominous. What do you mean, they all died?"

"It was her eighteenth birthday. They wanted to take her out to dinner, but my mother, she wasn't feeling well. She was depressed," Griff says, "all her life. Sometimes it was better, sometimes it was worse. I suppose, on that day, it was worse, and she wouldn't go. I don't think they really understood—I don't think anyone around here understood. So they went to the city without her, because they'd made the reservation. Probably wanted to teach her a lesson. Probably thought they'd come home, full and happy, and she'd regret being *difficult*." He makes the word soft but venomous, as if he's remembering it in the mouth of someone else.

I imagine depressed women are called *difficult* rather a lot.

"But they didn't come back," he finishes. "They were hit by a truck and died."

"Oh my God."

"So she was alone in the house—my house. She never told me much about that time, the time when she was alone, which means things were bad. My mum, when she wasn't well, she'd do anything to hide it." Griff's voice is soft, like a touch, like a hug. His eyes are distant, like he's seeing something else. "She used to tell me she had a migraine, and that she had to stay in bed. I'd be as quiet as I could, trying not to disturb her. But when I got older, I figured a few things out and realised it wasn't a migraine. Then I started trying to help—bringing her things, making her eat."

Our hands are side by side against the earth. I put mine on Griff's and squeeze. He turns it over, laces our fingers together, squeezes back. He even smiles at me, though it's a small, sad echo of his usual grin.

"It made her feel guilty, I think, when I tried to take care of her. But there was no-one else to do it—everyone treated her like a fucking pariah. She was that creepy girl who survived her whole family and walked in the woods at night and got knocked up at nineteen without a ring." He rolls his eyes. "Anyway, once she knew that I knew... she tried to hide it even more. We didn't argue much, but when we did, it was because she wouldn't tell me anything. She felt like, if I helped her, that was a burden on me. Like she was a bad mother for needing me." Griff holds my hand tighter, turning to look at me with a fierce challenge in his eyes. "But she wasn't. She was perfect, and I loved her, and she's the only person who ever loved me."

I let go of his hand to slide my arm around his shoulders. And then, somehow, we're lying back on the grass, and I'm holding him, and he's letting me. Resting his head on my chest, the greatest weight I have ever felt. I wonder if he hears my heart pounding out his name.

"No-one helped her. That's why she's gone," he says dully. "Because no-one in the whole fucking world helped her."

"You did." I kiss the top of his head.

Griff swallows. "I tried." Then he's quiet, and the sounds of the forest soak into my bones while I run my fingers through the raw silk of his hair. I feel the tension slowly leave his body. The sun is a little lower when he speaks again. "She overdosed a few months after my eighteenth birthday. She wrote me a letter and put on her pyjamas and got in bed."

I bite my lip so hard, faint copper floods my mouth. "Oh." Tighter, I hold him tighter, just in case he disappears. "I'm sorry." It feels pathetic. It feels like a shadow of a sentiment.

But Griff looks up at me with those solemn, midnight eyes and says, so seriously: "Thank you." Then he smiles.

He's the most beautiful thing I've ever seen.

"You wouldn't do a thing like that, would you?" he asks, and it seems so natural, so obvious that he'd know—of course he'd know—I reply without hesitation.

"I hope not. I haven't been bad for years."

"But would you ask for help?" he pushes.

In the past, the answer was always, *No*. But now I imagine my sister watching a stream with painful longing in her eyes, and I hope with all my heart that I mean it when I say, "I'd try."

He lies down again, as if satisfied. "That's all anyone can do, isn't it? Try."

Why do those words make my eyes sting?

"I have her ashes," Griff says after a while. "I meant to plant them with something, but I never have."

"Do you want to?"

"I do, and I don't. I haven't figured out where my head's at yet." A pause, a laugh. "It has been ten years. I should probably get a move on."

"What's the rush?" I frown, my hands tightening in his hair for a second before I force them to relax. "There is no *should*. Do what feels right, and if you don't know what feels right, don't do it."

"That sounded almost like wisdom."

"Makes sense," I say dryly, "since I'm very wise."

"Must be your age."

I smack him on the head and find myself snort-laughing like Theo and I used to do when we were back at school. Griff grins up at me, and then he's laughing too. It's like rolling around in sunshine. Right now, I don't think I recognise myself, but not in a bad way. It's just… I'm lying in the dirt—and God knows how many animals have shat here—grinning and grabbing someone, pulling his body over mine until he kisses me, kisses me, kisses me, his hands cradling my face, his calloused thumbs stroking my cheeks. Being me has never felt like this, so no, I don't recognise myself.

Our hearts are so close, I imagine I can feel Griff's thumping against his ribcage, and he can feel mine. He pulls back just enough to rub our noses together, and I smile as if I've never cried. I should be retching at all this cuteness, but I think this man could inspire me to heights of tacky and corny behaviour such as the world has never seen. In fact, I know he could.

Do I really have to leave?

"Do you have to disappear on me," he begins, and I have a what-the-fuck, he's-reading-my-mind moment before he finishes, "and see Mrs. Hartley tonight?"

Oh. Right. Yes. I'm absurdly grateful that he's not asking the more serious question, because if he was, I would tell him *Yes*. Yes, despite my frequent moments of hesitation and my strange, reluctant thoughts, I do have to leave Fernley. Which is why I can't let this attachment veer any further out of control.

"Yes," I lie, "I'm going home to Maria. I told her I would." But what I mean is, *I don't know if I'd ever recover from waking up next to you.*

"You're friends," he says, studying my face.

"I suppose so."

"Will you still be friends after you go home?"

There's a lump in my throat, one it takes me several ragged seconds to swallow. I hoped he wouldn't ask me this, and he isn't —at least, not for us. He's asking for Maria. "Of course we'll still be friends," I tell him briskly.

"So you'll come back?" he pushes, going for my jugular without even trying.

"That's not how I operate." I wish I could sit up, but Griff's still lying over me, his weight on his forearms. The fact that he hasn't pulled away, even though every word he says exposes how small I can be, is an awful sort of miracle. He's still looking me full in the face, still caging my body with his, and it doesn't even feel like a trap. It feels like permission to show him exactly how terrible I am. As if it doesn't matter, somehow.

"How do you operate, Olu?" His voice is quiet.

I know the wrong answer could hurt him. It's written all over his face, and for the first time, I wish he'd go back to being stone. He shouldn't ask me. He shouldn't ask me. Because right now, I look at him and think—why in God's name *wouldn't* I come back? But that's precisely why I have to leave on schedule, before all of this sours and the magic fades and Griffin stops smiling at me.

They always stop smiling at me.

"Maria," I tell Griff stiffly, "will have my number. If she wants to call me, she can."

"Right," he says softly, and for the first time in a long time I feel the twinge that means someone's disappointed in me.

But that's probably all in my head, fuelled by the sneaky tangle of guilt in my chest. That guilt reminds me that Maria isn't like my other friends, who can hop on a plane to reach me if it's urgent. She has three children and just enough money to keep herself in Earl Grey and red wine. She needs a real, supportive friend, not someone who sees her home as part of a quest toward self-actualisation. So I suppose she's another person I'll hurt when I leave.

I came here to escape my own shittiness, but it seems I've brought it with me and spread it around.

Usually, that thought would have teeth. But today, for some reason, it doesn't bite quite as hard. I remember my decision to hate myself less, and hear Griff's gravelly voice in my head: *"That's all anyone can do, isn't it? Try."*

I'm trying, I'm trying, I'm trying.

Finally meeting Griff's eyes, I tell him, "I don't know if I'll come back to Fernley. I don't go back. I'm not sure how to do it yet."

He stares at me for a moment, and I'm certain that this is going to ruin everything. That he'll lose patience with me—which would be understandable—and I'll lose all his quiet, steady warmth.

But that doesn't happen. Instead, he dips his head and presses his lips lightly to mine. He stays there as he speaks, so that I feel every word: "Let's go home."

13

GRIFF

I don't know what to do about Olu. But I don't think he knows what to do about himself, either, and I refuse to push him. Not when I could end up pushing him away.

Walking home, the lightness between us is replaced by something heavy and possessive and a little bit desperate. The air is a mixture of the storm of want in me and something... something in Olu that I still can't name. He has an edge to him, and it doesn't seem like my fault—but if he wants to wear that edge down on me, I think I'll let him.

Then we get inside the house, and he shoves me up against a wall, and I know I will.

He kisses me hard, bites my bottom lip. His eyes catch mine and he says, his voice low, "Okay?"

"Whatever you want, remember?"

"A lot," he tells me as he drags me through the kitchen. "I want a lot."

Climbing the stairs takes a while because we're kissing every five seconds, feeling our way up the steps with our eyes closed. He falls, and I catch him by his shirt. I trip, and he keeps me upright, although I'm not sure how. We sort of collapse onto the landing, and then he's straddling me and dragging his shirt off over his head.

He orders breathlessly, "Get naked, Griff."

"You're sitting on my chest."

"Excuses, excuses. Do as you're told."

"Get off, you prick." That's what I say, but what I do is roll us over until *I'm* straddling *him*. I'm not sure how our clothes come off in the end, but it's fast and it's rough and it happens. By the time we stumble into my bedroom together, we're both butt-fucking-naked and laughing. We stand face to face in the fiery glow of the sunset through the windows.

His smile shoots straight to my heart.

"Let's play," he says softly, his laughter fading. My dick jerks, hard and aching against my belly. I'm not sure what Olu's doing, because I'm trying not to look at anything below his neck. Me coming fast once seemed to flatter him, but if I do it twice, he might be concerned. This time, I'm going to last. Trouble is, the brilliant shit that comes out of his mouth really doesn't help my cause.

"Lie down and touch yourself," he tells me. It's an order, but a silky one, his tongue flicking off his teeth. If I do as I'm told, maybe he'll put that tongue on me. I can tell from the look in his eyes that he wants to put *something* on me.

Or in me.

I have this feeling that Olu wants to fuck me, and I'm only slightly bricking it—but my nerves are the electric kind that set my whole body on fire. Good nerves. Sex nerves. Because I've thought about it before, but no-one's ever wanted to try it—not like that, and not with me. So I sprawl back on the bed, my pulse thrumming hard through my dick.

He murmurs something under his breath, and for a second, I almost think he said *Beautiful*. But I don't know. I didn't really hear. He sits on the bed too, right at the foot, his green gaze dancing over my bare skin and kissing the tip of my cock. My balls ache. I'm biting my lip bloodless.

"Touch yourself," Olu says again. "I want to watch."

I lift my hand to obey, but a question leaves my mouth without permission. "Why?"

He arches an eyebrow, looking regal as fuck even while naked. I don't know how he does that. "Why, what?"

My brain catches up with my mouth, and I'm embarrassed. Tough shit; I asked, so I can't take it back. "Why do you want to watch me?"

Something shifts and softens in Olu's eyes, molten gold spilling beneath the green. He crawls over my body, and I feel the warmth of him everywhere, even though we aren't quite touching. There's the ghost of his chest above mine, the hum of almost-there heat in the air between our cocks, the faintest contact when his knee brushes my thigh. He looks me in the eyes and says softly, "I want to watch you because I love looking at you. You," he tells me quietly, "are gorgeous, Griffin. I want every inch of you. So show me."

I've never done anything like this before, but for him, I try.

———

OLU

I sit back while Griff lies there, bold and magnificent, lazily stroking himself with one big hand. I want to fucking *eat* him. I want to swallow him whole.

But I restrain myself, difficult as it is, and watch him take his pleasure with a slow deliberation that makes me want to lie down and beg. Not that I will; I'm in control right now. I'm in control, because I need him to be mine—and if he's to be mine, I have to take him. The thing is, Griff seems just as eager for this as I am, which I find… surprising, all things considered.

People never want me the second time as much as they did the first.

A little voice in my head, one that sounds like *me* rather than my father, demands, *Since when is Griffin just people? There is no-one in this world like him.*

I decide not to think too hard on that. Luckily, Griff's cock is the perfect distraction: it's as heavy as the rest of him, curving darkly against his stomach, the swollen head gleaming. He twists his fist over that head with each downstroke, his pre-come making a slick, wet sound as he glides, his jaw clamped tight on muffled grunts of pleasure. Those endless eyes crash into me as his hips jerk.

"You like me watching you," I say, tendrils of heat coiling around my limbs.

"Yeah." It's soft, faint, deliciously debauched. His hair is even messier than usual, his cheeks flushed above the line of his beard, his gaze almost glassy. He's losing it for me. This is just how I like him.

I reach over and run a hand down his powerful thigh. Then I grip his knee, pushing until his left leg is bent up against his chest, and I can see everything I want. The heavy weight of his balls, so soft and vulnerable, bouncing with each hard stroke on his cock. The meaty curve of his incredible arse and the shadow of all that it hides…

When I spread him wide, he groans, "Fuck, Olu," and his strokes speed up. The tight ring of muscle I've exposed is dark and sweet and tempting. I kiss the back of his thigh and a heavy breath shudders out of him. I bite, then suck, and he gasps, "Yeah, yeah, *yeah*," so I bite again. Harder. My eyes are still on that ring. I want I want I want, so I drag my mouth over his arse, toward his hole, and then I lick.

He arches his back so hard, I'm surprised he doesn't fly off the bed. The sound that explodes from his chest isn't really a word, or if it is, I don't understand it. After what he told me the other day in his shower—the way he said, *"Never done that"*—I wonder if this is the first rim job he's ever had. Or maybe it's not. Maybe he's just so desperate for it that he's gone from strong and silent to a gasping wreck, his hips thrusting at nothing, little teardrops of pre-come rolling down the veiny underside of his shaft. I watch one drop glide over his balls as I tongue him harder, getting him slick and wet for me. God, I love this. I love—

My thoughts are out of control because I need him.

I give Griff one last kiss before I rise up on my knees, my voice harsh. "Do you have—"

"Drawer," he chokes out, and reaches for the bedside, but his limbs seem slow and heavier than usual, like he's moving through syrup, and his expression is dazed. To see him like this, to *make* him like this, might be the definition of pleasure.

I catch his reaching hand, pushing it above his head instead. Then I lie over his body, my cock sliding through the slippery mess he's made of his own stomach. "Do you want this?"

"Yeah," Griff says softly and lifts his head to kiss me. His mouth is sweet and gentle, but below the waist, we're thrusting jerkily against each other. His free hand grabs my arse and squeezes, and I grunt into his mouth. I'm on fire again. I pull away, reach for the drawer, and rifle through a surprising amount of crap to find lube and condoms. When my fingers are slick, I lie over him again, looking into his eyes as he draws his knees up for me.

"Tell me," I say, and reach between us, my mouth against his throat as my finger circles his hole. "Tell me exactly what you're asking for."

"I don't—I can't—"

"You can talk to me, Griff. It's me. You do whatever you want with me." And I, it seems, do whatever I want with him. Because as long as our bodies are skin-to-skin like this, I barely remember what self-consciousness *is*.

He squeezes his eyes shut and relaxes against my finger. Teeth sink into his bottom lip, as if he's still trying to trap words inside himself—but then something in him buckles, and he gasps out a shaking breath. "I want you to fuck me. I do. Just do it, just do it, just…"

I push, slow and steady, until his body lets me in.

"God, yeah," he moans, his eyes wide open now, his lips parted. He looks as if he barely remembers his own name. I hope he doesn't remember to hide from me, either.

I bite into the meat of his shoulder as my finger strokes him carefully, tenderly—but Griff rocks his hips, screwing himself like he doesn't give a fuck about gentle. I should've known, really.

"More," he begs, so I give him a second finger. He sucks in a breath when I scissor them, stretching him open, getting him ready for me. "I can take it," he says, words coming faster now. "I want you. Kiss me. Olu—"

I do. I put my mouth on his and swallow every cry as my fingers push deeper. By the time my knuckles come to rest against his arse, he's gasping nonsense right into me. It feels as if we've swapped: I'm so full of need that I can barely speak, but everything in his head is spilling from his lips and it's glorious.

"You're fucking incredible," he swears, "so incredible. Just fuck me, just give it to me and everything will be fine, okay? Okay?" Even now, as Griff writhes beneath my body and babbles because of me, it feels as if he's soothing all my quiet worries. I don't know how he does that.

When I pull out my fingers, he sits up slightly and grabs a condom, fumbling with the foil, then grabbing my dick. He slides the latex over me, his hands warm and rough, this moment weirdly perfect.

I cup his cheek and look him in the eye. "Are you sure?"

"Didn't know I was this hard to read." He clears his throat and says gravely, "Olu. Please put your dick in me before I do it myself."

I'm still laughing when he falls back against the bed, dragging me with him. Even when we kiss, I'm laughing. Even as I add more lube, slicking his hole until it drips onto the sheets, I'm laughing—if a little breathlessly. But when I push the head of my cock against him and feel that slow, easy give, the laughter stops. When he takes it so fucking good with his fist shoved in his mouth and his face twisted with pleasure... oh, I'm not laughing then.

The hot grip of his body chokes the first two inches of my shaft, and I can barely breathe. Griff shudders beneath me, his hand digging into my hip so hard I know it'll bruise.

"Move," he rasps, and I think it's an order. He arches his back, working my cock deeper inside him, while I hold my breath and try not to come after thirty fucking seconds—which really shouldn't be so difficult. But he's deliciously hungry for me, so unexpectedly, openly eager, and so fucking strong. This is almost painfully good.

He impales himself on me with a low, satisfied moan that hits me like a drug. It's a miracle I can still think coherently, never mind speak, but I manage to choke out, "You're not supposed to top from the bottom."

Griff gives me a wicked smile I barely recognise. "Who said you were topping right now? They lied."

I've never laughed while fucking someone before.

"Behave," I order and grab a handful of his silky hair. Then I drag his head back, exposing the straining tendons in his throat, arching his body like a bow as I finally give him a hard thrust. He grunts, his incredible eyes on me as if he can't look away. His gaze is burning me from the outside while my own feelings burn me from within. When I turn to ash, I hope he smears me all over himself.

I drive into him again and again, slow and thorough because if I go too fast—if I pound into his hot, sweet body the way I want to—I'm absolutely fucked. Of course, I might be absolutely fucked either way. I'm drowning in him, and it's divine. When

Griff's eyes flutter shut, I tug on his hair and growl, "Look at me. Look at me while I fuck you."

He gives me what I need, his gaze holding me captive again, his skin flushed. "God, you're so fucking hot."

"Oh, really?" I'm not the only one. Pleasure attacks my best intentions, and I feel the last of my control slipping away. My fingers move between our bodies to circle the place where we're connected, his tight hole spread wide for me, stretched out and desperate for my dick. "Do you feel this?" I grit out, shoving hard into him.

"Fuck, *yes*." The words are a hiss.

"Do you know you're mine?" I must have lost my mind. But when he drags me down for a hot, frantic kiss, I have no regrets or concerns.

"*You* know I'm yours," Griff whispers against my mouth. "You do."

It doesn't sound like mindless sex shit; it sounds like the truth. Maybe that's why something shifts in me—or maybe it's just the wild pleasure of being with him. Either way, my mind shrinks to a pinpoint of consciousness that revolves around fucking Griff. Touching Griff. Anything Griff. He's so tight, I'm surprised I'm even moving. I'm surprised he isn't pushing me off and saying it's too much. I'm surprised I haven't disgraced myself and come seventeen times. I feel like I could. I feel, as I plunge into him with aching slowness, like I'm more myself than I've ever been. And *myself*, it turns out, is an animal.

He lowers a hand to his swollen cock, but I growl a warning. "Don't you fucking dare."

"Fuck, Olu, please—"

"*No*," I hiss, my balls slapping against his arse. "We both know you're going to come without it. I want you to understand how bad you needed this."

"Ungh." His eyes roll back in his head for a moment, and he bites his fist. Then he looks at me like he knows everything.

Things I'm only just learning. "Is this what *you* need?" he asks, spreading his thighs even wider for me.

"Yes." I rise up, putting my hands on his knees to hold him open, using him for leverage as I pound harder. "*Yes*." I barely recognise my voice.

"Oh, Christ," Griff moans, his hips shifting. "Do that again— what the fuck, what the fuck—" I hit his sweet spot, and his voice cuts out, his whole body jerking. A short spurt of his own come hits his stomach, and my satisfaction is almost violent.

"I've got you," I say as I fuck him through it, holding him down through sheer force of will while his come spills steadily. The sight of him dishevelled and flushed and losing it beneath me sends dizzy sensation glittering up my spine, but I grit my teeth to hold off the inevitable.

"Olu," Griff chokes out, "I don't know if I'm coming or…"

"Don't worry, love." I pause for a moment, leaning down to kiss him, and his uncertainty fades as his lips touch mine.

"More," he murmurs, arching his back, and I smile. Then I straighten up and rut into him like an animal. My eyes devour the way he's spread out under me, mindless and shameless and free.

"I told you," I pant. "You're losing it without a hand on your dick, because you love me pounding you into the mattress. Don't you?"

"Oh my God oh my God oh my God Jesus Christ." Griff grabs the sheets, twists them in his mammoth fists, bites his bottom lip. Then he grabs *me*, a hand around my nape, and drags me down and slides his tongue into my mouth. His muscles are tense and quivering, his come spurting hot against my skin as he rides out his climax. I wrap my arms around him and bury myself in him with a groan that feels like sheer peace. Sensation shatters into a thousand uncontrollable splinters, and I'm coming into the condom with shudders and moans and sweet, dizzying pleasure.

Griff holds me tight against his chest, nothing but stickiness and comfort between us. I am officially and utterly exhausted. He kisses my forehead and mutters, "Jesus, babe."

I laugh, or attempt to, anyway.

"If I knew I could have that, I would've tried years ago." A pause. "Then again, I suppose I would've had to wait for you."

There's something warm and soft inside me now, like a melting marshmallow. I suppose I've never had a melting marshmallow before, and I am suspicious by nature, so I study it for a moment. The hateful, insidious voice in my head tells me I should destroy it.

I tell the voice to fuck off.

For now.

———

OLU

My orgasm knocks me out, but I wake an hour or so later and stare at the darkened ceiling, sorting through my tangled feelings. I didn't expect to regret Griffin, but I'll be honest – I *did* expect to feel the way I always used to, after this: a little out of my own skin, a tad too naked. It's not a feeling I can describe accurately, but it existed even before the disgust.

Not with Griff, though. No; apparently all Griff causes is bone-deep satisfaction and near-giddy contentment. I'm like a child too high on birthday cake to go to sleep. The feel of his big body curving around me brings the strangest smile to my face—until I realise that his slow breathing and stillness don't mean he's actually asleep.

"You okay?" he murmurs, his voice a rumble against my spine. His fingers trace absent circles over my hip, and my smile widens. I don't know why I get like this with him when I have always disliked being needlessly touched.

I hope he never stops.

"I'm fine," I tell him. Then I correct myself. "I'm—great. I feel great."

"That's good, baby." I can hear the smile in his voice, and my feelings for him, whatever they are, tangle further. He nuzzles the back of my neck, and I shiver.

"Keep that up," I say lightly, "and you'll get *me* up."

"Oh no." Griff's utterly deadpan.

I snort and roll over to face him, poking him in the stomach. He grabs my finger with one hand, pokes me back with the other, and for some reason we both find that hilariously funny. By the time our laughter fades, we're wrapped in each other's arms again, foreheads touching, noses touching, mouths grazing in a way that sends butterflies flocking to my belly.

"I want to tell you something." It's only after I've spoken that I realise the words came from me.

"So tell me."

"You were right. I lied about why I'm here." I wait for Griff to stiffen, to draw back in suspicion, to assume the worst of me. But he doesn't move. His body remains utterly relaxed against mine, and I feel the kiss of his eyelashes against my skin every time he blinks.

"Go on," he says.

Well, alright then. A hint of the tension I'm carrying trickles away. "I'm not a writer." Of all the lies, that seems the most grievous, because it's a title I don't deserve to claim and one that feels so good to steal.

"For someone who's not a writer," Griff says, "you sure do write a lot."

I make an awkward hedging noise. "It's habit, the journal. You know I used to travel. Alone. But it's not—" Before I can say it's not *real* writing, he interrupts in that same calm, steady voice.

"And you talk about books a lot. And publishing. And passive voices."

"Voice," I correct automatically. "I only know about

publishing because I used to work for my brother-in-law. He needed help dealing with a firm he… acquired, so I took it upon myself to learn."

I hear amusement in Griff's voice. "Acquired?"

It's not exactly a funny story, but my lips curve too. "Acquired, took by force with the aid of my legal training—tomato tomato. Actually," I realise, "it's all part of the same story. It's all part of why I'm here."

Griff's hand curves around my hip. "Go on."

I must be high on my own orgasm, because I do indeed go on. "There was a man. Jean-Pierre. I cared for him, which made me happy. I thought that maybe—though it had never happened before—maybe I was falling in love. I'd always secretly wanted to, you see." I should feel like a fool, admitting that aloud, but Griff's thumb strokes back and forth over my hip, and all I feel is safe. Completely, overwhelmingly safe. "There's a lot I would've done for him. Apparently, the feeling was not mutual. He sort of… disappeared on me, and then a month or so later, I discovered that he'd photographed me during sex and sold the pictures to a rather prolific blackmailer."

The hand on my hip tightens, quick and hard, then relaxes in jagged degrees. As if Griff's forcing himself to calm down. But I can still hear the ragged tempo of his breaths, feel the drumbeat of his heart pounding against my chest.

"The blackmailer used those pictures to manipulate my sister, rather than me. My Lizzie." I wonder if Griffin fully understands how much it destroys me, even now, that it was Lizzie who suffered, Lizzie who dealt with that pressure alone for far too long until she came to me for help.

I think he might.

"You see," I continue, as if this is all a story rather than the worst thing that ever happened to me, "my brother-in-law is Isaac Montgomery."

It takes a moment for Griff to recognise the name. "Isaac… not the bloke who killed—?"

"Yes."

"And then he wrote those books about—"

"Yes."

"And then he bought out his own publisher?"

"He didn't buy out his publisher. The publishing house was owned and run by the aforementioned blackmailer, who was up to his eyeballs in debt and devised some convoluted plan involving my sister, seduction, and Isaac—"

"Hold on," Griff says suddenly, pulling back to look at me. "Does that mean your sister was the woman in the papers with all the—"

"Shut up if you want to live."

"*Hair*!" he splutters. "I was going to say *hair*. Jesus, Olu."

I scowl at him anyway, just on principle. "Yes, that was Elizabeth. May I continue?"

His slight smile says he knows I'm not nearly as annoyed as I seem. He kisses me on the forehead, which should infuriate me, since I'm trying to be intimidating, and then he cuddles me close again. Any irritation I did hold abruptly vanishes.

"Go on," he says. "Tell me."

"Before she saw those pictures, even Lizzie had no idea that I was gay. You see, our family—our family was not a good one," I say quietly, which might be the understatement of the century. "My father owns an oil company; my mother is of the English aristocracy…" I trail off and start again, this time with the parts that matter. "They are awful. Almost comically so; like caricatures of hateful wealth. Elizabeth is much younger than me, and I always knew that when I was old enough, I would take over her upbringing and get her away from Mother. But if our parents found out about me, they'd never have allowed it. So, from the moment Lizzie was born, my life revolved around making sure no-one found out. I suppose, even after she reached adulthood, it became a habit. An anxious, fearful habit. Something I hid for so long, I eventually forgot how to stop."

He squeezes my hip again, gently this time, purposefully, and I know what he's saying without words. I don't need to explain myself, not here and not to him. In fact, not to anyone.

"I wanted to choose how I came out, obviously. But in the end, I didn't get a choice—because Jean sold those pictures, and Lizzie found out, and then when she couldn't handle things on her own—she came to me, and we needed help, and so all of our friends found out, and... well." I clear my throat. "It wasn't exactly how I would've done things, that's all. It turned out fine in the end, I suppose—my friends still care for me. I was forced to come out to my parents and was promptly cut off. And, in the end, we got the blackmailer back and took control of his company by wonderfully questionable means, which I quite enjoyed. But..."

"But," Griff says, "that's still a monumentally shitty way to get to a happy ending."

"Yes," I murmur. *Yes. God, yes.* Then I realise that what should have been a confession of my purpose here has become an emotional trip down shit-hole memory lane. "Anyway," I say quickly. "The truth is, I came to Fernley to take part in the elder-flower harvest, because I needed some time to think. Alone. Away from home. But that sounds so bizarre, and then I bumped into Henry—which really was a coincidence, you know—and I felt as if I needed a normal explanation, so I said—"

"I know what you said, sweetheart. And I get it."

Hearing those words is like sinking into a warm bath of sheer relief. I realise that a tiny part of me worried Griff would hate me for the lie. Or else, that he'd hate me for the sad, aimless man hiding behind that lie. Yet he doesn't seem to care in the slightest.

"I love how you just... go places," he says, his fingers gliding over my hair now. "You just go places and do stuff. You want something, you want to be happy, so you go and look for it. Even if you think you'll find it in something as ordinary as elderflower."

I blink. I have only just decided to see that part of myself as positive rather than negative, and now, here Griff is saying exactly the same. Perhaps I'm not an entirely poor judge of my own character. And perhaps I'd do awful things to hear him say *love* again, so rough and tender.

"Thank you," I manage faintly.

We're quiet for a moment. Then he speaks again. "So. That Jean-whatever guy. He's why you were so nervous, isn't he?" For a moment, I'm not sure what Griff means. Then he kisses me softly, a loving nuzzle of his mouth against mine, and says, "What that bastard did. It shook you." And it clicks.

"He took me away," I say, a truth I haven't been able to articulate tumbling free. "He took me away from… me." That sounds so ridiculous, I should be embarrassed, but I'm not. I'm something else. Something that feels slightly defiant, actually, rather than sad and ruined. That's a surprise.

Griff kisses me again and whispers, "Do you really believe that, sweetheart? That he took you away?"

And I realise all at once, with slow, breathless relief: "…No. I don't. I worried about it, for a long time, but now I think—"

"What?" he prompts softly.

"Now I *know* there isn't a man on earth who could take me away like that." It's been a slow, painful lesson to learn. But it's one thing I'm certain of.

"Good," Griff says. Then he pushes me onto my back and rolls slowly on top me. His weight is balanced on his forearms, either side of my head, as if he wants to make sure I don't feel trapped— as if I ever could with him. I understand him now, from his silences to his impenetrable looks. Griff's stony gaze is the irides- cent kind, and when the light hits him just right, I see a rainbow of emotions. He bends his head and kisses me so slow, so deep, so true, that I'm caught halfway between wanting to crawl inside his skin and wanting to throw myself out of the window. I can't quite believe all the things I've just told him. I can't believe I want to tell him *more* when I already feel too much, when I'm in danger of overflowing. This can't be right; surely it can't be right.

As soon as he pulls back, I hear myself say roughly, "I have to go."

He doesn't miss a beat, blinking lazily down at me as if to say, *I know what you're up to.* My skin tingles, and I'm not sure if it's leftover arousal or panic. I want him to ask me why I'm leaving, so I can snap at him and we can argue. But he doesn't do anything like that, because he's a certified bastard.

He just says, "Okay, love," and then he lets me go.

14

GRIFF

I'm being weak with Olu and I know it. I'm letting him keep one last bit of distance between us, because I don't want to push and have him turn away from me. That'll bite me on the arse soon—I know it will, the way I sometimes feel thunderstorms hours before they arrive. But the rest of the week is so perfect that I don't give a shit.

In the day, I oversee the harvest, and he swings between helping and writing in his journal. In the evenings, he comes home with me and fucks my brains out—which is my new favourite thing—then lies around looking good and writing in a *different* journal. Yeah; there's two. In fact, I get the feeling there's more than two. Ever since he told me the truth about his work, I've been dying to know what's in these little leather books. If he's not plotting some boring nonfiction thing in them, what is he doing? Being himself, probably. It turns out that's exactly what I'm hungry for, but he never lets me read the damn things.

He never spends the night with me, either. But I don't think about that.

It's Friday afternoon, and I'm in a good fucking mood. First, because I plan to spend the weekend with Olu, and second, because the elderflower harvest has wrapped up faster than ever —which is down to Rebecca overhauling our 'online presence' (that's what she calls it, anyway) and snagging us the most volunteers we've ever had. I've spent the day doing the rounds, checking over all our land to make sure the job is truly done. It is. So now I'm heading back to the farm, looking for my man even though I have yield reports to write.

I can't help it. I'm hooked.

As I stride up the lane, I catch sight of Olu in the courtyard, along with Rebecca and... Henry? All of them, I realise, look incredibly pissed. Rebecca's waving her hands around, the way she does when she's furious, and Henry's blustering about something, I can tell. But Olu? He's silent. He's still. He's staring, completely calm, at Henry. Which says to me, loud and fucking clear: DANGER—but apparently, no-one else has figured that out about him yet, because they're not running for cover.

As I speed up, my sad, near-empty bin bag (there were a few elderflowers left) smacks against my back with every step. When I reach the gate, I shove it open and ignore the staff hovering outside their various buildings, wasting time and trying to subtly eavesdrop. Usually, I'd take a second to send them on their way, but right now I'm focused on getting to Olu before he flips and murders everyone within five miles. He has this look in his eye that tells me he's thirty seconds and one wrong word from blacking out and waking up with blood on his hands. I even know what he'd say after: "*Oops.*"

And now I'm mentally laughing at the thought of my boyfriend committing mass murder.

Wait—did I just call him my boyfriend?

Doesn't matter, don't think about it. I'm finally close enough to interrupt. My best friend, my boss, and my... Olu are all looking at me with expressions I can't read.

This is the point where I sweep in and heroically save the day, right? So I clear my throat and say, "What's going on?"

The temporary quiet dies. Henry and Rebecca start up again.

"Ms. Baird *seems* to have forgotten that she'll need *my* reference—"

"I haven't *forgotten* anything, I just expressed the *opinion* that—"

"—and since this is in fact *my* business, Rebecca, I fail to see what *credit* I owe—"

"—all due respect, *Henry*, I haven't seen your ar—*you* all bloo —all *week*, and—"

Their words merge into a mess I can't untangle. Just trying is giving me a headache. Plus, I don't think they're actually talking to me; they're glaring at each other like, if they look hard enough, one of them might burst into flames.

Good luck, Bex. I mean that.

I leave them to spit at each other for a moment and focus on Olu, who's staring at Henry like the man's entire body is made of maggots. Henry, luckily, doesn't seem to have noticed.

"Olu," I say, not sure if I should reach out and touch him. He flirts with me at work all the time, and the whole village is whispering about what we do after hours, but I don't know how he wants us to be, in a situation like this. We haven't talked about it, because we never actually discuss what it is we're doing.

I mean, I know what *I'm* doing. I'm falling in love with him, also known as happily ruining my own life. But I don't know what Olu thinks this is, and I don't want to ask, since I'm pretty sure the answer would hurt my feelings. For the same reason, I decide not to grab him in a courtyard full of my colleagues. Instead, when he doesn't respond to my voice, I say his name again. Soft, the way I'd like to touch him. Strong, so he knows I'm there. "Olu. Olu, look at me, would you?"

On the third try, he finally seems to hear me, blinking fast, like I just dragged him out of a daydream involving his fist and

Henry's face. "Griff," Olu murmurs. But Henry and Bex are still going at it, so I see the movement of his mouth more than I hear the word.

"You okay?" I ask, moving closer. Can't help myself.

"I'm fine." He must see my scepticism at that, because he gives me a smile—a real one, a beautiful one. It makes my pulse calm the fuck down, then speed the fuck up for entirely different reasons. Out of nowhere, I remember him on his knees in the shower last night, so vivid I have to clear my throat and look at the ground for a second. When I face Olu again, his smile has a knowing edge to it that says, *I see you.*

Yeah, he's fine, the little shit.

Now that's settled, I feel a bit more in control. I put a hand on Rebecca's shoulder to catch her attention, and when she goes quiet, I say, "Explain this to me like I'm five."

She flicks angry eyes at me, her jaw tight. "Henry wants to announce the end of the harvest on our social media."

I have no idea why that's argument-worthy. "You're the expert, but… isn't that what we're meant to do?"

"Yes," Henry insists, "it is. I've no idea why Rebecca is being so difficult."

Bex looks ready to bite his head off—I mean, *literally* bite his head off with her tiny mouth—so I squeeze her shoulder again. She satisfies herself with a murderous glare and turns back to me. "Of course that's what we're meant to do. But I wanted to film *you* announcing it."

Uh… "Me?"

She nods.

"Like… on video?"

She nods again. "You're the one who organised and oversaw the whole thing. And there's pictures of you working all over our accounts—people know who you are."

That's news to me, the sly cow. "They do?"

At least she looks a bit apologetic. "Er, yes."

"Bex—"

"They like you, Griff. I thought it would be nice."

"They like me?" I feel like I've swallowed a wad of cotton wool. "They can't like me. They don't know me. It's just pictures."

"They think you're cute and manly and good with plants."

"All true," Olu murmurs, and I know he's trying to make me blush. Thank God my beard is overgrown enough right now to hide the fact he's succeeding.

Even though I feel kind of good about this in a shy, awkward way, I have to admit: "But videos, and talking, and stuff—not really my thing, Rebecca."

"That," Henry cuts in, "is exactly what I said."

Just like that, Olu's expression is dangerous again. "No," he bites out. "You said something else."

Ah.

Now the situation is starting to make sense. There's not many things that get Rebecca this angry, but snide comments about me are, for some reason, up there. What I didn't expect is for Olu to feel remotely the same way. Clearly, neither did Henry—because he's finally noticed Olu's glare, and his pink face is full of pure, wounded confusion. If I know my entitled pricks, and sadly I do, the confusion will turn into fury soon enough. Next thing, Henry will say something awful, Olu will say something worse, and then he'll be banned from the farm for his last week in Fernley, which means we'll barely see each other. He might even go home early.

I really, really, *really* don't want that.

Just like I don't want Rebecca to go too far and wind up unemployed in York without a reference. So, before things can go any further, I say, "Doesn't matter. Okay? Doesn't matter." I look at them both in turn and try to speak with my eyes: *Just calm the fuck down*.

Olu and Bex are both as stubborn as each other, but lucky for me, they're also smart. Eyes narrow, jaws shift, body language changes as they each back down.

"Fine," Rebecca mutters.

Olu just turns and walks away.

I can see Henry watching his back with suspicion. Since Henry doesn't speak to common village folk if he can help it, he's always behind on gossip and probably has no idea that I've been drooling over Olu like a besotted puppy. But the man's finally taken his head out of his arse long enough to notice *something*, and I don't want him to take that something out on Olu. See, you never can tell what rich people might do. They don't think in straight lines. It's like, the more money they were born with, the fewer logic points they get.

I'm not sure why Olu got to keep his logic points. Must be because he's special.

"Henry," I say, wracking my brain for ways to fix this.

He looks at me like it's a chore.

"I think you're the better choice. You're... charming. Know what you're talking about. And customers will like seeing how involved the owner is." I am talking out of my arse. My arse has a mouth, a script, and a secret hope that it'll one day be the next David Tennant.

Henry goes from bored of my existence to impressed by my good sense in the space of three seconds. "Well, of course. I'm glad *you* see that, Griffin." He gives Rebecca a smug grin. "I suppose the dynamic duo share a single brain, and Griffin has custody right now? Ha! Ha! Ha!"

I give Rebecca a look that says, *Don't smack him on the head with your camera.*

And she gives me a look that says, *Why?*

It was expensive, I send back.

Fair point, she agrees, and bares her teeth in what's supposed to be a smile. "Alright, then, Henry. My mistake. Let's find the perfect spot and get started."

They walk off, and I'm left standing in the courtyard,

surrounded by nosy staff members who watch me like I'm road-kill and they're crows.

I say, "Work light this afternoon, then?" and they scurry off, which isn't as satisfying as I'd hoped. Once upon a time, the little slice of power I had here at work was enough to make up for the outright fucking nastiness in this village. Now, it feels pathetic. I wonder if that's because Henry laughed me out of his office and proved how fragile it all is, or if I'm getting used to someone other than Rebecca treating me like a person.

Speaking of, I need to find Olu before he does something fantastic like piss on Henry's desk.

I follow his footsteps into my building, take a quick look into Henry's office just to make sure, then move on to mine. And there Olu is, sitting on my desk—not *at* my desk, but on my desk—tapping his fingers against the wood and glaring daggers at the wall.

I shut the door behind me. "Don't."

"Don't what?" he snaps, but I know he's not snapping at me.

"Waste the energy."

"I hate him." Winter fir eyes land on me, ice-cold. "I hate him quite a bit."

Love me instead. "Stay here while I finish up my admin work?"

The last of Olu's irritation slowly fades, and he gives me a tiny, reluctant smile. "What's in it for me?"

"I'll take you home with me tonight."

"You always take me home. You're astonishingly easy." He has this look on his face like he's glad.

"Easy, yeah?" I try to sound offended. Not sure if it works, but I try.

He slides off the desk and walks toward me. "Oh, dear. Why do I have the feeling I've just royally fucked myself?"

"Dunno. But you should practice that, because I won't be doing it anytime soon."

We both laugh, but the fact is, I haven't done it at all. Which is not to say we've been saints. We haven't. And it's not that he's strictly a top, because we've talked about it, and he's not. It feels like I spend half my life thinking about sinking inside this man, but I haven't even tried yet, because…

I just want to be sure that he's okay. That he's always, absolutely okay.

So I'm taking my time.

Eventually I get on with my work, and it goes fast, which is a surprise. I thought Olu would distract me, sitting there all gorgeous and maybe-mine, but whenever I mutter my frustrations out loud, he says things that clear my head. Things like, "Why, yes, spreadsheets *are* the devil," and, "You're not stupid, Griffin. Don't say that."

My thoughts untangle. I'm done before I know it.

There's a powerful pull between us as we walk home—but then, there's always a powerful pull between us, and the fact he's leaving in a week makes it more intense. I force myself to think about that for a moment, just so I won't go into total shock when it happens. *He's leaving soon, he's leaving soon, he's leaving soon.*

It hits me, when we reach my house, that I don't want to spend all the time Olu and I have left rolling around in bed—most of it, ideally, but not all. So, once we're inside, I tell him, "We're not having sex."

He gives me a strange look. "I didn't mean it when I called you easy. Frankly, I don't see that sort of thing as a negative."

"I know. Don't worry."

"Then what's wrong?"

"Nothing's wrong. I want you so bad I feel like I'm dying."

He laughs, but it's a little uncertain, his hands jammed in his pockets and his expression awkward. Beautifully awkward, but still; I would never have guessed, the first night I laid eyes on him, that he could ever be this uncomfortable over someone like me. The map of fine veins on his forearms rises and falls as he flexes his fists out of sight.

"I just want to spend time with you," I say softly. "Doing stuff. Normal stuff." I've made a mess explaining this, but he gets it. He gets me. His tension fades, I see it happening, and then his smile is so real it hurts.

"Okay," he says, and he sounds warm. Happy. I think I just made him happy. Nothing's ever felt better.

I nudge him toward the kitchen counter, then take everything useful out of the fridge. Olu stands there, blinking his impossible eyes while I pile fruit in front of him.

"What are we doing?" he finally asks. Slow, like a man waking up from a dream.

"We're going to make cordial," I tell him. "Our own recipe."

"We?"

"I'm going to teach you."

I expect an eyeroll, a smirk, some wry muttering, but what I get is his face lighting up like the sun. Still, he plays it cool in a way that makes me want to kiss the fuck out of him. "Alright," he shrugs, looking around the room like he's barely interested.

"So, first thing's first: choose your ingredients."

Olu's eyes flicker over everything I've laid out like he's a computer running through data. "Aren't you afraid I'll steal all your recipes?"

"Yeah," I say dryly. "That's why we're making a new one."

He snorts and reaches out to touch a bowl of glistening raspberries, but stops before he makes contact. "Maybe you should write a recipe book or something."

"Are you sure I'm even literate?"

His laughter is low and rich. I want to run my thumb over the curve of his mouth, but if I get distracted, cordial will go out the window. And I think he's way more into cordial than I realised. Or maybe—I don't know—*maybe* his interest is a sign that he's into something else.

Not enough to stay.

Whatever.

"After all the work you did this afternoon," he says, "yes, I'm sure you're literate." Before I can melt at the fact that he sounds *impressed* by me, Olu picks up a grapefruit. "Would this be too difficult?"

"Nah. Just gotta pulp it."

So we do. Then we strain it to remove the seeds, because Olu frowns, "Who wants *bits* in their cordial? Not I." And when we start boiling sugar and water, he says, "That's rather a lot of sugar, Griff. Let me see your teeth." And when I ask if he wants to infuse it with anything, go for a more complex flavour, he murmurs, "Simplicity is the essence of sophistication, country boy." Then he adds the raspberries and picks out three different herbs and a red chili pepper.

I mutter, "Simplicity, yeah?"

He says, "Speak up, darling," and bites me on the shoulder.

By the time the cordial is ready, he has swipes of rich pink and yellow all over his cheeks—I never realised how much I touch him—and my own face is sticky too. It seems Olu never realised how much he touches *me*, because his eyes keep flicking to his sugary fingerprints all over my skin, then fluttering away. He smiles a little bit every time.

I wish he'd stop being so perfect.

"This is going to taste terrible," he says, "isn't it?"

"The herbs have to infuse, yet."

"Don't mollycoddle me."

"Like I'd bother," I lie.

He grabs the front of my shirt and licks my temple. Even though my stomach hurts from laughing, and my head aches from grinning, and the thought of him leaving sticks at the back of my mind, that tongue is all it takes to get me hard.

Olu's blinking up at the ceiling and licking his own lips, acting oblivious. "Hmm," he murmurs. "Not bad." Then he goes up on his toes to lick my forehead. I realise he's tasting smudges of almost-cordial off my face, and I know, from the light in his eyes, that he's being so fucking… *gorgeous* about it on purpose.

"You're a brat," I tell him.

"You've gone all growly," he says back. I might be embarrassed if he didn't sound so pleased.

"You're *licking* me."

"But not anywhere interesting. I'm not allowed." He toys with a button on my shirt and looks resigned.

I put a hand on the back of his head and say, "I've changed my mind. Make it interesting." How he even understands me is a miracle, because I sound like my vocal chords are made of stone. All of me's made of stone, in fact, tense with the effort of holding back—and my cock's the hardest part. Olu smirks and undoes the first button, kissing my chest as he spreads the fabric. Another button, another kiss, again and again, until he's kissing my belly. Until my shirt's hanging open, and he's on his knees. I shove off the fabric and watch him with my heart in my throat, because I'm pretty sure he's about to put my dick in *his* throat, and he's damned good at it.

He yanks my belt aside like it's his worst enemy and rips open my jeans like he's launching an attack. I'm giving myself a pep talk about restraint when he drags down my briefs and slides my stiff, aching shaft into his mouth.

"Holy fuck," I hiss, my hands cradling his face, my hips jerking because I can't control myself right now. He sucks me so hard, so wet, and those eyes, those eyes—I hit the back of his throat, and he swallows. My knees are weak. My vision's starting to blur a little bit. I slide a hand from his face to his throat, so I can feel the muscles working my cock, and he moans like he likes it. I know he likes it. So I squeeze a little bit, and Olu sucks some more, until his face is pressed against my body and I'm buried in him. I could pass out right now.

Instead, I watch as he pulls slowly back, leaving my dick cool and glossy. His lips are slick, and he's breathing hard when he lets me go—but it's only a second before he sucks me deep again.

The next time he comes up for air, I whisper, "Let me."

He opens his mouth, and I feed him my length, inch by inch. His eyes are green fire, wide and wild, his pupils blown like he's high on me.

"You're beautiful," I tell him. My thumb strokes his face. My cock slides over his wet, eager tongue. I can hear him gagging on it, just a little, and I murmur, "Do you like that?"

When he moans again, I feel the vibrations down to my balls.

"You want me to take you upstairs?"

He nods around a mouthful of me.

I take a risk because time is running out and I want, I want, I *want*. My voice cracks as I ask, "You want me to fuck you?"

He pulls back, taking a single breath before his words tumble out. "You can fuck me anywhere."

"Good," I say simply, but inside I'm all relief.

If I had it my way, I'd spend the rest of my life bending Olu over kitchen tables or taking him outside and shoving him against trees. But what I have is a week, a rare opportunity, a handful of soon-to-be memories, and a man who doesn't know I love him.

Because I do. I pull him to his feet, and he gives me one of those precious, private grins and kisses my cheek with the mouth that just sucked my dick, and I absolutely love him. I love his ice and I love his fire, I love his distance and I love his trust, and I love his sharp words and his secretly soft heart. I love him, and if I told him, he'd probably have a heart attack and run a mile.

I tow him upstairs and shove him onto the bed—the same bed where I'll lie alone after he leaves, haunted by the scent of him and the memories. But I won't think about that now, not when he's here and hard and grabbing me with hands that shake. Hungry; he's hungry. I know it because I feel it too. We stumble out of our clothes, and then I'm on top of him, sliding my cock against his, aching with possibility.

"Tell me how you want it."

"Hard," he says.

"Do you think—?"

He grabs a fistful of my hair and growls, "*Hard.*"

Alright; that's what I'll give him. But I'll take care of him too. I find the lube, a condom, and then I flip him over. "Your ribs," I start.

"Are fine," he insists, and the bruises do look faded. So I pin him, giving him my weight because something tells me he'll like it. Moving down his body, I press my forearm tight against his lower back as I get him wet and ready for me. My slick fingers glide over his arse, his skin gleams and his body arches, and every moan he makes goes straight to my dick. I ease a finger into him and feel his heat pulling at me, dragging me deeper. My head dips, my teeth sinking into his hip while he chokes out my name, and I've never felt as fucking good as I do in this moment.

"More," he pants. "Griff—"

He's okay. He's okay, so I give him another finger, and another, fucking him open fast and reckless. Like he wants it. Like he trusts me to give it to him. "Tell me," I order, because I need to know. "Tell me it's good."

"It's fucking good, Griff. You're—good—for me." He probably meant to say that all sharp and in control, but it comes out breathless and needy in a way that ruins me.

"You are so fucking perfect," I tell him, and it's only the truth. "You're perfect, Olu." I curve my fingers inside him and rub at his sweet spot until he can't say another word, until every exhalation sounds more like a sob. Then I pull out and spread him wide, look at how I've wrecked him.

"Alright," I murmur. "Now you can have my dick."

He reaches back with one demanding hand, grabbing my thigh and dragging me closer while I fumble with the condom.

Finally, I'm wrapped up and splayed on top of him, my cock gliding between his slick cheeks. For a second I wonder if I'm too heavy—

"Hold me down," he orders, no room for argument. "I want…"

"You want to feel me, babe?"

The way he whispers "*Yes*," does something dangerous to my heart.

His head is turned to the side, and I press his face against the pillow with one hand, pinning his hip with the other. "Arch your back." When he obeys beautifully, I tease his hole with the fat head of my dick, giving him just the tip until he's almost spitting.

"You fucking bastard," he growls, bucking beneath me. But I'm bigger than him.

"This is what you want," I tell him, and he doesn't disagree—he can't disagree. But he *can* call me an evil shit and swear that, "If you don't fuck me now, Griff, I will *ruin* your life."

"I find it really hot when you threaten me." My dick pulses like it's testifying.

"Fuck me, then," Olu snaps, but there's a desperate edge to his voice, and he's rutting against the sheets like he can't stop. "Fuck me." This time he's begging, and that's more than enough to break me.

When I finally give in, it's bliss. His body is all tender, demanding heat, clenching around my cock like a fist. I press my face against his shoulder and shove the last few inches of my shaft inside him, hearing his breath hitch as I thrust. He's chanting my name into the pillow like I'm a god. Sometimes he makes me feel like one. And even though it's reckless, even though it's fucking pointless, I can't stop myself from whispering into his skin, "I love you."

For a moment, every inch of him freezes—but there's no ice to it, somehow, and a second later, he's relaxed again. He lifts his hips and fucks himself back on me, and we both make this low, strangled sound of pleasure at the same time. Being inside him is like touching the centre of the earth. Being *with* him in any way is like dying and going to heaven. Olu is everything.

"I love you," I say again, biting out the words like they're a crime or an insult. That's how he'll treat them. Maybe that's why, a moment later, I grab his hips and fuck him hard. If I give him this, give him what he asked for, he won't have a chance to catch his breath and tell me I'm a twat. I go up on my knees and pound him into the mattress, and he grunts with every thrust, slamming his palm against the headboard so hard it reverberates through the frame. He's skin and sweat and salt and right now he's *mine*, all mine. He's holding on to me so tight, grabbing any part of me he can reach with a desperation that feels like being loved back. Every beat of my heart is twice as powerful now and twice as important, because it works for both of us. Everything I am is cradled in the palm of his hand, and I can't even make myself be afraid.

So when Olu comes with a low, drawn-out moan that shivers like surrender, what am I supposed to do? I lose whatever threads of control I had left, grab his shoulders, and drag him closer as I fuck him deep. It'll never be deep enough—I want to live inside him, the only place in this world I could ever be safe, even if I'm too big to fit. Three hard thrusts, and my release bursts over me like a shockwave. The pleasure's so intense it's almost painful, and then I'm lying halfway on top of him—so I don't crush him too badly—kissing the perfect curve that is the back of his head.

As we lie there, messy and weak and gulping down air, I say for the third time, "I love you." Three times makes it magic, that's what my mother taught me.

Finally, he responds, and he sounds achingly sad. "Don't." But he turns in my arms and kisses my jaw, my cheeks, my temple, again and again and again. "Griff. Don't."

How can I not?

15

OLU

That night, I sit at Maria's kitchen table feeling like a lump of clay. I suppose it's better than feeling like an alien; at least clay is from the earth.

"Are you alright, darling?" Maria asks, giving me an odd look from her place at the kitchen sink. She is scrubbing her daughter's football boots. Watching her makes me think of Elizabeth, and the nights we spent dyeing pink pointe shoes brown.

"I'm fine," I tell Maria and myself. I simply miss my sister and all the friends I've been avoiding. Or perhaps I'm dehydrated because Griff drained every last drop of come from my body. I should take a sip of the cordial we made together, which I've brought round to share with Maria, but every time I taste it I remember licking raspberry juice off Griff's forehead, and I hear him saying in that gravelly voice, *"I love you."*

No, no, no, no, no. I cannot think about that. I refuse.

"You don't seem fine," Maria says, and I wonder if the easy bluntness of Fernley residents has something to do with the north/south divide.

"Well, I am," I insist. "Why don't you sit down and let me clean those boots?"

"Every time you come here, it's, *Maria, let me wash your dishes. Maria, let me mop your floor. Maria, let me wipe your arse*. Behave yourself!"

"I just like to help," I mutter.

"Relax. How's Griff?"

Well, that was a subtle subject change. The woman has all the finesse of a brick wall. "You mustn't ask me questions like that."

"And why not?" she snorts.

Because they make me feel guilty.

But that's ridiculous. I have nothing to feel guilty about. I didn't tell him to fall in love with me, and really, who falls in love with me anyway? He has only himself to blame. He really, truly, does. Besides which, I highly doubt it's a permanent condition. He'll be fine as soon as I'm gone.

Maria is watching me over her shoulder with too-sharp eyes, so I decide to change the subject. Unfortunately, it seems my mind has become one-track. "You do know I'm leaving soon, don't you?"

"Of course I know. You live in my flat."

Ah. Yes. I wince a little, though I'm not certain why.

Until she adds, "Although, that's not why it's been on my mind."

I cock my head. "On your mind?"

"Yes. I don't particularly want you to leave." She puts a squeaky-clean football boot—not that they were especially dirty to begin with—on the draining board, and turns around to face me. "I do realise you have to go. But I will miss you, love."

"Miss me?" I echo, sounding woefully confused. It's just that... well. I think Maria's rather wonderful, especially in all the ways I'm not, so the fact that she likes me in return is something of a surprise.

But then I catch myself and think—*Why?* I have wonderful

friends, friends I pacify with the odd text when I'm down and distant, friends who let me do that but make it clear they'll be there the instant I call. I have the respect of people I respect in turn, countless times over, so it suddenly seems illogical to believe I don't deserve it.

My fingers flex, searching subconsciously for a pen. I need to hash this out in my journal. But first I have to tell Maria that, "I'll miss you, too. I really, really will."

She smiles, the sort of encouraging smile I've seen her use with her children, which makes me think I might be missing something. When I stare blankly at her, clearly not grasping what, she laughs and rolls her eyes. "That's nice to hear, Keynes— but I'm assuming we'll still be friends, after you go, and I'll see you again." Perhaps that's supposed to be a question, but she says it rather firmly.

And it's easier than I expected to reply, "Yes. Yes, of course we will." I sit back, pleased with myself. That felt rather like progress.

Then Maria ruins it all by adding, "Or maybe you'll fall wildly in love with Griff and stay here forever."

I pick up my glass of cordial from the worn kitchen table, trying to cover my reaction. That reaction being: *pain*. Burning, intense pain. "You are grossly overestimating the depth of my relationship with Griff." It's the biggest lie to ever leave my mouth, but I can't admit the truth, now, can I? I can't say that staying with him sounds like a fantasy, or that the reality scares me. I can't tell her that watching Griff know me better and better, and love me less and less, would end me. The knowledge is carved into my tired, useless heart, and that's enough. This happiness I've found with Griffin is as sweet as sugar, and it will dissolve just as fast. Happiness tends to do that, I've found.

"How disappointing," Maria frowns. "I was hoping I could keep you."

"I'm afraid not. But you have my number. If you don't call

me," I say darkly, "I *will* call you."

"That was ominous," she smirks.

"It was supposed to be."

Her laughter warms me right through. There in my friend's quiet kitchen, I feel a little bit strong. But later, when I crawl into my bed alone, I find a thousand weaknesses waiting to devour me. *You don't have to leave this behind. You don't believe Maria will wake up one day and find she despises you, so why believe it of Griff?*

I tell the weaknesses sternly, *Empirical research.* I can't make foolish choices just because my feelings about myself have started to improve. Friendship and intimacy are two different things, and one of those things has consistently proved beyond me. But the weaknesses swear that Griff isn't like everyone else, that we're something entirely different together, something precious, never-before-seen under this sun. Something perfectly us.

———

GRIFF

Time slips through my fingers like fine soil. It's running out. He's running out. We're running out.

I spend most of the weekend with Olu, and every work day after that, and it's bliss—but he never stays the night. I love him as hard as I can, and I think he drinks it down through thirsty roots, but his petals stay curled up tight. He's my shy rose, or he would be, if he were my anything. But he's not, because he's still leaving.

I know he cares about me. I *know* he does—I feel it in his hands, the way he traces his fingertips over my skin when we lie together. So why can't I open my mouth and ask him what will happen to us?

On Sunday, his sister calls him while we're walking home, and his face changes completely when he hears her voice. I thought he was golden before, but with her, he's the centre of the fucking sun. He says *Elizabeth* the way my mum used to chant spells under the moon, he asks about the baby so desperately, I know he wishes he was home, and it's painfully clear that I will lose this war no matter how hard I love him. Olu has an entire life I'll never touch, and he'll never ask me to.

The reminder makes me wonder what, exactly, *I* have. More and more, the answer feels like 'not much'. Rebecca shows me furniture and job listings, and I help her choose patterns and draft cover letters. It turns out that the harvest was incredible, but my satisfaction is a gnat bite; I am not fulfilled. I tell Henry about it, and he shows up on Wednesday to hold a staff meeting congratulating us—but mostly he congratulates himself. He avoids looking at me all together, like the sin of asking for credit has turned me see-through, and I realise that a lot of people look at me like that. As if I'm see-through.

Thursday night, I take my mother's ashes to the woods and try to put her in the earth. Just like ten years ago, I can't. Olu rubs soothing circles over my back and takes me home again, and the way he holds me in my bed should make me happy—but all I can think is that it should be our bed. There should be an *our bed* and there never will be. I want to punch Henry's smug face in; I want to roar at every villager who looks right through me; I want to shake the ones who watch me as if I'm a rabid dog.

I want to burn the woods Mum used to love, because I walk through them now and I can't even see her ghost anymore.

Have I always been this unhappy, or is Olu drugging every cup of tea he makes me? Maybe there's dissatisfaction sitting right under his tongue, and I've been drinking it like cordial.

Oh-fucking-well. I'll spend the rest of my life remembering how good he tastes.

———

Olu

As my last week in Fernley slips past, I should be irritated by Griff's charged silences, by the way he looks at me when he thinks I won't notice—with this dull, hopeless pain that rips my heart to shreds. I should be lashing out at him the way he'll inevitably lash out at me.

But I'm not.

I soak in all his little hurts, and they feel like mine. They *are* mine, though I'm much better at hiding them. For such a quiet man, Griff now wears his heart audaciously on his sleeve, and I wish awfully that I was brave enough to touch it. But I suppose that's what it all comes down to: I'm not.

On our last Saturday morning together, I show up at his door like the desperate thing I am, hiding my growing panic behind a pathetic smile. Lately, my mind is sharper than ever, emotions painfully intense rather than cotton-dull. Blame it on the pills; I certainly am. This is what I wanted, but it feels like being infected by rogue programming. I keep having thoughts I didn't authorise. Thoughts like, *Leaving him isn't smart; it's cowardly*. Thoughts like, *You should love him enough to take a risk.* Thoughts like, *Are you sure forever isn't standing right in front of you?*

Griff opens the door and drags me into his arms, scattering my confusion. When he kisses me, all I can feel is *perfect.* Then he lets me go and reality returns. "So," he says, and I can't read his expression. "Tomorrow."

Ah.

Behind him, his kitchen is cool and fragrant as ever, rich with green things. I can see by the raspberries and sliced lemons on the counter that he's busy, can smell the sugar on him, and want to run my tongue over his skin in case I can taste it too. In an ideal world, I would join him and mess up whatever genius recipe he's devising. We'd shower together when we were done, and doze the afternoon away, and maybe I'd take him somewhere in the evening. Somewhere far away from here, so he could see things I don't think he's seen before. In an ideal world, I would be and do whatever Griffin Everett needed. In an ideal world, I'd be brave.

In this one, I hold his gaze and repeat, "Tomorrow." The word is broken glass in my mouth, because tomorrow, I leave. I have to. I want to see Liz and restart my life, to keep all these good changes going. But I also want to be Griff's, to know that it's safe and it's forever and it will never come back to bite me.

In short, I want the impossible. How greedy I am.

"Can we go for a walk?" he asks me.

I do believe I'm about to be ceremoniously dumped, which is a relief. The alternative was to leave my heart behind in this place, dangerously far from my body—which I would've done, if Griff would've let me. But, since he clearly doesn't want to keep it, at least I'll have something to hold on to when I no longer have him.

He leads me through now-familiar streets toward a green space where I've seen people playing fetch with their dogs—using sticks, of course, because balls are just so *city*. I want to laugh at this place the way I did when I first arrived, but I think I hate it now, hate it like an enemy. It will always be the place that has what I want: Griff.

There are no dogs around right now, though I'm sure some will appear soon. We sit in the grass, me checking for crap, Griff apparently confident in the villagers' wholesome commitment to keeping Fernley clean. All around us, there are daffodils brighter than butter, airy dandelion clocks, and delicate daisies with petals coloured like clouds at sunrise, pink edging into the white. Griff sprawls amongst it all, and he seems...

He seems, undeniably, to fit. His big body could have sprouted from the earth, his strong, careful hands are as lovely but resilient as the daisies, and his face, as he tips his head back beneath the sun, is beautiful. Gorgeous. Like everything I never knew I wanted.

He looks at me, and I hold my breath, waiting to be left.

But all he says, in the end, is, "Let's be lazy."

My exhalation tastes like relief. "Darling, you've never had a better idea."

He laughs and plucks a daisy, holding it out to me. It smells of fresh, sweet nothing. Like us. I push it into one of my shirt's open buttonholes, and Griff smiles as if that was exactly right. My hands itch to cup his creasing cheeks and kiss that smile off his face, but I don't, since tenderness will only make this worse.

Perhaps he disagrees, or simply doesn't care, because he murmurs, "I'd make you a daisy chain, if I could."

"You can't make a daisy chain?" I put a hand over my heart. "I'm shocked. Shocked, I tell you."

"I could when I was a kid. But my hands—"

"Do other things now," I cut in, before Griff can insult the slow, deliberate fingers I adore.

His smile is a tiny dart to my chest.

I hold out my own hand and say, "I'm certain *I* could make one, if I received the proper instruction."

"Yeah? Teamwork?"

"Indeed."

"Like this, then," he says, plucking a daisy at the very base of its finely-furred stem. "Length. Okay?"

"Okay." I pick one just like he did, choosing the longest stem. He nods, and I keep going.

"Now," he says after a while, "Use your thumbnail—here." He talks me through slicing a fine hole and looping the next daisy through it, slow and delicate so as not to rip the bond wide open. Rinse and repeat. It's a satisfying cycle.

"You never did this as a kid?" he asks while I fall into a rhythm.

"You know what my childhood was like," I murmur, because we've talked of so many things, these past few days, that he does. Griff's heard all about my wealth and my obedience, the ice I lived with and the infrequent burn of the cane over my palms.

Just as I've heard about the times his mother smiled and the times she couldn't. That's a connection as fine and beautiful as the floral chain I'm building, but just like this chain, it will dry out and die. It has no roots. "I'm glad you've taught me," I say, "since I'll be an uncle soon." But what I mean is, *since I'll be leaving you soon.* Going back to who I really am: a friend, an uncle, and a man who disappears sometimes because no-one's earthing him.

I don't want to believe that's all I'll ever be, but until I know exactly how to change, hope seems arrogant. I can't stay with Griff, *be* with Griff, based on nothing but hope. He deserves more than that.

"You'll be a fantastic uncle," he tells me.

"You can't really believe that."

"Why not?"

I look up, find him watching me as if he truly doesn't understand. And it strikes me, all at once, that he doesn't. I've been so much better, and so determined, here in Fernley. He has no idea what a mess I am.

"I'm unreliable," I begin, my voice quiet. "I can't predict, from day to day, how I'll be. Who I'll be."

"Baby," he says softly.

But I'm not finished, and I don't want him to make this feel better. I want it to *be* better, and no-one can give me that but me. Every time he tries, it hurts us both. "I'm cold," I say, because it's often true. "I run away when things get difficult. My temper is ridiculous."

"And you think you'd lose it with a child?"

I can't answer that, because once he eases a concession out of me—once I say something that makes me seem good, like, *"No, of course I wouldn't"*—he'll think that he's won, that he can convince me I'm wrong. So I steamroll over him and get to the part that matters.

"I'm going to leave you here without a backward glance," I say. Even the words hurt. "That should prove I'm not good enough to be with you." Now Griff is looking at me like he's never seen me before, which makes sense, since I'm not sure he has. My chest tightens. There's an anvil lodged in my ribcage, heavy and sharp, because this is it: the moment when he finally figures out who I am. He'll see, and he'll stop loving me, right on track. Which is a good thing. It's a good thing.

"Olu," Griff says finally. "You don't have to leave me."

The anvil moves from my chest to my throat. Of course, since it's an anvil, it's far too big for my throat, and things are tearing. "I do."

"You *don't*." The expression on his face, I realise suddenly, is pain. I want to flinch away from that—from the fact I'm hurting him—but I think it needs to be this way. He asks me abruptly, "You don't seriously think you're not good enough, do you?"

That's his issue? What, does he want me to repeat all the worst things about myself, as if it isn't hard enough to hold them inside me? My emotions are a cauldron, hot and poisonous, so intense I can't think clearly enough to respond.

"Olu," he says, "I can't tell what you're trying to... Is this what you *want*? Or...? For fuck's sake, talk to me."

Through gritted teeth, I snap, "You don't decide when I speak."

"I know that." Carefully, Griff takes my growing daisy chain from my hands. I should push him away, but I don't. I'm furious, but I'm frozen. I want him to touch me. I need him to touch me. Since this will be the last time.

He sets the daisies gently aside and drags me onto his lap. "You are absolutely good enough, Olu. You're better than enough. I promise."

Before I can say that he doesn't know what he's talking about, and that frankly, he's getting on my nerves, arguing with my perfectly sensible conclusion—Griff kisses me. His mouth is soft and slow and sweet, as if to tell me without words that I can stop him whenever I want. But I already knew that. So I pull him closer, *hard*, and we topple over. I cling to him like a vine and let his weight crush me into the grass, and he doesn't falter or hold back. He slides his tongue into my mouth, sends electric shivers dancing through my veins, his hand sliding to cup my nape. Anyone could see us, but I don't care. I'm not worried. I'm not panicked. I love him. I love him so much I can barely breathe.

He pulls back and says, "Stay."

"I can't."

"You can," he insists fiercely.

"I *can't*." He doesn't know how messy things are in my head, but if I stay long enough for him to figure it out… I don't want to see how he reacts. "Just let me go," I say, "and spend the rest of your life thinking I was someone else, and this was a perfect holiday romance." I sound pathetic, but maybe that's okay and maybe I don't care. Maybe, right now, it's not shameful to be devastated.

Because what I'm doing is devastating.

"You know we wouldn't last, if this was real," I tell him, forcing iron into my voice. "Say you know that."

His hands tighten on my hips. "Stop it."

"We'd give things up for each other and resent it. Or try long distance and drift apart because this was only meant to be a fling. Forcing something is never worth it. So I'll leave now, while you still think you love me—"

"While I *think*? Olu, shut up."

"Why?" I ask, and my voice is so empty it almost scares me. The emotion that was overflowing a second ago is gone, hidden inside me where no-one can see, because it's private. I'm breaking myself right now, and it's private. "Why?" I ask again, when Griff remains speechless.

"You aren't leaving like this." His voice is a tangle of disbelief and dawning anger. *Finally*, anger. "You aren't going to feed me this bullshit about—about how we're just too much effort, and then fucking disappear."

"I am."

He pushes me away and asks, "*Why*?"

"Because I'm a piece of shit, clearly."

"Stop *saying* that." His eyes screw shut as he tugs, frustrated, at his own hair. Then he stops, opens his eyes again with something like realisation. "Of course," he murmurs, "of course you can't stay here," and the pain in my chest is almost violent. But I don't flinch. Then he continues, "I have to come with you."

This must be a hallucination. "You have to—what?"

"You can't stay here in the middle of nowhere. Your sister—and—no, I have to follow you home." He reaches out and takes my hand like we've just solved everything. "Okay? Say it's okay."

"But you don't want to leave Fernley. You said you'd never leave."

His shout rings through the clearing. "That was before *you*!"

I didn't even know Griff could raise his voice. He looks rather surprised, himself. For a moment, I want to laugh and kiss the shock off his face. Then I remember what I'm trying to do here.

I'm trying to leave him.

And he won't let me.

I imagine Griff abandoning everything he's ever known. I think about him quitting his job, selling his family home, turning his back on all the places where he sees his mother's ghost, to follow a generally good-for-nothing man ten years his senior, whom he's known for three weeks, to London. I see him, in my mind's eye, sitting in my sterile, shining apartment in the city, wilting every day and learning exactly who I am. How I am. The way I think and feel and act in real life, when I'm not cocooned by the slice of escapist fantasy that is a place like this.

I feel sick.

"I'll come with you," he says, sounding nervous now. "I mean it. I will."

My response is the absolute truth. "I don't want you to."

16

GRIFF

Days pass. Part of me—the part Olu woke up, the part that hopes for things—believes he might come back. That he'll tell me he's sorry, he didn't mean it, he wants me like I want him. That we *meant* something. So on Monday, I keep an eye on the front gate at the farm, half-expecting to see him leaning there like nothing happened, an apology only I would notice in his eyes.

That doesn't happen, obviously, but I hope for it on Tuesday, too. On Wednesday, I'm less hopeful and more miserable. By Thursday, I decide to hate him. It doesn't exactly work, but I do my best.

Now it's Friday morning, and I'm on my hands and knees, yanking out the dandelions by my office building's front door and imagining they're all Olu's tongue—the same tongue that tried to let me down gently before losing patience. Ever since he left, his words have been ringing louder and louder in my ears. I would've given him anything. I put my heart and my world and my entire fucking *self* on the table, and he said, *"I don't want you to."*

I almost wish he'd said what he really meant: *"I don't want you, Griffin. I came here to escape something, and you helped, Griffin. But did you really think I'd fucking keep you, Griffin?"*

I should've known better. No-one keeps me. No-one.

"What *are* you doing, dear boy?" The voice floats to me from somewhere over my head, the accent and the lazy surprise reminding me of Olu. He'd ask the same question, just like that, as if he were too cool to be truly shocked by me scrabbling in the dirt—too cool to be shocked by anything at all. But that's not true, no matter what he pretends in public. He has real, raw feelings no-one would ever guess at, and for a while, he let me see them all.

Stop. You're hurting yourself.

I dump the weed in my hand, sit back on my arse, and look up. It's Henry talking to me, obviously. He has this pompous quality to his voice that Olu doesn't—probably because his whole cut-glass thing isn't entirely natural. When he was younger, he had a bog-standard Leicestershire accent like the fucking rest of us. Bet he thinks I don't remember that, since I'm supposed to be slow.

He's staring at me now as if I'm not just slow, I'm bonkers. I know that look, even if I don't know much else. And now I hear Olu's voice in my head, soft and secret: *You know all sorts of things, Griff, so stop being awkward.* When he said that to me, our legs were tangled together beneath my sheets.

Stop it. Stop it.

I've let the silence between Henry and I stretch too long, the way I used to. "Just weeding," I grunt, and drag myself to my feet.

He arches an eyebrow. "Griffin, you are my production manager. Please leave the menial tasks to Peter."

Menial, I can tell by his tone, means *shitty*. Henry says it as if he and I are on the same level: *Leave the shitty jobs to the shitty people, Griff, and we'll go to my office and eat caviar.* Which is exactly how Henry normally behaves, only... not with me. I have no idea what's going on, and it's pissing me off.

When I don't reply, he shifts back and forth, then clears his throat like he's about to give a speech. "Well. How are you, my boy?"

What is this *my boy* thing? "Fine."

He gives me a look that tries to be sympathetic but just comes off as slimy. "I hope you don't mind me saying, Griffin, that I've heard reports to the contrary. Apparently, you now spend your nights roaming the woods like—"

My jaw tightens. "Like a monster in the dark? Or maybe just like my mother."

Henry's mouth flaps soundlessly.

"Nice to know everyone in this village is still incapable of minding their own fucking business," I snap.

He finally recovers, holding up his hands. "I hope you don't think of it as prying, Griffin! It's not. Just healthy concern for one of our own."

I have never, not *ever*, been *one of their own*. I don't even know who *they* are.

Henry leans closer, like we're sharing secrets or something. I can see his pores. I don't want to see his fucking pores. "Between you and I," Henry whispers, "I'm rather missing his presence also."

"Missing who?" My words are so hard, so flat, so obviously a brick wall of *fuck off*, that I don't think anyone on earth would have the balls to keep pushing.

But clearly I'm fucking wrong, because Henry does. Which makes me wonder how he fits his massive nuts into his corduroy trousers. "Keynes, of course!" he says cheerfully, not realising I'm seconds away from stomping him into the ground. "I know the two of you were close—though it seems you've, er, perhaps drifted apart." He must see something in my eyes, because he backtracks again. "Not that I'm attempting to pry! No, simply showing concern."

If he says *concern* one more time, I will throw him over my shoulder and climb to the top of the tallest tree in this village like I'm King fucking Kong. And then I'll drop him.

"Now, as for myself," he goes on casually. "Well, Keynes and I are the sort of friends who go through years of separation, you understand. We bump into each other, have a grand old time, and then it's off to our own worlds again! But at this point in my life —and I'm sure you agree, Griffin—I'd like to hold on to my friends a little more tightly. And Kate feels the same. She absolutely adored Keynes at our dinner party a couple of weeks ago— he is so charming, isn't he?"

I am going to punch Lord Henry Breton-Fowler in the face. That must be obvious, because he looks at me with alarm and takes a massive step back. When he starts his rambling speech again, the words come a bit faster.

"You see, it occurred to me, Griffin, that you may have collected the elusive Keynes's contact details, which—" He breaks off and does this tinkly little laugh that makes me want to rip my ears off. "Which I *quite* forgot to snag for myself. The number on his card seems to be outdated. An oversight, I'm sure."

There's a weird rushing in my ears, like an ocean thrashing just before a storm. I'd like to drown Henry right now, that's for fucking sure. Because apparently, he's actually trying to act like we're best friends so I'll give him Olu's number.

The fact that I don't even *have* Olu's number is the icing on the shitty fucking cake.

My blood burns like the rivers in hell. "You really do think I'm thick."

Henry's head rears back. "*No*, Griffin, of course not!" He laughs nervously, like I'm the one who's being unreasonable. "I simply—"

"You know what?" I cut in. "There is no-one on earth as useless and arrogant as you. What is that like? To be so sure you deserve whatever you want—but, at the same time, to be so painfully fucking *shit?*" I'm shouting. Somehow, I'm shouting. Staff members are milling awkwardly around the courtyard or peeking from the blinds that cover their office windows, eager to see the fuss. This is the part where I calm down and apologise and try to melt into the furniture.

Fuck that.

"Olu didn't give you his contact details," I say to Henry, "because he doesn't fucking like you." He told me that himself, but I'd know, even if he hadn't. Olu doesn't care for people like Henry. He doesn't enjoy being around smug, snide pricks who look down on others, who use and manipulate them. No; he befriends people who are kind, and he worries about injured foxes, and he tells me how smart and capable and worthy I am, over and over again, even when I ignore him. That's what Olu does. And the memory of it—of *him*—smashes through every chain that's ever kept me here in Fernley. Every chain that's ever kept me quiet.

I'm so sick of this place.

I thought it was enough, staying here to feel close to my mum, collecting whatever scraps of respect I could get through work or whisper-thin connections. But it's not, is it? It's not. Bottom line is, I deserve better than this. I deserve better from everyone and everything. And I'm going to get it.

Henry's kicking off, of course, his pale cheeks mottled as he spits, "Now, you watch what you say to me. I own this place!" His venom becomes a shout. "You wouldn't have a job without me, you great, lumbering oaf, and I'll thank you to remember that. I could terminate your employment for such shocking behaviour as easily as breathing!"

"But you won't," I snap back. "You won't. Because then who'd do your fucking job for you?"

Henry sucks in his cheeks, shaking silently with rage—like it's all trapped inside him, but he can't let it escape—which is how I know I'm dead on. It took me years of hard work to reach this position, but now I'm here, he's finally noticed I'm too good to let go. Who'd fill the gap?

He's about to find out. The hard way.

"I quit."

His jaw drops. "You—what?"

"I fucking quit, you piece of shit." I turn away, then stop, turn back, and say, "I know you lied about my recipes. *You owe me.*"

His skin turns as white as the clouds above us.

"But don't worry. I'm not going to collect, because I don't need to." Also, because I'm too fucking exhausted to bother, but he doesn't need to know that. I tap my head and say, "I'm the one with the talent. I'm the one with the brain. There's way more where that came from." And I really believe it's true.

Then a familiar voice—a beautiful voice—a voice I fucking love, cries, "Yeah!" Rebecca appears out of nowhere, slightly breathless like she's been running, and jabs a finger in Henry's direction. "You're a shithead, and I quit too!"

Even now, she makes me want to laugh. Under my breath, I ask, "Didn't you already hand in your notice?"

"Shh," she whispers. Out loud, she says, "Fuck you, Henry." Then she hooks her arm through mine.

We leave.

―――

OLU

For roughly a week after leaving Fernley, I do nothing.

Well, that's not entirely true. I sleep—but only on the sofa, because my bed no longer feels right. I drink water when my head aches. I get too hungry to ignore, and start to miss the sun and the wind, so I pull a hat low over my face and leave the house. At the shop around the corner, I pick up twenty packets of frozen pasta bake and pay at the self-checkout machine. And once a day, when Elizabeth calls, I pick up the phone and pretend to be fine.

But on the seventh day, Sunday, I make a mistake. When the phone rings that afternoon, I pick up automatically, but Lizzie's voice doesn't answer my cheery "Hello, darling!" Someone else's does.

"Keynes? You sound... off."

Shit. It's Theo. My best friend, who was once very easy to fool when it came to emotional things, but has become much trickier since he got married.

"Hi," I say, rather inanely.

Theo pauses. "I'm surprised you picked up the phone."

"Why?" As if I don't know.

"Because you've been off on one, that's why. What's wrong with your voice?"

"Nothing's wrong with my voice." It's hoarse because I haven't used it since yesterday morning, the last time Elizabeth called. I clear my throat. "What do you want, Theo? I'm busy."

"Too busy to help me with something?"

I'm not, but the thought of dragging myself up and pretending to be fine as I help him is just... nauseating. Rather like the prospect of running a marathon after days of starvation: anticipating how shit it will feel is enough to make me dizzy. "I'm sorry," I tell him, pressing a hand to my stomach. "I can't."

"Really?"

"For fuck's sake, Theo, I *can't*." I'm not ready to be around people yet; not when Griff is still in my blood. Not when I can't forget the look on his face when I pushed him, once and for all, away. He never told me out loud that he feels constantly rejected, that it digs into his skin like a burr. I noticed that fact on my own, and then I used it.

Now I tell myself it was the right choice, but how can it be?

How can it be, when I have never hated myself as much as I do right now?

"Alright," Theo says. "Listen; I'm in Spanish Town."

Well, that catches me unawares. "Spanish Town, Jamaica? What on earth are you doing there?"

"I'm on holiday. It's a thing people often do with their spouses," he says dryly. "So I can't come to get you."

I pull back and stare at the phone. *Come to get me?* When I put my ear to the receiver again, Theo's still talking.

"…check on you instead."

"What are you saying right now?" I snap.

His response is worryingly serious. "Sometimes I wonder if you realise how much you help me."

"Theo, what are we talking about?"

"We're talking about the fact that you've been avoiding my calls, your sister told my sister you're acting weird, and then, for the first time in our *lives*, Keynes, you just claimed you were too busy to help someone. You, who almost missed your final tort law exam because you were helping your next-door neighbour bury their ferret."

"For Christ's sake, will you ever stop bringing that up? I assure you, I really didn't want to."

"But you did it anyway," he says. "Don't tell me you're fine. I don't believe you."

My jaw drops. "You don't need help at all, do you? Did you just… entrap me?!"

"Yes," he says, annoyingly pleased with himself. "I wish you'd take your pills, Keynes."

"I *have* been taking them, thank you very much." Which is presumably why I've spent the last week feeling as if my lungs have been dragged out of my arse. Not so long ago, all this agony would've been muffled and distant, easy to compartmentalise, as if it happened to someone else. I almost miss that.

But not quite.

"Hmm," Theo says, and I imagine the slash of his inky eyebrows. "Well, whatever it is, we should talk about it."

Talk about it. For once, something in me leaps at the opportunity to do just that; to voice the doubt that's been ripping my mind apart ever since I left Griff behind. Because Theo's sensible, logical, trustworthy. He'll tell me if I chose wrong, and I'll believe him. "Okay," I say. "Okay. We'll talk." I take a breath and gather my thoughts. "If Jen"—his wife—"ever felt like all the good parts of herself were submerged, and only the worst parts floated to the top, and she wanted to work on that, to feel more balanced, but she didn't quite know how…" My words slow down, then grind to a cautious stop. Because, even as I ask this question, the answer is crystal-clear. I know exactly what Theo's going to say.

"What?" he prompts me. "Go on."

But I can't. I can't even ask, because it would be an insult. If depression or insecurity or shitty, hateful parents—or anything else in the world—ever made Jen feel like me, there's only one thing Theo would do. He'd love her anyway, because all her good parts would still be there, and all her not-so-good parts would still be *her*. Because you don't give up on someone when they're drowning.

Griff wouldn't give up on someone who was drowning. I know that for a fact.

"Olumide," Theo says, which means he's trying to be serious. "Speak."

Right, right. I've been coming to some sort of epiphany while he sits there in Spanish Town, worrying his pretty head about me. "Nothing. I have nothing to say."

"What? You can't stop there."

With complete honesty, I tell him, "I don't need to ask the question anymore."

It takes an unholy length of time and a mammoth amount of reassurance to get Theo off the phone. It's a bit of a shock to realise that he thinks I'm far worse than I am; he's trying to seem casual, but I think he's actually concerned for my safety. In the end, I convince him that I'm not on the edge the way I was a month ago; I'm just fucking miserable.

And, I'm starting to fear, completely brainwashed when it comes to my own self-worth.

When we finally hang up, he mutters awkwardly that he loves me, and I decide that in the future, I'll believe enough in that affection to tell him when I'm struggling with myself.

I'll try, anyway. The love of my life once told me that trying's all we can do.

When I'm alone with my silence again, I find myself doing something I've never done before. I go to the glass sideboard in my living room, opening the doors to reveal every journal I have ever finished. I rifle through the layers on layers of little books until I find the section filled by smaller, black ones marked *F.* Then I choose the very first one, and I start to read.

———

Olu

Almost two hours later, I'm on my third journal and have, thankfully, stopped crying. It seems awfully self-absorbed to sob over the story of yourself.

But if these were someone else's journals—if I were reading about a different young man who tried to do good, who heard over and over again that it wasn't enough, who decided in the end to stop fucking trying and accept that he must be something awful—then I might cry over the words for hours and hours. Perhaps.

The good news is that I am feeling far more confident in my ability to stop hating myself: all I have to do, it seems, is let go of everything my parents ever taught me. I know. Likely impossible, but I'm pleased to have a goal. The bad news is that I am feeling less confident about explaining all this to Griff. How, exactly, does one say, *"I assumed you would stop loving me if you found out how depressed and anxious I am,"* without making it sound as if you think the other person's a bit of a prick?

Then I stop and remember that Griff understands how certain worries can eat someone alive. In fact, Griff tries to understand everything, because he is kindness itself. And he's told me in a thousand different ways that he'd never punish me for my demons. It's probably time I listened to that.

But before I can grapple with my growing urgency to see him, to fix this, the phone rings again. And this time, it really is Elizabeth.

I answer with a smile that's almost real. "Darling. How are you?"

"Very well, thank you," she says briskly. *Brisk* might be Elizabeth's defining characteristic. "And you?"

"Absolutely peachy!"

"I think you're lying," Liz tells me calmly. It takes a moment for me to absorb her meaning, but when I do, my mouth actually hangs open. I am awash with shock and indignation. Did this little brat just call me a *liar*? How dare she disbelieve my carefully constructed falsehoods! I expend all this energy on faking happiness for her, and she simply *calls me out*? Children are so ungrateful.

"I'm not sure why you'd think that, Elizabeth," I say firmly, "but I assure you, I'm very well."

"Really?"

Is it me, or is her voice getting louder? After a moment, I decide it's a psychological effect of my guilt. "Yes, really."

"Then you won't mind answering the door, will you?"

"I beg your pardon?"

The bell rings, and she says sweetly, "Theo called me, by the way. Do let me in, Olu. My back's killing me." Then she puts the phone down.

Bloody bastard *Theo*.

I shoot out of my nest of stale blankets on the sofa and curse until the air turns blue. Then I roll the blankets into a ball and shove them into a cupboard along with my journals, fluffing the sofa cushions to smooth out the indent left by my miserable arse. My thoughts are almost as frantic as my hands: *Lizzie's outside, can't keep her on her feet, where the bloody* hell *is her husband?* I collect empty glasses of water and packets of unfinished biscuits, dumping the debris into the cupboard under my kitchen sink. And then, finally, I go and answer the door.

It swings open to reveal my tiny but formidable sister, leaning against her massive husband's side with a frown on her pretty face. She looks as if she's smuggling a bowling ball under her dress, and her golden-brown skin glows as if she's swallowed the sun. In short, Lizzie looks wonderful, which means I can be annoyed with her instead of worried or concerned.

"You didn't tell me Isaac was here!" I scowl.

I expect some smart comment back, but instead, she looks me up and down, biting her lip. "Olu, what on earth has happened to you?"

Only then do I remember that I'm wearing a stained T-shirt and greying pyjama bottoms. "Nothing," I say firmly.

"Bullshit," my brother-in-law tells me. "Now move."

A few minutes later, we're all sitting in my living room, pretending not to notice the signs of disarray I failed to hide. Well, Lizzie and I are pretending not to notice; Isaac stares openly before giving me a lizard-like look that I believe I'm meant to find intimidating—and many people might. But those would be people who've never seen his wife use him as a literal stepladder to put up Christmas lights.

"I've been ill," I say into the silence, holding my cup of tea close to my chest. "That's why I didn't come to see you as soon as I was home."

Isaac snorts. "You didn't come to see us because you were waiting for your face to stop doing that."

Oh, God. "For my face to stop doing what?"

"Being honest," Lizzie says softly. "Olu, you look so sad."

"*Do* I?" I'm horrified.

"Also," Isaac adds helpfully, "you smell, and you need a haircut."

"Excuse me, Mr. Montgomery, I am speaking with my sister." Still, I run an absent palm over my head and realise he's right.

"What's going *on*?" Lizzie demands. "What happened to you in that *awful* northern place?"

Isaac makes an odd, choked sound. "I don't think Leicester-shire's north, Liz."

"Well it's not home," she snaps, and something in my chest constricts.

Before I can stop myself, I'm muttering bitterly, "What is home, anyway?"

"I *beg* your pardon?" Elizabeth stares at me as if she might be moved to violence. My sister is small and round, with dark curls she now keeps in a pixie cut and whiskey-brown eyes that take up half of her face. She is also frequently terrifying. I'm proud to say that I contributed to the aura that makes her so; however, it still occasionally works on me.

"*This* is home," she says, quick and sharp. "*We* are home. I certainly hope you don't think otherwise."

"We are home". The words strike at something in me, reverber-ating through my chest, and I stare from my sister to her husband and back again. They're home. But then, as if she's reading my mind, she says, "You too, Olu. All of us. We're home."

I open my mouth. Close it. Open it again. Sheer brilliance falls free: "Ah."

Lizzie huffs out a laugh. Then she shuffles forward in her seat, hesitates, and raises a hand. Reaching for me. This is not the sort of thing my sister and I do, except in emergencies. Typically, of course, the emergencies are hers, because I keep my own to myself.

But not today. Today, I raise a hand too, and she twines our fingers together. I stare at the carpet and try not to pass out through the stress of emoting.

Gently, she asks me, "What happened, Olu?"

For a moment, I can't reply.

Then Isaac says, "Bet you any money it's a fella."

I scowl. "For fuck's sake, Montgomery, disappear."

Lizzie puts a hand over her mouth. "Olu! *Is* it?"

Oh, Christ. "Fine. Yes. I ran away to some ridiculous village and started carrying on with a bloody fruit farmer and ultimately realised, after ruining everything, that I have serious self-esteem issues to work on. Are you happy now?" I snap.

"Yes," Lizzie says, utterly matter-of-fact. "I've been meaning to talk to you about family therapy, since the baby's coming, and you suddenly seem much more receptive."

I splutter.

"Well, I'm not happy," Isaac interjects. "Who's the farmer? Are you going back to him, or what?"

The words are out of my mouth before I can think twice. "I intend to try, if he'll have me." I pause and stare down at myself, as if my body might not be my own. That was alarmingly candid. Since I appear to be on a roll, I look at Liz and say, "Family therapy sounds bearable, if you insist."

"For the sake of the child," she tells me.

"It is arguably our responsibility."

"You two," Isaac snorts, rolling his eyes. Then he holds Lizzie's hand and kisses her knuckles.

"Well," Elizabeth says. "Now that we've dealt with the most imminent issue; Olu, you're on notice."

This conversation is not so much a rollercoaster as a wormhole. "Erm… I'm sorry, Liz. For what?"

She gives me a severe sort of look that works very well on her students and will doubtless work even better on her child. "Did you think I didn't know you've been struggling?"

Oh. Ah. Hm. "Yes?"

"Well, I did. And all I wanted to do was help, but you're always so protective of me. It was only after you left last month that I talked to Theo and Aria and realised, you aren't letting *anyone* help. So, you're on notice, Olu: that's not going to work anymore. We've all made a pact, the whole group."

"Wonderful," I drawl. "It's a conspiracy." But there's something warm in my chest.

"For a long time," she says, as if I haven't spoken, "you were the only one loving me hard enough to make up for everything else. You were the one who kept me safe from all my demons. You have been everything to me, Olu, all my life. Now you *will* let me look after you."

I want to say something pithy, but I find I simply... can't. All I'm capable of is a stiff nod, because if I speak, my emotions will overflow. Loving Lizzie has always been the most natural thing in the world, and I never understood where I learned how to do it. Our parents certainly didn't teach me. But now I realise that Lizzie taught me, from the moment she was born. Being there for her has always lit up the shadows in my life, so I shouldn't be surprised to learn that she's there for me, too.

"Alright," I say finally. "I suppose that doesn't sound too bad."

She gives me a little smile. I give her one back. And a part of me that I didn't realise had been missing slots neatly into place.

"So," Isaac says. "Now we've done the touchy-feely family bit, will you come back to work?"

"I left the company," I frown, "because my being involved was nepotism, plain and simple. I assumed you were joking when you asked me to come back."

He stares. "All twelve times?"

Has he really asked so frequently? "It *was* becoming a tired joke, if I'm honest."

"Jesus Christ, Olu, you do my head in."

I know I'm feeling better now, because I give him a wink.

"You saved my arse, back when we got the company," Isaac goes on. And I suppose, now he mentions it, he's right. But he was just finding his feet back then, and I had business and legal experience, which applies itself to any number of things. I shrug, and my mind wanders to Griff. Griff, who I might eventually be with. Griff, whom I am determined to see again, since I owe him an apology. He seems to expect good things from me, so I shouldn't throw away his faith. I'll do what's right and tell him I'm sorry. That's all. Then I will nobly and humbly leave.

"You handled all the technical shit," Isaac's saying. "Taxes, payroll, renewing contracts, managing the transition with the staff to keep everything moving…"

Of course, it's possible Griff won't *want* me to nobly and humbly leave. Maybe he'll want to tell me what a tosser I've been, in which case, I will certainly let him. But I'll also make it clear that I won't try to hurt him again, and that I'm working through a series of epiphanies with regard to, ah, self-image, and—

"Did you like it?" Isaac demands.

I blink back to the present. "Hmm?"

"Working at Montgomery Publishing. Being my right-hand man. Did you like it?"

He does ask the silliest questions, sometimes. "Of course I did. It was the best job I've ever…" My sister and brother-in-law are watching me like cats watching a mouse. My words trail off as self-consciousness fills me, but then I push through. "It was the best job I've ever had," I admit.

"Great," Isaac says. "You're hired."

I straighten in my seat. "Here, now. You can't hire me for a job I already—"

"Shut up. I'm giving you two weeks off to get your shit together. Come on." He rises to his feet. "Let's sort your hair out."

"Piss off."

"You going to see your fella or not?"

I hesitate, ignoring my sister's smile. After a moment's thought, I admit, "Perhaps I would like to regain my usual style."

"There you are, then," Isaac says. "Maybe you should shower, and all."

"For fuck's sake, Montgomery." He's not entirely wrong, though.

17

OLU

Nine days after leaving Fernley, I'm back. But I know something's wrong when Maria winces as she opens the door to me.

Usually, that wince would be an arrow to my heart. I would assume the worst—that Maria didn't want me here—and choose a mask designed to hide the fact that I'd even noticed, never mind that I cared. However, I am now embracing this new-fangled concept called vulnerability (only around friends, you understand). And, since Lizzie and I went so far as to contact a counsellor—which means I have essentially admitted to a complete stranger that I might possibly require some assistance with my, ah, self—I am, at this point, committed.

So I grit my teeth and ask awkwardly, "Is everything alright, Maria, darling?"

"Oh, yes," she nods, the sun flashing off her strip of white hair. "Everything's fine. I mean, I'm fine. And you're looking well, Keynes. And I'm very happy to see you!"

"I'm happy to see you too," I say truthfully. "Sorry I didn't call ahead, but I was a bit distracted"—*nervous, anxious, shitting myself*—"and it completely slipped my mind."

"Oh, don't be silly. I expected you'd be back, anyway."

"You... did?"

"For Griffin," she says, and the wince is there again. She leans against the doorframe. "I'd invite you in, only—"

"Only?"

"I think you're about to leave again."

I do believe I'm sweating. And in a linen suit, too. "Maria, darling, please be direct. You're making me quite miserable."

I think my honesty shocks her, because for a moment all she can do is stare. Then she pulls herself together and says, "Griffin left the village days ago."

There is a ringing in my ears. My heart is not beating so much as it is flying around my chest, smacking into my ribs every so often with an *Oof*. "I beg your pardon?"

"He left. Gave Henry Breton-Fowler an earful and quit his job, apparently—the village was all atwitter. Then he goes, that very night. House is locked up, and only little Rebecca Baird has the key. No-one knows where he went."

Right. I see. Well, no need to panic. No need, no need, no need. I'm sure Griff is fine. He's probably just gone off on some twenty-eight-year-old sort of adventure, like he should have long ago.

Of course, the timing seems rather suspicious, and my skin is too tight for my body, and I'm worried, worried, worried—

No. I'm calm, I'm thinking, I'm handling it. I adjust the cuff of my shirt and say, "I'll be needing Rebecca's direction, then."

Maria looks pleased.

My journey to Rebecca's house is faster than expected because, after the first minute or so of walking, I start to run. I don't care how undignified that is, and I don't care about the dog walkers who turn in the street to watch me with expressions ranging from alarm to astonishment. Wanting Griffin, it turns out, is rather like being with Griffin: I forget to worry about things that don't matter.

Rebecca's house is, as Maria described it, *The little white one on the corner just past the church.* I pound at the front door, and someone tall, thin, and very much not Rebecca opens it.

I really don't have time for this.

"I'm looking for Griff," I say without preamble, "or someone who knows where Griff is."

The man gives me a slow, sceptical look up and down.

"Quickly," I snap.

The fine lines on his forehead become deep furrows. "So," he says. "You're the bloke, are you?"

I sigh. Then I shout at the top of my lungs, "Rebecca!"

It does the trick.

A few seconds later she's there, a ball of blonde energy, pushing the thin man aside. "Christ's sake, Lewis," she mutters, "don't go sticking your oar in." Her hair is piled on top of her head, her cheeks are flushed, and she's wearing shorts and an oversized shirt covered in dust.

I raise my eyebrows. "Moving going well?"

"I'm packing up the loft," she says, "while His Highness here answers doors."

The man's voice comes from the hallway she just shoved him into. "Oh, come on, Bex—"

She steps into the garden with me and shuts the door behind her. "Alright," she says briskly. "I'm not best pleased with you—"

"I'm wounded."

"Quiet, would you? I'm trying to have a helpful, fairy godmother moment, here."

I do believe that aligns perfectly with my goals, so for once, I shut my mouth.

"Good. Now, I can't tell you where Griff's gone because friends don't give friends' whereabouts to men who brutally rejected them."

Ouch.

"But, just in case you had a good reason, which I'm hoping

you did..." She gives me a look that says I'd better. "I feel comfortable telling you that he's gone to France—"

"He's gone *where?*"

"To learn about making wine without grapes."

I stare. "He's gone to... wine without... what?" Then a memory slots into my mind like something from a slideshow: Griff and I, lying fully clothed on my bed, watching dust motes dance in the sunlight and talking about a wine hotel in Alsace.

Rebecca is watching me closely, her lips curving into a slow smile. "That mean something to you, does it?"

"I hope so," I murmur. "I really hope so." Because if I'm wrong, I'm about take a pointless bloody flight.

———

GRIFF

It's hotter in France than it is back home. You'd think that'd be common sense, but we're so close, right? As countries, I mean. There's just a little strip of water between us, and we've spent centuries in and out of each other's business. So, even though I knew things would be different here, I still wasn't prepared.

I'm happy to be surprised, though. Happy to find myself in a place I couldn't have imagined on my own. Next time, I'll go somewhere even further away—and yes, there's going to be a next time. Turns out, planes aren't that intimidating, and people don't stare at me as much as I thought they would, and my savings account is fairly healthy. I like it here, doing things I've never done, seeing things I've never seen. Like my view right now: I'm sitting on one of the benches placed throughout the hotel's grounds, watching the sun set over the hills. Hot orange spills across neatly arranged vineyards, and for a moment, I don't even mind how overpriced this place is. I'm too proud of myself for taking a risk, and doing it alone, too.

Without Olu.

Although, sometimes it doesn't feel that way. I sort of see him everywhere. Like, when I arrived here, I remembered the way he'd described it and compared everything I saw to the memory of his voice. Even now, I see someone walking toward my bench from the corner of my eye, and some awful, hopeful voice in the back of my mind says, *That's Olu*. The fine hairs on my arms stand up like an electric charge has washed over my skin, as if it's actually him.

Then he says, "Griff," and I almost fall off the bloody bench.

My head snaps to the side, and there he is: in a creased, pale blue suit that looks way better than it should, striding down the lane toward me, the sun's last efforts lighting him up like a god. I freeze like I'm a rabbit and he's headlights. What the fuck is he doing here? How is he here? *Why* is he here? My tongue feels too heavy to ask any of that, and my hands are grasping the bench tight enough to ache. I sort of want to throw something at him and run away, so I don't have to face how much I love him or how much it hurts. But judging by Olu's expression, if I really wanted to avoid him, I'd have to throw something pretty damn big.

Because he looks determined. And, even though I'm supposed to be furious with him, I can't be. I just can't. I've given up trying.

"Griff," he says again, his voice hoarse. "You're here."

I set my jaw as he comes to stand beside me. "Obviously." Snarky feels good right about now. I think I'll keep it up.

He doesn't look put off, though. Just hesitates, as if to make sure I'm not going to storm off, then sits down. There's enough space for a whole Rebecca between us. And, now my brain's working again, I'm pretty sure Rebecca is how he found me here —she's a traitorous genius. But *why* is he here, when I'm so certain he only ever saw me as temporary? The words are stuck to my tongue, trapped inside my mouth.

Seeing Olu up close after trying so hard not to miss him is sort of like being hit in the gut. I lose all my air. He has dark circles under his eyes, and he seems thinner than usual, his suit not fitting quite as perfectly—but he's still as beautiful as I remember. Wish he'd fucking stop that.

"I'm sorry," he says. "I'm not really sure how to do this, so forgive me if I get it horribly wrong. But it seems pertinent to start with the fact that I'm sorry."

I want to say, *For what?* but I might have stopped breathing.

Good thing he's still going. "And now, of course, I'll illustrate what I'm sorry for, so you'll know that I—that it—that I know." He's staring at me so hard, I think I'd feel it even with my eyes closed. He takes a breath and rubs his palms against his thighs unsteadily. A soft, sweet feeling floods my chest, soothing the wounds that formed when he said he didn't want me.

"I pushed you away," Olu says. "I lied to you, when I said we were too much work. I'm sorry for acting as if there was nothing between us, when there's everything. And I am so fucking sorry for hurting you, Griff." His voice doesn't waver, and neither does his gaze. "I want you to know that I only did it because—because I was struggling with myself, and I couldn't believe that you might love me anyway. I'm not sorry for feeling that way, exactly, because dealing with those feelings is… part of me," he says, as if the words are brand new and he's still learning them. "So I can't apologise for that. But I am sorry it made me lash out at you. Sorrier than I can say."

Oh, fuck. My heart is aching like he just punched it, because suddenly, I don't think Olu used me. I think he needed me more than I knew, and I was too hurt to notice. I replay the things he said to me that day, the wild look in his eyes that screamed *Escape*, and I see everything a little differently; it's like pouring light into a shadowed room and watching the monsters melt back into furniture. The thing that looked like rejection was Olu's pain. I always knew he had it, but in that moment, I didn't *see* it.

Maybe I shouldn't try this just yet, but I reach out and hold his hand. "Okay," I say. "I'm sorry too. I'm sorry I believed the worst of you for even a second."

Surprise flares in his eyes, and a tiny, cautious smile warms his face. "Oh. Really? I thought more grovelling might be required."

The idea makes me scowl. "I don't want you grovelling to anyone."

He laughs. "Okay. Alright. I see. Well, then. Next up is the, er, request."

I wonder if he's written this down somewhere and spent a plane ride frantically memorising it. The thought makes me hold his hand tighter, maybe too tight. He doesn't wince. He squeezes back.

Why does touching him feel so fucking good?

"I need you to know," he says, "that I adore you. In fact, I—I love you. A lot. A ridiculous amount, really, but who am I to argue with, er, feelings?" He winces. His discomfort is a weight on my chest; the kind that comes from a huge dog trusting you enough to fall asleep there. "I love you," he repeats, firmer now, "and you're brilliant, you're gorgeous, you're perfect—for me. I think you're perfect for me. So, I wanted to ask if you'd possibly give me another chance. Because I want you. I mean, forever. I— okay, that's enough." He nods sharply and presses his free hand into his thigh.

I can *feel* the force of his hope, his nerves, his regret. But beneath all that, I can feel myself: I'm stunned. And so happy I don't know what to do with it. What happens when you're over-flowing with more fucking joy than you've ever felt in your life? It's like an ocean in me, made up of *I love you* and *You're brilliant* and *Will you give me a chance?* All the things I've ever secretly wanted, barely dared to hope for, never quite got around to expecting.

But I should've known to expect a lot from Olu.

"Griff," he says suddenly, and his foot starts to tap. I think he does that when he's nervous. "Do you want me to leave?"

"What? No!" I blurt.

"Oh." The tapping stops. "Right. You just looked…" he laughs. "You're thinking ferociously again."

My smile is sheepish. "Sorry. No, I don't want you to leave. I want you to know that I love you. And then I want you to kiss me."

He sits up straight like I shoved a hot poker up his arse. Those winter-fir eyes, warm whenever they look at me, widen. "Oh. Well, then, I suppose I'd better—"

"Yeah, you'd better." I grab him by the back of his neck and drag him closer, right where I want him, *oh fuck that's perfect*. His thigh presses against mine and his hands grasp my shoulders, strong fingers twisting at my T-shirt. Then his mouth is there, hot and sweet and cautious. A *hello* kiss, the whisper-soft brush of skin on skin. An *I missed you* kiss, holding still and breathing each other's air.

I whisper into his mouth, "Please don't leave me again."

"I won't," he says. "I won't."

"And I won't stop loving you when things get hard. Please try to believe that. Because I'm going to prove it." I press our foreheads together, let him feel my lips move against his. "You're not a burden, Olu, not to anyone, and especially not to me. I know you're depressed. I know you have bad thoughts sometimes. I *know* all that, and I love you as you are. I want you to feel better, but I love you as you are."

His next breath shudders out of him. "And I love *you*."

"It's not a competition," I say solemnly.

"If it was," he tells me, "I would absolutely win."

Now we're kissing and laughing, and Jesus Christ, I've missed this. I've missed this so much that I drag him onto my lap—I was right, he *has* lost weight—grab fistfuls of his clothes, and suck at his bottom lip like it's my favourite fruit. Peaches, that's what he is. Soft and sweet for me. We probably shouldn't be crawling into each other's skin on a bench at a fancy French estate, but then again, I think Olu knows the owner, so hopefully we won't get arrested for public indecency. Because he's mine, and he's kissing me, so obviously I've become indecent. Luckily, his body hides the bulge in my jeans.

But not for long, because he comes up for air, his pupils blown and his brown sugar skin reddened by my beard. "Take me—"

"To my room?"

"I was just going to say *somewhere*. Anywhere. But your room is probably a good idea."

I kiss the grin off his face.

We might pass a thousand people on our way to the hotel— I'm really not sure, because I can't see anyone or anything but him. We run through the grounds like reprobates. We shove through fancy old doors and stumble up the stairs. There's a burning coil in my belly that tightens every time I look at him, every time I touch him, and that coil is connected directly to my dick. While I fumble with the key to my room, Olu slips his hands under my T-shirt, his mouth hot on my throat. My cock gets heavier in my jeans. Before, my heart ached for him, which was very noble and emotional and shit, but now he's *in* my heart, so the nobility has gone, and it's my balls that ache instead. I'd feel awkward about it, only, from the feel of his erection against my arse, he's on the same page.

Good.

I finally get the door open, drag him inside, and slam it shut. "Fuck," I mutter. "Need a condom." Then I order, "Take your clothes off," over my shoulder while I open and shut every piece of furniture with a handle. Surely French hotels provide free condoms. They're *French*.

"You don't have any?" Olu asks.

"I didn't come here to screw a herd of dancing girls; I came to learn about wine and mope about you. I forgot I had a dick, to be honest. I hope you're taking your clothes off." I open the last available drawer, find absolutely jack, and throw up my hands. "No condoms."

"I get tested every time I have sex," Olu says. "Or I did. I haven't since you."

"I haven't been tested since 2017," I say.

"That's rather irresponsible, darling."

"Which is the last time I had sex before you."

"Oh. Really?"

I turn around and scowl when I find him fully dressed. "*Clothes*, man. And yes, really. Pickings were slim."

"I bet," he mutters, but there's a little smile on his face. "Alright, then. No condom. How thrilling." He's trying to be sarcastic, which means this is a big deal for him. "Since I also forgot my dick worked, here." He produces a little tin of Vaseline and throws it on the bed. "We're DIY-ing it today."

We could be stuck on a desert island with nothing but spit and a prayer and I'd be happy. I don't say that, though; don't want him getting a big head. Of course, the fact that I walk over and strip him probably has a similar effect. I shove off his jacket, start unbuttoning his shirt, and press my thigh against the thick line of his cock through his trousers.

Olu groans, shudders, drops his head against my shoulder. "Griff." He doesn't sound precise and in control right now. He sounds slow and heavy and slightly dazed, just how I like him. His hips jerk forward, chasing the pressure of my thigh, and lust races up my spine like flames along a line of gasoline.

"Remember the first time I got your shirt off?" I ask him, slipping buttons loose one by one. "In the kitchen. You were all shy."

"You made me uncomfortable," he says, his hands gripping my hips. Hard. Like he owns me.

"Why'd I make you uncomfortable?" I whisper the words into his ear as I finally push off his shirt. Then I run my palms over his hot skin, my thumb brushing the place where he was once bruised, feeling the slight bumps of his ribcage.

"Because I wanted you," Olu rasps, dragging off my T-shirt. He throws it aside, dips his head, swipes his tongue over my nipple. "I hadn't wanted anyone in forever, but I started to want you, and it felt so odd. Felt so... different. I wasn't sure of it." We're both reaching for each other's flies. Our hands should tangle, but we move like a well-oiled machine.

"Are you sure of me now, baby?" I ask him.

"Yes." The word is soft. He leans forward and kisses me as if he'll never stop. Then I shove his trousers and his underwear down, and he groans.

"Take my cock out," I urge him, and he does, dragging at my clothes the way I did his. Eventually, finally, we're both naked. His shaft is thick and gleaming against his abs, making my mouth water. My own dick is so stiff it hurts, and when he grasps us both with one hand and squeezes, all I can do is moan my desperate, wordless pleasure.

"Did you miss me?" Olu asks lightly. "It feels like you did."

"Yeah, yeah. I'm about to fuck you legless. Let's see if you can be smug then."

"I can always be smug, darling." But his tongue slides out to wet his bottom lip, and his hands are hungry.

"I bet." I turn and push him onto the bed. He sprawls on his back like some gorgeous, arrogant prince, all heavy-lidded eyes and an *I dare you* smile. One leg bends at the knee, and my attention is torn between the firm curve of his arse and the crude way he cups and lifts his own balls.

"Shameless," I tell him, coming to kneel on the mattress. "Aren't you?" I can barely string a sentence together.

"Do you mind?" he asks archly.

He knows full well the answer is "Hell fucking no." I lean down and lick a long, wet path across his dick. His whole body jerks, the breath forced out of his lungs. Then I take the head between my lips and suck.

"*Fuck,*" he groans, his hips shooting forward. "Fuck, Griff."

I grunt around a mouthful of him and suck harder, wetter, deeper, until his next breath sounds more like a sob. Then I release his swollen shaft and lick down to his balls. Grab his arse with both hands and push, lifting and spreading until I see that tight little hole. I thrust my tongue between his cheeks, pushing as deep inside him as I can.

"Jesus," Olu pants, tugging at my hair. "Come here. Just fucking—come here. I need to see you. I need you in me."

I give him one last lick and straighten up. "Well, since you *need* it so bad…"

"Actually, never mind. Get my dick in your mouth again so you can't talk back." But his actions don't match his teasing words. As soon as I sit up, he's on his knees, straddling my lap and reaching for my cock like it's a grand prize. His fingers are slippery now, the little tin open beside him. He sinks his teeth into my shoulder, licks the bite, then lifts his head to look me in the eyes. While I'm tangled in all that intensity, he fists my cock without mercy and strokes. *Holy fuck.*

I kiss him hard, with tongue and teeth and all the love I'm too breathless to spell out. He kisses me back until my blood is burning through my veins, setting my heart on fire. And then, because I can't wait anymore, because I'm about to blow in his hand, because I need us to be connected, I find the little tin amongst the sheets and slick my own fingers. Slide them over his arse, circling that tight ring of flesh. Push slowly, firmly, into him. Olu shakes as I split him open.

"Yeah," he breathes, arching his back, his cock nudging mine as I finger him deeper. "*Ah*, Griff."

"You like that?"

He nods, nipping at my bottom lip.

"You want more?"

"I want you."

"Be patient." I use my free arm to keep him upright as two fingers become three. He pulls at my hair and fucks himself back on me until I think I'll come just from this: the feel of his body against mine, the little moans he can't quite swallow, the tight clasp of him around my fingers. Yeah, he wants it. He needs it. He needs *me*.

And I need him. This is heaven. This is us.

I slide my fingers out of him and move us around a little, until my back hits the headboard. He's still straddling me, reaching past my shoulders to grip the polished wood.

"There," I tell him. "Now sit on my dick."

His grin is wicked, his eyes almost delirious with lust. "You're going to make me do all the work after such a long flight?"

"It's ninety minutes, you big baby." But no, I won't make him do all the work. I just want to watch him try.

Olu bites his lip on a smile, then rises on his knees. "Give me a hand," he murmurs, so I hold my cock while he sinks down so slow and easy, I almost forget my own name.

"Jesus *Christ*." My head falls back, my eyes closing as everything flickers for a second. He's so tight around my dick that the pounding of my blood feels almost painful. I'm so fucking hot for him I can barely breathe, and it gets worse once he takes me all the way, deep enough that his arse touches my thighs. He grunts, his abs flex, and a stream of come spurts from his cock to paint a hot stripe over my skin.

"Oh God," he pants, his voice thin. "Oh my God."

"Good?" I manage.

"*Yes*."

The minute the word leaves his lips, I'm kissing him. I jerk my hips up, he clenches around me, and my head spins. A bead of sweat drips down to the base of my spine. Then he rises up, up, up, until just the tip of me is inside him, and sinks down again.

I don't even know who I am anymore. Suddenly, all I know is

Olu. I push him back onto the bed, following until my weight's sprawled over him. Then, when he's pinned beneath me, spread open around me, begging for me with every breath, I fuck him hard and deep.

"Shit," he chokes out, his fingers tangling in my hair.

"You like it?" I pant in his ear.

"Yes, fuck, yes, don't stop. I'm about to come."

"Yeah?" I grab a handful of his arse and squeeze as I thrust. "For who?" I need him to say, I need him to say—

"*You.*"

"Whose are you?"

"*Yours,*" he growls. "Oh, Christ, Griff, I'm coming. I'm—" His words dissolve into a moan, his come spraying wet against my stomach. I hold him tight and fuck him good, and finally, when he's got what he needs, the last of my control slips away.

I spill everything I have inside Olu, and burning, star-bright satisfaction turns my vision black. Slowly, the pleasure fades and reality bleeds back in. I roll off him, flopping onto the mattress like my battery's run out, and maybe it has. I don't know what comes over me when I'm in bed with this man. I like it, the hunger and the words I can't control—but now, when all I want to do is lie here quietly and hold him 'til we fall asleep, it makes me laugh a little.

Luckily, Olu's right here with me, laughing softly, too. I sling an arm across his body, so he won't get any bright ideas about moving. Then I say, "I love you."

"I love you," he replies. So easy. So honest. Swapping those words feels like making a miracle.

———

Olu

Griff and I spend the rest of the evening lazing around, talking about nothing, and defiling his hotel sheets. By midnight, we're freshly showered and right where we belong: wrapped up in each other. His strong chest and soft belly are a comforting wall against my back, and his fingertip draws a figure eight over my bare hip. The smile on my face can only be described as *loopy*. Thank goodness it's dark in here. I want to tell him I love him, just so he'll say it back again and I can melt into a pile of sappy goo, but I'm trying not to come on too strong.

Of course, I already spent an extortionate amount on a flight to Alsace and confessed my undying love, so perhaps that ship has sailed.

His voice lazy with the happy exhaustion *I* put there, Griff says, "I can't believe you didn't bring any luggage."

"I was in a rush." His arm tightens around me, as if that makes him pleased. I decide I've played it cool more than enough in my life. Griff deserves all the messy devotion I can give him. Rolling over to face him, I litter his cheeks with kisses. "Do you see how desperate I was to come and fetch you, darling?"

"Fetch me?"

I thread my fingers through his hair and rub my nose against his. "Certainly. I'd like to take you home."

Slowly, softly, he repeats, "Home?"

"I've been thinking," I say, refusing to feel nervous. "It seems you've rather outgrown Fernley."

He snorts. "Something like that."

"And I believe London isn't quite doing it for me, either."

He goes still.

"Especially because I'd like to be somewhere you can grow things. You're rather good at that."

After a pause, he says, "I'm unemployed now, you know."

"Yes, I heard. Apparently, the whole scene was quite thrilling."

"You'd have loved it."

"Oh, I'm sure," I murmur.

Another pause. Then he says, "I was thinking I'd start a

company of my own. But it'll be bloody difficult, so I reckon I'll be poor as a church mouse for a while. Even if I sell the house."

"The house? Griff—"

"It's okay." His lips brush mine. "It's okay. I think I want to."

I swallow hard. "You do?"

"Yeah. I brought Mum's ashes here, you know."

"You did?" I appear to have lost a considerable portion of my vocabulary.

"The owner, he's a nice bloke—"

"Gustave?"

"Yeah," Griff says. "He let me put some by the south vineyard. Which made me think, maybe we could travel to all sorts of places, and show her. Because she never left Fernley either."

"I like that idea," I say. "I like that very much."

We're silent for a while. Then he whispers, "You never said if you'd be alright, shacking up with a church mouse."

"Well, that was an oversight," I say immediately. "I'd be happy to. In fact, I'd be rather proud to, since it's you."

His grin practically glows.

"As long as you wouldn't mind us staying close to my sister. Oxfordshire. Somewhere green, I promise."

"Of *course* we'll be close to your sister," he says, as if it's obvious. As if he already knew. Which he did, I suppose, because he knows me.

"And we'll visit Rebecca," I add, because I know him too. "Rebecca and Maria and… and everyone, everyone we love."

"Sounds perfect."

My smile is slow and dreamy. "Griffin."

"Yeah, sweetheart?"

"I think everything's going to be fine." And when I wake up beside him the next morning, I know I'm right.

EPILOGUE

FOUR MONTHS LATER

OLU

My stomach is a lead weight. My lungs are cinched too tight to breathe, and there's a roar waiting to rip from my throat if someone doesn't *tell me what I want to hear* within the next five minutes.

"This is really good, Olu," Griff says. Which, incidentally, is *not* what I wanted to hear.

But I can't bite his head off, because I love him, and I'm trying not to do that anymore. So I just mutter, "Thanks."

"I mean it," he says.

"You're just trying to distract me."

"That too."

Well, at least he admits to his nefarious ways. Similarly, I can admit that I like hearing about his favourite parts of my journal, which I always do, regardless of the circumstances. Letting people read my writing is one of the things I've been working on, these past few months. I need to get used to the pressure because I've set myself a goal: one day, I'm going to write a book and try to have it published. When that day comes, I need the emotional fortitude not to murder anyone who criticises it, so I have firmly instructed my loved ones to be brutally honest.

Griff's honesty is my favourite kind, because he loves everything I write, and he really means it. But right now, all he gets from me is a quick smile before I go back to burying my face in my hands and trying not to die.

I hear him sigh, and then he rubs soothing circles on my back. Even though we're in a very busy hospital corridor, I don't flinch away from contact that reveals my emotional state. Fuck, *I'm* revealing my emotional state, carrying on like this. I'd like to say it's 100% growth, but a good 50% is the fact that I'm losing my mind with worry.

"You need to relax," Griff says. "I know it's going fine."

"No, you don't. Neither of us *knows* anything because we're not in that room, and until we are, as far as I'm concerned, my Elizabeth could be—"

The door in front of us opens and frantic sound spills out. I hear sobbing, and I'm on my feet before I register Isaac looking dazed in the doorway. "She did it. They're fine. Everything's fine. You can—"

I shove past him, and next thing I know, I'm standing in the delivery room with its dark, rain-spattered windows, its lamps turned low, and my sister crying her eyes out on the bed.

"Lizzie!" My heart cracks right down the middle.

Then she looks up, and I see the biggest smile on her tear-stained face, all the happiness in the world glowing from her dark eyes. She lifts the bundle in her arms toward me. "Look. Look!"

Hours of tension drain away so fast I feel dizzy. There are little rainbow dots dancing at the corners of my eyes.

"You look wonderful," I tell her, but my gaze is already on the baby.

"Stop," she tuts. "I've had more than enough lies from my husband." Isaac is hovering behind me—Griff, too, because he and Liz get on beautifully. We're a family, all of us, and here's the newest member, with an impressive scowl and a head of thick, dark curls.

"Oh, well done, Elizabeth," I murmur. "Well done."

She starts crying again, tears streaming silently down her face as she beams up at me. Then she hands the baby over, and I think I'm crying too. How awful. How wonderful. I love this child.

An hour later, Lizzie is asleep in bed, and Isaac is seated by her side, their hands intertwined. I'm holding baby Benjamin, watching the way his lips move over his toothless gums. He's like an old man. An old man I could balance in the palm of my hand.

"I remember," I say absently, "when Elizabeth was born. She looked just like this. But I wasn't allowed to hold her or get too close." I dip my head to the baby's hair and breathe deep. "I bet she smelled like this, too." Lovely. Perfect. Tiny. Is it possible to smell tiny? Clearly, the answer is yes.

"You like babies," Griff says, sounding very pleased with me indeed.

"I do believe I've mentioned that before, one way or another." My eyes don't leave Benjamin.

"You have. But it's one thing to hear it. This is…"

"What? This is what?"

He kisses my cheek. "Something else." The words are soft, like a touch. I smile. Then he says, "Want one?"

Which snatches my attention completely from my nephew.

"Want—? A—?" My mouth works as my mind reaches for a yes, hesitates, then flinches away. "I don't know if that's a good idea." And I mean it—I simply don't know. But I want it to be.

Griff must see that because his gaze holds mine steadily, quietly understanding. "Will you let me convince you?"

I take a breath. "Perhaps." The shock fades, and hope glitters. I flash him a smile and add, "If you can."

He huffs out a laugh, because there's one thing we both know:

Griffin Everett could convince me of anything. But all he says is, "I'll do my best."

After a pause, I decide, "So will I. To be brave, I mean."

"Together."

"Together." I lean into Griff's shoulder and kiss my nephew's head.

The End

AUTHOR'S NOTE

My first full-length (-ish) novel was *Bad for the Boss*, in which Olu's best friend Theo wooed his now-wife Jen with the contract Olu describes in this book. It was exactly as messy and sexy and romantic as it sounds. It was also a learning curve and a turning point for me. If it weren't for that book, I might not have the career I have today—and if it weren't for that book, I wouldn't have written *Work for It,* which might be my favourite project ever.

Olu sprang into my head fully-formed from the moment Theo first calls him in *Bad for the Boss*. And now here I am, almost two years later, finally telling his story in this spin-off. It's been a while, but that's okay because this book needed time to brew. It also needed a level of experience I didn't have back then. Even now, I doubt I've done Olu and Griff complete justice, but I've definitely done my best. I hope you agree.

If you are struggling with depression, anxiety, or any persistent moods, thoughts, and behaviours that affect your life negatively, please know that you are precious simply by virtue of existing—you don't have to do anything else to matter—and that you should look after yourself by seeing a medical professional.

There is no shame in taking care of your mental health; it's arguably the most important aspect of health there is.

If you are looked down on, diminished, bullied or mistreated, never feel silly or childish for being hurt by it. Never feel as if rejecting or avoiding that treatment is an overreaction. You deserve kindness and respect at an absolute minimum.

If you are struggling with coming out, please know this: how you choose to express yourself in a world that doesn't deserve you is no-one's business but your own. You have no-one to answer to. Your identity belongs to you alone, and anyone who tries to take that from you is both monstrous and doomed to fail.

All my love,

Talia

ABOUT THE AUTHOR

Talia Hibbert is an award-winning, Black British author who lives in a bedroom full of books. Supposedly, there is a world beyond that room, but she has yet to drum up enough interest to investigate.

She writes sexy, diverse romance because she believes that people of marginalised identities need honest and positive representation. She also rambles intermittently about the romance genre online. Her interests include makeup, junk food, and unnecessary sarcasm.

Talia loves hearing from readers. Follow her social media to connect, or email her directly at hello@taliahibbert.com.

Printed in Poland
by Amazon Fulfillment
Poland Sp. z o.o., Wrocław

62456638R00162